I0723870

Books by Vincent Michael Ives

THE ZOMPIRE SERIES
Children of the Apocalypse

Coming soon:
Hunger of Death
Echoes of Humanity

Children of the Apocalypse

VINCENT MICHAEL IVES

www.VMIbooks.com

**Get your free e-book short story set after the events of this book by joining the Vincent Michael Ives email list.
http://eepurl.com/ipOjtA**

by Vincent Michael Ives
Copyright © 2021, Vincent Michael Ives.
Published by VMI Books, VMIbooks.com

This is a work of fiction. Any similarity to actual persons, living or dead, or actual events, is purely coincidental.

...but who can say it won't all happen like this someday?

Copyeditor: Leigh Ives
Cover Art/Designer: Creepy Duck Design
Interior Designer: Vinnie Duyck
Interior Graphic Designer: Matt Statton

ISBNs: 978-1-961018-00-6 (paperback), 978-1-961018-01-3 (ebook), 978-1-961018-02-0 (audiobook)

To those suffering great loss,
that you may find the good
that comes only through suffering.

Chapter One

Leo's alarm moaned to life. He rolled over and thwapped the button to turn it off, but it continued to sound in his half dream state. He swiped his hand at it again. The sound persisted, but something about it struck him as wrong. The hair on the back of Leo's neck prickled as the noise pinged its way deeper into his head until it plucked a string of recognition. That wasn't his alarm. It was something else, something he had not heard in a long time. The unmistakable moan of a zombie.

He shot upright in his bed and sat still, suddenly fully awake, his ears hyper-sensitive to the old familiar sound. It was not coming from inside, or at least not from one of the rooms adjacent to his bedroom. He tilted his head, focusing one ear toward the open window. The sound was definitely coming from somewhere outside the complex and not from within the walls, likely from the street-side of the building. He rose, letting the blankets slide off his skin into a pile on his bed. The morning air wrapped its icy fingers around his body, snapping him awake. He swung his legs off the bed, which was just two mattresses stacked on the floor, no needless bed-frame that would eventually break.

The chill in the air made his legs bloom with goosebumps. The only thing covering his bare, freckled skin was an old pair of yellowed underwear, pinned at the back since the elastic had given out years ago.

He hoped to find a new pair someday soon, or at least a pair that hadn't been worn and washed enough times to the point of being little more than paper-thin netting. He had given up on his dream of ever finding a pair that still had functioning elastic. All things existing in the world were old, and Leo felt the age in his own body.

Leo lived in one of those two-story apartment complex deals comprising thirty-five separate apartments built around a central courtyard lazy tenants used to let their dogs pee and poop, though none of that happened anymore. Leo was the only person living at the apartment complex, he didn't have a dog, and it had been a couple generations since the world ended. Though it wasn't fair to suggest the world itself ended, but the zombie apocalypse had been a fairly defining moment in terms of human history.

Leo made his way through the makeshift doorway in the wall, though calling it a doorway was a bit of a stretch when, in reality, it was a sawed out chunk of wall merging the adjacent apartments. His parents had done that to every wall in the complex, making it one giant suite.

He lived almost entirely on the second story. *Never trust the first floor.* Sure, the inner area was closed in, keeping stray zombies out, but you just couldn't trust the ground floor. That was engrained into him from an early age. The windows and doors on that floor were boarded up or barricaded, but an extra level of caution never hurt anyone. The four stairways to the second floor were blown up or cut away with a torch decades earlier. That was the only way he'd known the place. He could see where the bases of the poles that held up the metal and concrete steps used to be. Zombies could climb stairs, so remove the stairs (that was just prudence). They couldn't do ladders, ropes, or thin ramps made from small planks of wood, as zombies were historically not great with balance. So those were the methods for humans to get up and down from the second floor. Good practice for Leo, bad times for zombies.

Leo lumbered through the holes in the walls to the apartment space on the front of the building, where a ladder led to a hole in the ceiling. He opened the ceiling-hatch and stepped out onto the roof. A shiver moved down his spine from either the cold air, the zombie moans, or a mix of the two. It was strange for him to hear the sound again. It had been so long since the last time he had encountered one, it almost seemed like a dream. He zig-zagged his way to the front of the building, stepping around and over the random bits of detritus strewn about the rooftop.

There it was. A rotting, walking corpse, ambling its way up the street. Leo watched its meandering route. Its feet awkwardly slapped against the grass-strewn pavement with each mindless step. He pitied it and he hated it. Leo's stomach gargled as it too was waking up and sought sustenance. Annoyed at being woken up before his alarm, Leo whistled at the thing shakily making its way down the street. It wobbled its head, searching for the source of the sound. Leo waved and whistled louder. The rotting mass clocked the motion and trained its dead milky-black eyes on Leo. It stumbled onto the curb toward the building.

Leo stretched his arms as he walked to the north side of the building, ignoring the zombie below. He would deal with that thing in a moment. Right now, he needed to stretch and wake up his own body. After cracking his neck and rolling his shoulders around in their sockets, he grasped the top of a long pole that leaned against the north side of the building. He lifted it, surprised it was much heavier than he remembered. It really had been quite a long time since he had to use it. He removed the pole from a hook that held it in place. Leo hoisted it just enough to swing it around the front corner of the building. He let it fall back to the ground, thunking the bottom into the dirt below. Leo held onto the pole with one hand and walked the top of the pole several feet further along the front edge of the building. He lifted the pole again, swinging the bottom like a pendulum further along the roof edge, thunking it into the dirt a few yards ahead of him. He moseyed along the roof edge, stopping right above where the bottom of the pole sat buried in the dirt below.

The zombie ambled its way closer to Leo, stumbling over a broken chunk of sidewalk. Leo wanted to yell down at the zombie to hurry it up, but he knew any words were just a waste of energy. Its ears could hear, but its mind was deaf. The zombie plodded toward the building at the only pace it would ever move. Its nature was base, and Leo's job was clear. Eradicate every monster he could.

Leo shivered again. The sun had peaked over the horizon before he woke, knocking back the chill in the air, but he was unaccustomed to being outside in just his ratty underwear and he was itching to get on with his day. After more mindless plodding, the zombie finally made it to the front of the building just below Leo. It padded its rotting fingers against the cracked stucco wall in a fruitless attempt to get at Leo two stories above. Leo sighed. These things were as predictable and annoying as mosquitos, but not quite enough to be completely boring. Leo grunted at the inconvenient creature below him, then hoisted the long pole skyward, hand over hand, until the sharp spike at its base sat poised a few yards above the ground. His shoulders ached from the weight. He had done this hundreds if not thousands of times over the years, but he honestly could not remember the last time he had needed to perform the task. *When exactly had he gone from spiking several zombies a day in his youth to having the whole endeavor become a rare, yet annoying treat?*

Leo wondered if he should add practicing lifting the pole to his daily routine to keep in shape, but then again, not having to use it in forever negated the entire point of practice. Either way, as the zombie below swatted a hand against the building, Leo thrust the pole downward and loosened his grip, letting gravity take over as it slipped through his hands. The spike drove straight at the zombie's upturned head directly into its eye socket. Nice! Leo thought, still got it. The zombie crumpled into a heap on the ground as the pole drove itself further into its head, scrambling the poor creature's brain on its descent. After making sure there was no more movement, Leo lifted the pole again, withdrawing it from the heap on the ground and swung it back towards the north of the building, thunking it down into the dirt again, effectively cleaning the zombie's brains and viscera off the sharp spike on its bottom end. He walked the pole back along the wall and around the corner of the complex, nestling it back into its hook along the north face of the building.

Leo glanced back at the zombie folded against itself on the ground. "Well," he said to no one in particular, "guess I'm awake."

Leo made his way down the ladder back inside and through the holes in the walls towards his bedroom. He stopped at a mirror beside one of the portals between apartments. His beard was getting long again. He'd have to trim it soon. *At least it's still got some red in it*, he thought. His hair used to all be bright red, but decades of outrunning zombies had taken its toll. Grey hairs worked their way through his beard, destined to conquer the whole thing. The hair on the top of his head had long since given up the ghost, which only made body maintenance easier, and he could avoid getting burned by just wearing a hat all the time, though it didn't stop his freckles from coming out in full force every summer.

The sound of Leo's alarm echoed through the complex. Leo continued to the room with his bed and pressed his alarm off, breathing in the moment of silence. Like his dad used to say, you gotta find the joy in small moments. Waking up at all in the morning was a small joy in itself. *It could always be worse.*

Leo remade his bed. The blankets were still warm to the touch, a siren call for him to return to their sweet embrace, but there was much to be done. He always felt it a waste to leave a bed perfectly warm, only for it to become cold again when he re-entered it. He finished making his bed, dressed, and walked to the kitchen, which was two apartment holes away.

Breakfast was simple; a fried egg on buttered toast. Leo had been trying out a new recipe with a rosemary bread. He wasn't sure he liked it, but he enjoyed having it as an option. Variation was a privilege. Not one to sit in the morning, Leo ate his breakfast while walking back to the roof. Now that he was fully dressed, the morning felt nice. Sunny with a few clouds. Warm, but not too hot. *The breeze will be nice later on,* he thought. *Another moment to enjoy the world.*

Leo walked to the front edge of the complex to begin his rounds. All was still clear on that front, aside from the crumpled heap he had left earlier, no other movement. The south side was the same. West, also clear, as usual. That area used to be the carports where tenants parked their cars back when that was a thing. Leo used it as storage for non-perishables, and to keep his bike protected from the sun and rain. It was a powder blue Schwinn, but time and rust had different plans. He was proud of his Schwinn and imagined it was an illustrious name in bicycles.

Its gears worked well enough, which was the second most important part. The seat being the obvious first in the hierarchy of importance on any bicycle. Every day was leg day, but only so far as his ass wasn't sore, then every day was sore ass day. Looking down on the bike under the ever tired carport, Leo reminded himself to add another layer of padding to the seat. He had a lot of riding and deliveries to do, and it would be great if he could sit down without having to take his time breathing through the literal pain in his ass.

Leo continued on to the north side of the building—also clear. He felt like there had been more days like that lately. That, or he was just an optimist. He remembered growing up having to use the long pole he kept on the roof to spike a zombie every morning. Though he questioned if he was remembering accurately or if nostalgia had distorted his mind. Either way, he'd take it as a sign that it would be a good day, *'cause why the heck not think positive?*

Having finished his breakfast and feeling good about life, or as good as he *could* feel, anyway, Leo climbed back down into the apartment, sealing the roof hatch behind him. He packed some snacks and meals in his bag and slid down the rope near the back of the complex. He opened the metal gate blocking one of the first floor apartments to check his cistern. It had been a while since it rained, but there was enough water in it to satisfy him. He filled a couple of water bottles that had seen more than their fair share of wear. It would be a long couple of days, and it was always a good idea to have enough water. *Either that or die.*

After going through the gate at the back of the complex, Leo latched it shut behind him and walked to the carport. He brought an old shirt he used to like, which had since yellowed out into its current state of retirement. Leo wrapped it around the bicycle seat, tying it to itself underneath in a couple of places until it stayed snug.

He backed his Schwinn up to a cart and attached it to the rear wheel fork. It used to be the frame of a stroller people would attach to their bikes. Leo couldn't remember ever riding in it as a child, but then again, he never remembered a time when he didn't know how to ride a bike himself. He wondered if his dad ever pedaled him around in one of those. He was certain he'd never ridden in the cage of that one, anyway. He found it funny how people never remembered the early years of their own lives. It seemed unfair to have lived and lost that time, especially with the world as it was. His dad must've spent so many hours doing literally everything for him every single day, and not a second of that time was even a dream in Leo's mind. All those moments of connection, somehow disconnected forever, lost like smoke in the fog of the past.

Leo hooked up the cart to his bike. The part of the cart where you would expect to see fabric or a child's seat was replaced by a flat base and surrounded by wire-mesh forming a mobile cage. That was more to protect what was inside from getting out than it was for keeping what was outside from getting in. It all depended on what the cargo was, though, which would be a lot of things in the next few days.

He rode down the old driveway and stopped at the gate, checking again there were no surprises for him on the other side. All clear. He opened the gate, walked the bike and cart out, then closed the gate behind him, double checking it was secure. If you forgot to cover your butt, or got in a hurry, you could really ruin the rest of your day. Leo knew to enjoy the small things in life because they were also the things that could wreck you. He mulled on that as he left his bike and walked to the crumpled zombie on the ground. Spots of thick black goo spattered the wall, resembling a rooster tail a few feet above the ground, right where the spike had driven itself into the zombie's head. Leo left it, knowing the next rain would wash the wall clean.

Leo knelt and grabbed the nearest arm of the thing, trying to only touch the moldy sleeve and avoid the skin entirely. The cold deadness of those things always made his skin crawl. No matter how common they had been, they were always unsettling, especially up-close. Leo dug his fingers deeper into the fabric, wrapping the sleeve tighter around the zombie's arm. He dragged it across the overgrown grass up the street. There was an open area two lots north with a burn pile Leo and his parents used to burn all the corpses they had either found or had made over the years. The old property on the lot had burned up before Leo was born, so he had only known it as "the burn pile."

Leo paused, releasing the zombie's arm onto the ground and stretched. His shoulder ached. In the past, he had used a flat-top cart to wheel the bodies to the burn pile. It had been very useful through the years. That is, until the wheel went flat too many times and the rubber had worn away to nothing. Luckily, that had been around the time the zombie herds had thinned to barely anything. Leo ended up burning that cart in a fit of anger years ago. He forgot exactly what pissed him off so much that day, but some days, even the tiniest things could set him off. Other days, nothing could faze him. A small part of him regretted throwing the cart into the fire, but mostly he smiled at the thought of not requiring its use any more. Other than times like this one when he was dragging a wet skin-sack.

He grabbed the sleeves of both of the zombie's lifeless arms and dragged its corpse the rest of the way to the burn pile. Those things stank. They'd only gotten worse through the years, their bodies susceptible to the same decay Leo's would eventually, as had all people before him. He hated their smell even more than their appearance. He flopped the body on the pile of ashes and walked away, ready to breathe in some fresher air. He'd have to wait to burn the body for some other day before a deep rain to prevent the flames from jumping to other areas. In the meantime, Leo wiped his hands on the grass. He hadn't touched the thing, but its stink would linger, at least for the first bit of his journey.

The streets were long deserted, but not void of life. Decades of nature had slowly reclaimed the world. First, weeds and grasses sprouted in the tiny cracks here and there, and the seasons of heat and cold grew those cracks into fissures. Small bushes followed, then trees. Forests filled several streets in what used to be called downtown, complete with undergrowth, canopy, and wildlife. It would be a beautiful sight if one could let down their guard and ignore the few zombies ambling about, searching for their next meal.

The fact nature just didn't care about people scared him. Nature attacked humanity back in the day with every sickness it could think of. Every few years a mutated wave of some flu or whatever infected its way around the globe. Each one would attack people in different ways. Some said having that many people living so closely together caused them. Leo could almost imagine what it was like having so many people walking shoulder to shoulder down the streets, those rusted out hulks called cars sitting brand new, motors running, carrying people from wherever to who the heck knows. He'd never seen a group of people larger than sixteen in one place, much less hundreds or even thousands. Traffic, as a concept, blew his mind as unimaginable. There had been so many people they couldn't even move past each other. *Then they got sick and died, which at the very least, solved the traffic problem.*

There used to be billions of people roaming the earth. There was no way to know how many remained, but he knew some of them weren't people anymore. They were *whatevers*. Leo called them zombies, because that's what his parents called them. That's how he'd known them. Seen too many go from alive to that in between place and had to carry several of them the last few steps on their journey into eventual death. "Man," He thought aloud, "the world is messed up sometimes." A moment later, he continued the thought in his head. *Other times it's a forest taking back its home.*

Leo headed south towards the old city. It was an uphill climb, so his focus turned to that effort. Every push down on the pedal, every breath. It was a climb he'd done many times before, and always dreaded, but found thrilling as he approached the peak. He couldn't wait for the other side when he could just coast downhill. It was funny how it surprised him every time how far he could coast. He knew it, he'd done it before. He assumed all the grass and plants would slow him down sooner every time, but he always glided farther than he expected when he let himself. He enjoyed that moment every time, and he knew it was coming up.

"Hey there, stranger." A voice called out, snapping Leo back to the moment. "Doing your chicken run?"

Leo looked up and saw Anna sitting on the tall cement divider on the side of the highway. "How'd you guess?" He called out as he neared her, coming to a stop at the top of the hill. He knew it meant he wouldn't get to enjoy coasting down the other side of the hill as much, but it was a suitable moment to take a rest, anyway.

Anna was somewhere around fourteen years old with big curly hair and a giant smile. "Just figured it was about that time. I'm running tools, myself. Some parts my daddy made for the power plant."

"Ah, makes sense. Gotta keep 'em running. But yeah, that's one stop, anyway." Leo looked at Anna, suddenly realizing she was much younger than she acted. "You out here alone?"

"Yep." Anna said with an air of importance. "Daddy's got a lot of work, so I'm making the run myself. I know the way, so it's nothing." She tossed her hair, giving off an air that she clearly knew her task was of utmost importance.

"Wow, glad to hear you're movin' up in the world." Leo said.

"You gotta watch out down the way, though. You know the cement wall is c--"

"Crumbled, yeah I know." Anna grunted. "I can walk too."

"Oh, I know you can, I just want you to make sure you're safe."

"I'm not a baby, I can get there and back myself. Plus, daddy says there's not many of them out here anymore."

"Well, he may be right, but still..." Leo hated to see Anna glaring at him, "I just want to make sure you're ok."

"Hey, I'm all the way up here. *You're* the one who's closer to those things if they pop out of somewhere down there on the ground." Anna said, done with the conversation.

"You're right, sorry. I gotta stay alert too." He hoped Anna would be okay with that. She covered up her annoyance well enough. "You know, I'll be stopping by the power plant myself, I can deliver that if you like."

Anna glared at Leo. "No. It's my job. Roll away, now." She flicked her hand, dismissing Leo.

He smiled at her precocious tenacity. "You're right, can't be late. Take care Anna, hope to see you on my way back or something."

"Yeah, gotta go too. Important stuff." Anna stood and dusted off her rear, balancing her way along the top of the cement divider. "Take care, Leo." They waved each other goodbye.

Leo pedaled until gravity took over and carried him down the hill toward the city. He just wanted to check on Anna. Their upbringings weren't that different. Both were trained to always be vigilant or die—or worse. *Oh well*, he thought, he'd done his part. Anna would do exactly what she was going to do with or without his words. She was a good one. She's got a fire in her, his dad would say, a fire that burns hot.

Zombies were simple. Nature was straightforward. People could be difficult.

CHAPTER TWO

First stop for the day was still several miles ahead in the old downtown sector. Leo pedaled past carcasses of old cars and trucks scattered like dead ants. For about a hundred years they were the lifeblood of a civilization, propelling people all over the city and country like red blood cells oxygenating a thriving system. Then suddenly, extinction. Well, not suddenly, but it wasn't gradual, either, based on what he pieced together from stories he heard growing up from his parents and the other people willing to sit and talk.

Life before the first pandemic must've been crazy. It's difficult to imagine millions of people gathering without a care. Based on the TV shows and movies he'd been able to find, it must have been full of crime, police, and lawyers. A world out of control. With all those people spread across the globe, everyone had less responsibility and personal connection to the world around them. However the world used to be, the pandemics came and mucked it all up. People locked themselves in their homes, which must've been weird. The world as it was for Leo, generations after the previous one ended, locking yourself in your home was just basic survival. Only a few people like Leo, and now Anna, would travel the wilds.

Leo learned the delivery and survival trade from his parents.

His mother packed the right gear, and his dad always figured a way to make things work. It must have been nice for them to fit so well together.

A pang of sadness slowed him as he remembered he never heard the full story of how his parents met. He asked them about it once when they were all eating dinner together. His father coughed and almost choked on the piece of chicken he was chewing. His mother laughed and said she saved him from being trapped with some weirdo. His father shook his head and waved his finger for them to wait for him to recover and swallow the bite. He said, "Xavier wasn't that weird, he was just really into end-of-the-world stuff right before the world ended, which was not only convenient but damned prescient, too." Leo's mother rolled her eyes so only Leo could see and said that Xavier set up an underground bunker and wanted Leo's father to join him in his hole when everything fell apart. She touched his father's hand, and they shared a gentle smile. His father kissed his mother and said, "Thankfully, your mother distracted me and we made our way west, and eventually settled down here, otherwise you might not exist at all, so it worked out in the end."

About a year after his mother had passed, Leo finally asked his father how they met, but he only teared up and gave Leo a big hug before retreating to the garden, presumably to cry alone. His father mentioned Xavier one other time after that, crediting the man for teaching him their method of reusing and filtering their water. His father got very silent after mentioning him, and Leo never followed up with questions about the man or how his parents met after that. It seemed like a basic story Leo should know, but it was just too late for him to learn the truth. It was too late for a lot of things, and too late to feel bad about it, either.

Leo passed the ruined firetruck right by the highway exit he'd take to get downtown, the old red rusting itself into a dull red. Leo could hardly define what he rode on as a highway. It used to be a highway and over the years had turned into a green mat punctuated by bushes and the occasional tree sprouting through disintegrating car bodies discarded on the sides of the road.

Moving all those cars must have been a huge endeavor in the past, making room for whatever vehicles people thought necessary in a crisis. People just abandoned their cars, or perished inside, sick from the last pandemic, a plague on humanity. Based on the old shows and movies, Leo felt like they must've had it coming.

Leo pedaled down the ramp into darkness under another road that was too narrow and blooming with nature for him to use anymore. The darkness was his least favorite part of the journey. *You can never truly trust what you see in the light, and exponentially cannot trust what the darkness may hide.*

He pedaled fast to get through that section, relieved to come out the other side. Every time he made that journey it seemed like he'd emerged in an old growth, where leviathans of steel, concrete, and a few stubborn bits of reflective glass grew from the ivy and vines sprouting at their feet. It must've been magnificent to see the city used as intended, full of towering walls of shiny glass and busy people. It also must've been scary. The might of humans saying "Look upon my works ye mighty and despair." Or whatever Ozymandias said centuries before the rest of the world caught up with him.

Leo wheeled down Fourth Street, swerving around the nature that reclaimed the world. Much like Ozymandias, nature must've known what was coming, lying in wait all those years while people burned and tore it down, just waiting and more than eager to return the favor to those tiny, pesky creatures. That also became the path for those who survived, and more so for their children, hunkering down and biding their time, waiting for their chance to live. Leo wondered if the world would ever go back to what it had been before he was born. The more he mulled it over, the more he concluded that once entropy struck, it didn't stop, like uneating an apple or uncooking an egg. Much like Fourth Street, life was a one-way street.

Movement. As he passed the corner with the plum tree growing out of an old food cart, he caught something in his peripheral vision. He stopped peddling and let the momentum carry him forward as he searched, seeing a rotting lurker lying on the ground. It was an old, ruined zombie, staring at nothing, flaccidly lifting its arm. It didn't seem to look in Leo's direction, or notice him at all. Leo kept watch on its every non-move to the last second before rolling past the street corner. The lurker looked to be near its last stages of non-life. Aside from that morning, it had been so long since he'd seen a zombie he could almost forget they were still potentially everywhere, but he never truly forgot, just almost. It was the very human kind of wishful thinking that nothing could truly hurt them that led to society's great demise.

Two more blocks and he'd arrive at the farm, but the smell was already strong. An acidic tang filled the air, making it feel heavier; thicker. The building itself did not differ from the ones surrounding it, a multi-story office building that used to be flat glass and steel on all four sides straight up to the sky. The people who lived there now had converted it to a giant chicken farm. Leo had never been inside. They had made a simple pulley elevator outside the building to lift and lower supplies. The pulley topped out at the fourth floor. Leo assumed the first two or three floors were all blocked off to repel zombies and humans alike. It was the most likely thing to do; it's what Leo would have done if he had lived there. They must know they'd attract all sorts from the smell alone, not to mention the sound. There were hundreds of chickens inside, their errant clucks echoing around the buildings blocks away. They were a simple animal to breed and grow, and their farmers were kings in the area.

Leo parked his bike and called up to the building, "Caw caw!" It was a call his dad used. It must've been a way to call for someone's attention back in the day, or maybe he was making a joke about the chickens. It's how he let people know it was him before they could see him, Leo adopted it as his own. Like nature, old habits died hard.

Blake leaned out the open window on the fourth floor. He was older than Leo, maybe in his early fifties, hairless, and had an extra chin that moved a half second behind the rest of his face. He cocked his head, searching the street below for Leo, much like a chicken himself. "Oh hey, been waiting for you! You ready for me to send you down some?"

"Yep, cage is empty!"

Blake disappeared inside the building. It would take him a few minutes to get everything ready. Several rope bridges and catwalks connected the roof of the chicken farm to the surrounding buildings. Leo always wondered exactly how their operation worked. They must use the roofs to grow feed, which meant they must have a good water source and pump to get it all the way up there. Then what did they do with all the poop? Was it good fertilizer? The whole place smelled terrible from the ground. How bad must it smell to Blake and whoever else lived there?

Leo knew Blake had a boy, he'd seen him look down from a window on occasion. Leo tried saying hello once, then the kid popped his head back inside. Another time when Leo waved at him, the kid stared back for a solid minute, probably debating if he should wave, but a sound inside startled him and he again disappeared back inside.

Leo opened the back of the wire cage on top of his cart. He kept glancing down the street, assuring no zombies followed him or were attracted by the omnipresent clucking. He lifted a piece of wire mesh up that covered the bottom half, securing it with wire to the backsides of the cage. He pulled out a pair of well worn and holey leather gloves from the bottom.

The rope wiggled as Blake rotated the wench arm out over the street. The confused clucking of a few dozen chickens in the cage got louder as they swung out four stories above. After a moment, the cage descended as Blake lowered it. As it neared the ground Leo called up "Almost. Five feet. Two. We're good!"

Leo opened the top of the cage. This was his least favorite part. He put on the gloves and rolled his sleeves down to protect his arms. As he reached in the cage, the chickens pushed against each other, but there was no escape for them. He grabbed one with his right hand over the beak, left hand on the legs, lifted it up and put it in his bike cart. The chickens were deafening in Leo's ears. He scanned the street between each transfer. He fought the urge to rush and took his time with each one, ensuring he did not hurt them. He got them all in his cart and closed the mesh, securing it with wire, making sure the chickens couldn't escape their new cage. He unloaded several flats full of eggs lining the bottom of Blake's cage. He set them on the top mesh shelf of the cart, making sure they wouldn't rattle around too much. His tongue watered as he thought about tomorrow's breakfast.

"All right, all done!" Leo yelled.

Blake leaned out the window, having watched Leo load the chickens. "So. Tomorrow?"

"Yeah, tomorrow's the plan." Leo yelled.

"Good. Good." Blake nodded. "The usual, right?"

"Yup. The usual."

Leo looked up at Blake, who stared back. They stayed like that for a moment until Blake waved a goodbye. Leo waved back. Blake was an odd creature, even more awkward around people than Leo. Sure, Blake was reliable, but odd. Leo lifted the kickstand on the bike and straddled the seat, checking one last time for signs of danger. He said "alright" to himself, and started off down the street thinking *as weird as Blake is, how much stranger is the person who lives inside my next stop?*

It was a longer ride to Leo's next stop, made even longer by the confused clucking behind him, a dull din that crescendoed every time he hit a bump, which was almost every twenty feet. He assumed the roads must've been smooth, but decades of raw nature had eaten them, eroding them, declaring itself in every crack.

For millennia earth just existed, minding its own business, then some upstart genus cut it, burned it, drilled into it, filled the sky, ground, and water with poison, and for a hundred years (or longer depending on how one measures things), ruled supreme, paving over every inch, then over the course of a few years nature regained control. It broke the people, and it broke the pavement, eroding the buildings; they became monuments to a time that was an uncomfortable blink for the earth, and a fatal nanosecond for the humans who lived on it.

"Then what does that make right now?" Leo said aloud to the chickens. "If earth and nature returns to its dominance, is the time of humans over for good? Or is this the over-correction where we learn our lesson and come back to live in harmony with the world, if that's even possible?" He pointed to a crumbled grand central station. "Or is this just in our nature? Must we dominate as a species?"

The chickens clucked.

"I dunno. Maybe I'm just one shiver in the death throes of humanity. Man, that's depressing." Leo pedaled in silence, listening to the clucks echoing around him.

"You know, I've never seen this city, or the world, for that matter, as it was meant it to be. Sometimes, like now, I kinda wish I was alive then, or everyone else was alive now so I can understand. But you know, maybe the city never really was as they meant it to be in the first place. On the shows there's so much crime and violence, and homeless people. Was that really a thing?" He rode over a bump where a tree worked at uprooting the pavement. The chickens give a large, exasperated cluck. "Yeah, I guess I won't know for sure, but maybe cities were built for one thing, but became something else."

"Cluck."

"Yeah, like your cage." He passed over the middle of a bridge spanning a former railway. The sides surrounded by metal fencing, rusting and peeling away. "Or this cage. My cage."

As he neared the industrial district, he moved away from those thoughts. They wouldn't serve him there. He hated the area, full of large warehouses and vacant lots, like carcasses of dead giants, strewn about the fields of an ancient battle. He presumed it felt the same way back when there were people around, just noisier and smellier.

He approached the power plant from the east. Its entrance was on the west, so he had to pedal around the south side of the complex. The outside was a solid concrete wall, filled with patches, braced up in one spot and secured with metal beams welded into place. One good thing about whoever ran that place—which Leo still did not know his or her name and assumed he never would—is that they liked things clean. The streets were plant-free, an attempt to keep nature from encroaching too close to the building as protection both from cover for outsiders, and from destruction via the slow route of nature's way. Those streets were the last few smooth patches of road Leo had ever seen. That alone made whoever ran the power plant worthy of respect.

Steam rose from the stacks, billowing in the air, relaxing and dissipating into the sky. There was a constant low hiss surrounding the area, a byproduct of whatever process they used to create electricity. It was faint, but with nothing else going on in the world, it was noticeable.

Leo stopped at the outer gate, the first step in the process. He pushed the button, which buzzed someone inside the complex. He waited. After a few moments, the metal gate clanked and slid open. Leo walked his bike through the gate into an enclosed area, about twenty feet wide and twenty feet straight ahead to the next door, made of solid metal with a little slider at eye level that always remained closed. The gate behind him rattled as it closed, locking him in the square. He imagined it must be like a drawbridge for a castle. More than just for show, but still more than was necessary.

"Enter." A voice rattled through some hidden speaker, the

sound quality lessened over the years.

Leo took a deep breath and walked to the metal door in front of him, opening it. He'd done the same delivery hundreds of times, but it never stopped feeling ominous. It was a clever and well-designed conceit to protect whoever was inside. Nothing left to chance. Inside the door was a smaller room with a matching inner door, a semi-airlock between the outside world and the power plant fortress. A small cage sat in the middle of the room. Leo grabbed it and brought it outside to his bike. He unloaded half the chickens into their third cage for the day. They weren't any more or less happy about it. Leo placed the cage inside the metal room along with two dozen eggs. Happy to be finished, he closed the outer metal door.

After a moment, the door gave a sharp buzz and clang as it locked. He knew the door was locked from the click, but he never tried to test it. He'd thought about it, but figured it more prudent to not piss off the person who provides electricity to keep his refrigerator working and watch his TV at night. He'd gone without electricity for months at a time in the past for various reasons, but he still preferred having the convenience of electricity, especially when using his air conditioner in the summer months. *One thing humanity got right.*

Leo heard the inner door open and the chickens give an outburst of clucking as their cage was moved inside. A moment later the inner door gave a muffled clang as it closed. Another solid minute passed before the outer gate started rattling open. No fanfare or thank you, just a basic transaction. *Nothing wrong with an uncomplicated life.*

Leo pedaled out. It was late afternoon, and he had the hardest pedaling ahead to his last stop for the day.

CHAPTER THREE

It was all uphill. Up, up, and up block after block. The rotting industrial area gave way to tired and collapsed houses, then transitioned to what had always been a park area, but had since become wild. The smell of cow manure greeted Leo as he neared the stadium. He wanted to get inside before the sun dipped below the horizon.

Two rows of fences surround the stadium, put there in some past quarantine time, maintained and repaired over the years by the family who lived inside. They were both wire mesh, the outer gate sat eight to ten feet away from the inner gate, creating a safe distance for someone to walk in the middle, out of reach from anything reaching through either side. The inner fence was another six feet from the wood wall surrounding the stadium—an old baseball field. It fascinated Leo that in their busy lives, people would gather in such large numbers to watch other people play a game. So much effort put into building a cathedral to a long-lost sport. People could be funny sometimes.

Leo coasted to the outer fence gate and picked up the plastic cone and kazoo sitting there. He hummed a song into the kazoo inside the cone, amplifying it enough to be heard inside. He looked at the sunset across the former parking lot, pocked by small bushes.

Sarah ran around the corner to greet him. She was one of his oldest and dearest friends. They got on well the first time they met. Leo tried to do the math on how many years ago that might've been. He figured they'd known each other for at least twenty years, probably more. Back then he had had a huge crush on her, and he thought she might've crushed on him too at one point, but their passions never worked on the same schedule. Like two hands of a clock, they might've worked in tandem, but most of the time they pointed in different directions.

"Hey there, stranger!" Sarah exclaimed with her slight southern accent as she unlocked the inner fence. Leo smiled, surprised at how glad he was to see her. Her short sleeves put her strong arms on full display along with their dark tan from countless hours working in the sun. "Cutting it a little close today."

"Yeah, guess I took my sweet time, but I'm here now." They walked alongside each other to the outer gate, separated by the fence. The inner and outer gates were offset twenty feet apart as an added measure of security.

"Just in time to eat dinner, but not help make it." She grinned, focused on unwrapping the chain.

"I come bearing gifts." Leo gestured to the chickens, with a flourish.

"That's not nothing, I suppose." She looked up at him, the sunset reflected in her eyes as it neared the horizon's edge, giving them a depth that immobilized him. In a moment he became lost in her eyes, in the person behind them, the girl he met when he was just a boy, but with something else in there he couldn't find a word for, something nameless that reached out to him, drawing him deeper into the pool. He knew he was staring, but also felt there wasn't anything else in the world but the two of them. She smiled and looked down, removing the chain. "Did I miss anything good out there?"

Leo took a sharp breath in, shocked back to the moment by her question. "Not really, no. Just the usual. It's been pretty boring lately, actually, which I'm not complaining about."

"You'd complain more if you were stuck in here all day with my family. And the cows. At least you get to see things," she said wistfully.

"You have a great view from the roof."

"Nah, I mean up close. I imagine it's an enormous world out

there when you're not looking down on it."

"The world's a lot smaller than you might think." Leo's words landed in his stomach. Sometimes it seemed like he was living in a small corner of a much larger world, but where else could he go if there was no escape from the existential threat zombies imposed? They would always be more persistent than people, they were everywhere, and they would never suffer death, only a fate far worse.

Leo pushed his bike through the inner fence opening, and Sarah secured the chain. They walked together in silence, indulging in their own thoughts as the sun faded into the evening.

Years ago, before Leo ever met the Jacksons, they (or someone) had replaced the astroturf covering the baseball field with real soil and grass. The north side of the bleachers got the most sun and shone green with cornstalks in a step garden that stretched from the top of the stands to the field. The field was green and fenced off; cows pastured in one quarter of the grounds. It seemed the cows would eat at one section for a time while the other three sections grew. It was quite an operation, justifying the Jackson's large brood to help get all the work done. Next to the calves and heifers on the far side of the field sat a small run to hold the chickens Leo brought.

"Let's head down for dinner, the chickens can wait." Sarah said.

Leo set the kickstand on his bike. They walked towards the tunnel under the grandstand. Leo wiped his shirt with his hands to get off any dirt he might've gotten on his ride. Sarah laughed.

"What?" Leo said.

"Nothing. Just you, trying to look good."

"I just wanted to—you know—I don't wanna get dust in there or anything."

"Right."

Sounds of the family and scraping chairs echoed out into the field, the twins laughing at some inside joke between them, no doubt.

"Look at what the cat dragged in." Sharina said as she set a dish of mashed potatoes on the large table. She was the matriarch of the house and held firmly to her robust southern accent. A strong head, a strong body that fit in with the rest of the family, and an even stronger heart. "Come, give me a hug, you."

Leo went to Sharina's open arms. She had always been kind to him, and not just out of her self-professed southern hospitality. He realized years before that she grew fond of him shortly after his own mother's death, but he was also keenly aware of the fact that four out of their five children were girls, which he thought played a powerful part in her affection towards him. He knew he was a bit of a favorite, a fact Sarah had also been aware, and not-so-secretly jealous of.

The twins laughed and made fun of Leo behind their mother's back. They weren't actual twins, but born less than a year apart and affectionately referred to as "the twins." Leo overacted to how tightly Sharina squeezed him with a mock pained look on his face. The twins giggled.

"Let me look at you." Sharina said, holding Leo's shoulders and pulling him in front of her. "Oh my, aren't you gettin' older?"

Leo wasn't sure how old he actually was. He'd never had a reason to keep track of how long he'd been alive. In the very least, he knew he was a few years older than Sarah. He shrugged, adding "a few decades can do that."

"Is that all? You look a LOT older!" The youngest girl said.

"Shush Dinah." Sharina said with a glance. "Don't listen to her, Leo. The gray hairs in your beard make you look distinguished," she said with a pat and went back to the kitchen. "Grant. Grab the steaks and let's eat."

When Grant entered the room, everyone found their seats at the table. He had always been one of the strongest looking people Leo had ever known. Leo assumed he worked out besides all the labor he did around the farm. He wondered if it was a bit of an addiction to find muscle groups heretofore unknown to humanity, though most likely he used it as an escape from the rest of his family. Everyone needed time to themselves, and to counter his stadium full of women, Grant spent his time expanding his muscles, though he clearly encouraged all his children to be strong and at their peak.

Many years ago when the middle twins were the youngest in the family, one of them (Tina, who let everyone know she was the elder of the two) told Leo that Grant's father used to be a professional baseball player, when that was still a thing. That's most likely the primary reason they set up the farm on the field. Perhaps he had tried to escape the zombie outbreak in the early days, and a full-blown farm was just the inevitability in an uncertain world.

Leo loved listening to the Jacksons around the table. Grant did not have any discernible accent, and the children adopted Sharina's twang in varying degrees based on how much time they spent with her versus with their father.

Grant placed a large platter of thick steaks in the middle of the table nearest his seat at one end.

Dinah looked disgusted. "Ugh, again? Can't we have the chickens Leo brought?"

Sharina shushed her. "Dinah. Company."

Grant smiled at his youngest daughter, unaware how clear it was to everyone else that she was his favorite. "We will, honey, just not tonight. Right now Leo needs a steak. It's been some time since you've had one, I imagine."

"Oh, it has, and I'm looking forward to it."

"See?" Grant said straight to Dinah who harrumphed and crossed her arms, looking down at her empty plate.

At Grant's cue, they all held hands and bowed their heads. "Lord," Grant said, "we thank you for this food we have before us, thankful for the feast you provide, and the fit weather to grow the crops necessary to sustain us. We thank you for the opportunity to do our work today, and to celebrate your love at this table. And we thank you especially for Leo's safe journey here and the gifts he brings, and for the gifts we will send with him. We say this in your name. Amen."

"Amen," the family said in unison, then dug straight into scooping potatoes, beans, and steak onto their plates.

That was always a fascinating moment for Leo, one of the few times he could observe how a group of people not only interacted, but how life must've been in the before times. That frenetic clamor, mixed with love and annoyance, must have been what normal was like back then. He looked at Sarah, waiting patiently for her sister to finish scooping mashed potatoes so she could put some on her own plate and pass them on to her little brother, the only other male Jackson aside from their father. *Sometimes the world seems small*, Leo thought, *but it can be so much bigger in its smallness*. Leo attempted to recognize and enjoy the moment, but was interrupted by Tina, the elder of the twins pushing the platter of steaks inches from his face.

After dinner, the younger kids played in one of the old locker rooms converted into a bedroom. There were enough beds for twice as many children than they had, a sign of the hope Grant and Sharina carried for a large family, and a sign of the struggle that came with trying to make that dream a reality. There used to be two more children in the family, but they passed away years earlier from two separate incidences. One from a zombie attack outside the stadium, the other from an infected scratch, both reminders that no matter where you were, danger existed. The Jacksons had known the pain that came with those dangers. They'd also shown that no matter what, hope also exists.

It seemed to Leo that only the best people survived. He knew there were also a few in the world to look out for who only had their own interests in mind at any cost, but the bulk of humanity who had remained through the trials of time seemed to be those who were thankful and helpful, how his parents taught him to be. Those who helped became those who lived.

"Wanna try some of my new batch?" Grant said as he got up, continuing before Leo could respond. "It's an IPA, my best one yet, I think." He left, yelling from the other room. "Sarah, take him to the roof, I'll meet you up there."

Sarah gave a shrug that read *what are you gonna do* and rose with a nod, and led Leo outside to the field. They climbed up the steps on the south side of the stadium to the ladder at the top of the stands. "It's a little sharp-tasting if you ask me, but it's important to him, so make sure you look like you like it, okay?"

Leo gave a sharp laugh. "M'kay. Never really understood the stuff, always tasted bad to me."

"Yeah, that's how sane people like you and me think."

They climbed up the ladder to the roof, Sarah going first and flipping open the hatch. Leo looked up, watching her climb above him. A moment later he realized he was just staring at her butt through her jeans and looked at the wall in front of him, hoping she hadn't noticed, embarrassed at not knowing how long he'd been checking her out.

He joined Sarah on the roof and they walked towards the edge and sat down next to each other. The stars were out en force. The city itself looked like a black void devouring the night sky; a silhouette of nothingness, aside from a faint light coming from the window of another one of the city's residents. Leo tried to place whose light it was. He knew most of the inhabitants at least through hearsay if not having met them in person.

"You ever make it any farther?" Sarah's question snapped Leo's mind back to the rooftop.

"You mean, away from the city?"

"Yeah. You said you wanted to try. Maybe see some more natural nature." She glanced at him out of the side of her eye and looked back into the darkness.

"Not really, no. The devil that you know, and all." He'd forgotten that years earlier he wanted nothing more than to escape the city, throw everything away and start fresh somewhere, make his own life. "I dunno, that's an old dream. I got it all figured out here now."

After a moment, Sarah sighed, "Oh."

Leo looked at her. For the first time in years, he saw sadness on her face. It must've been there the whole time, growing in plain sight, but he'd missed it somehow. Perhaps he had the city figured out, but apparently not the people in it.

"You wanna get away, leave all this?"

Sarah raised an eyebrow at him. "You asking for company?"

Leo looked into her eyes. The sun was long gone, but a piece of it remained, reflecting at him, still. They searched each other's faces for answers. He felt the nameless thing he'd seen in her eyes inside his own mind. It had crossed over into him and taken root. It stubbornly remained nameless, which annoyed the crap out of him. He hated not knowing what it was, like an itch in the middle of his back he couldn't scratch no matter how much he twisted himself around.

The sound of footsteps on the ladder jolted them to both shift an extra inch away from each other, just like when they were younger. Some things died hard.

"I'm tellin' ya, I'm getting better with each batch. Grew the hops myself up on the scoreboard. Gets plenty of sun, and the wind rarely blows the smell towards the living quarters—Sharina just hates the smell." Grant handed three open bottles to the other two and harrumphed his way into sitting.

"She prefers the cow smell?" Leo asked.

"It's been with us so long she doesn't even notice it's there anymore." Sarah said, looking down.

"We can all be thankful for that." Grant said, grabbing his beer from Leo and clinking his bottle. "Well, except for you, I guess. You acclimatized to it yet?"

"It takes a while, but each time I do a run I know exactly how close I am and which way the wind's blowing."

"At least you have that." Sarah said and got up. "I'm getting tired, gonna head down and read."

"Oh, I thought you'd wanna—you know—keep our guest company? He's not here every day, you know, not like your books."

"I don't think either of us is going anywhere, anytime soon. Goodnight." Sarah kissed her father on the forehead and climbed down the stairs.

"Night, sweet pea." Grant yelled after her, then leaned toward Leo "She doesn't like my beer. She acts like she does, but I think she just didn't want to fake enjoying it. Sorry about that, my bad for trying." Grant sighed and looked off. "But how are you doing?"

"Oh, I'm good. You know me."

Grant nodded in silence. "Hey, weird question. I don't suppose you've seen any, I dunno, strange acting—you know—zombies?"

Leo scrunched up his face and turned to Grant. "What?"

"Oh, just checking. It sounds silly, but there was a guy on the road coming from the east. You know I like to sniff out new people, make sure nothing's up. Anyway, I headed in his direction and he hid—so he's seen some things. Obviously. I told him it's ok, I was unarmed—I wasn't, but you know. Anyway, I asked him where he was headed and he said away from whatever's going on behind him. Sounded like he was a traveler, never really settled down. You can never fully trust that type; but he asked if there was a rush of zombies here, I said it's been pretty dry on that front lately. He said to keep my eyes on the east, that something was spreading. Who knows though, right? Just words from some vagabond livin' on the road. Anyway, I made sure he kept going and didn't follow me back here. That was a few days ago. Haven't told Sharina or anyone, so you know, keep it to yourself. Just wondering if you might've seen anything. To be sure, you know?"

"Yeah, no, I get it." Leo said. "Can't say I've seen anything out of the ordinary. Like you said, it's been dry like that here lately."

"Well, that's good to hear." They both took swigs from their bottles. Grant's was deep and satisfying. Leo took a sip and swallowed as if it were a large pill. "Well, just keep your eyes out, okay? Just in case."

"Yeah, always." Leo hiccuped.

Grant looked to him. "It's good, huh?"

"Oh yeah, best I've had."

Grant smiled and looked off into the night.

Leo ran back over the day in his head, questioning whether he should've stopped and taken care of the zombie he saw earlier. *It would've been easy, just a wasted away corpse.* Not much of a threat and unlikely to be a trap, as he'd been down that street before and didn't know of any new people living in that area. Though it would've put him behind schedule and he had just barely arrived at the stadium before the sun set. Mulling it over, he took another sip of beer. It wasn't as bad the second time. It wasn't good, by any means. The sour aftertaste lingered much longer than he would wish on anyone; the same was true for Grant's warning from the stranger.

INTERLUDE ONE: SARAH

S arah couldn't sleep. Her body always woke up before her alarm, as if it knew when it was required to be fully functional and needed to warm up her systems first. That part of her body vexed her. She was annoyed with her body for a lot of things it did without consulting her first. She lay in bed a full hour before having to milk the cows. The sun wasn't even up yet, but her body didn't care. She rolled onto her side and stared at the wall, looking at the old paint slowly chipping away off the slats, showing its bare wood underbelly.

Is this to be my life, she wondered? Yes, the farm animals needed a regimented schedule, or they'd get mastitis or some other illness, but every day it felt more and more like she was the livestock penned up inside the stadium, a prisoner in the panopticon. The giant oval ring of the stadium reminded her more than a little of that giant prison, God at its center, always watching, or maybe ignoring her the times she wanted Him there the most.

Like the calves, she was born into her fate, unable to leave. She wondered if that was why Leo annoyed her so much the previous night, the fact he could come and go as he pleased and didn't even appreciate his freedom. She held the key to the gate, knew where it was, could open it any time and walk right out, which meant she was the real jailer in her scenario. She hated that thought more than all the others. She rolled over to look at the clock. Only one minute had passed when she was certain it had been at least fifteen. She grunted at the clock, indignant at time's cruel strokes.

What does it really matter? Sarah asked herself. *Every day is the same.* Wake up, milk cows, eat breakfast, do her chores, eat lunch, do more chores, milk cows, eat dinner, avoid her family, go to bed, repeat. *No*, she thought, *that's not fair.* Sometimes she really loved her family, loved playing games with them, it was just that they could get under her skin so bad and so fast sometimes. She rolled onto her back and did the math for the last time she'd been outside the complex. *How long ago had it been?* That she had to think about it so hard annoyed her to no end. *Maybe a year or so?* Technically, two weeks before she rotated the compost pile, which was outside the main walls, despite still being fenced in and shouldn't count, anyway. *So yeah, it's been a solid year since I've seen anything outside the stadium walls. That's depressing.*

She looked back at her clock. One more minute had passed. It just didn't seem right. Time must work differently inside the walls, like it was just as trapped as she was. She'd wasted her life there. She was surprised to find her hands had worked themselves into fists. She shot her arms up and slammed them down on the mattress, shooting her frustration into the bed. It helped a little, but she still felt the anger and frustration swimming around her chest. She got up and put on clothes.

The rest of the rooms were quiet. She was the only one up. She tip toed to the room where Leo slept, leaning into the doorframe. In the dim light she could discern the outline of his body under the covers, gently rising and falling as he breathed. He didn't know how lucky he had it. She wondered if he even appreciated his life, his freedom. The anger returned. She knew he was interested in her many years ago. It was so obvious then. She remembered being flattered but annoyed at the same time. Then when she came around and found herself wanting to try being with him, he'd gone cold. *Why?* Why couldn't he have felt the same way for her when she was ready? Had she become invisible, or merged with the rest of her family like they were one organism, which, she admitted, was not far from the truth.

They'd talked about leaving the city together. She was

disappointed that she'd ever given the idea actual weight. She knew it would never happen, she would never let herself out of her cage, and Leo was just as stuck in his ways as she was in hers. She left the doorway and moved down the hall to the kitchen.

Sarah filled the kettle and put it on the stove, then realized the fire was out by that hour. She didn't want to start a new one, so she sat on a stool along the counter separating the cooking side of the kitchen from the cleaning side. Sarah rested her head on the palms of her hands and stared off at nothing in particular, thinking how that's exactly where her life was going: nowhere in particular. She didn't know how long she'd been there when she jumped at the sound of a voice behind her.

"Mornin' sweet pea." Grant whispered. "Oh, sorry, didn't mean to scare you." He added after seeing her jump in shock. "You up early too?" She nodded.

He slid the stool next to her out and sat down, leaning his arm on the counter. "What's up?" He asked, "other than us, I mean." He chuckled at his joke. Sarah smiled out of politeness.

"Oh, nothing, just couldn't sleep." Sarah said, and turned away to get up, annoyed that her father could read her so well. *I wish I could hide.*

"Wait." Grant said, and ran his nails down Sarah's back. He'd done that since she was a child, it always seemed to relax her. She looked ahead, leaning her body against her father's hand. "You can always talk to me. I might not know the right thing to say, but I'm here for you. So's your mother. You know that, right?"

Sarah nodded and looked down. "I know." More mouthing the words than saying them.

"Life's hard sometimes. Your yoke is... not always light. Sometimes it's just heavy for no reason. I wish I could make things different for you," he shrugged "but we just gotta do the best with what we have, I suppose. Let go and let God."

Sarah appreciated her father's efforts and felt annoyed by them at the same time. She hated having so many conflicting feelings in her all the time. *Why can't anything be straight forward?* She smiled and nodded at her father. He pulled her in for a hug, wrapping his enormous arms around her. He was warm against her, his warmth enveloping her, then he patted her on the back, countering some of the warm feeling. They leaned apart. "Thank you. I know. Don't worry about me, I'm fine."

After a pause Grant said, "Ok."

Sarah knew he wasn't convinced. It irked her she couldn't just have her feelings in peace. "I was thinking I should rotate the compost today. It's about time, right?" She figured it was best to distract them both by focusing their minds on the day. *No use swimming in regret.*

"Yeah, that needs a doin'" Grant said. "I'll help you with that after breakfast."

"No thanks, I'll do it myself."

"I know you can, but... I'd just rather help is all. See how it's doin'."

"Dad. I can do it, I'm not a child anymore." Sarah's words hit both of them harder than she intended. When her father was her age, he was already a dad with children running around the farm. She wasn't a child, and never would be again. She was also running out of time to have a child of her own, she'd devoted her entire life to the farm, treating her siblings as ersatz children of her own. She wondered why she was cursed with being the oldest child. She knew her younger siblings weren't burdened by the same weight she had to carry every day. She was glad of that for them, and also jealous at the same time. *Again with the opposing feelings.*

"Sorry, sweet pea. I know you're a fully capable adult of your own." He gave a nod, then got up and made his way to prep the morning milking.

Sarah remained on the stool. She felt guilty for making her father feel bad. She knew he could only do his best, however limited that best may be. She shook her head, angry at her own thoughts. He was a great father and raised her and all her siblings to be strong, hard-working people, and her mom showed them all how to be strong inside and out. She really did have a special place on the farm.

The world outside the stadium could be dangerous, and her family worked hard to keep them all safe inside the walls. Yes, the paint was peeling from those walls, but they still kept them all safe. She rose and headed out the hallway, up the slight rise of the ramp as it opened onto the field. The brisk morning air surprised her with a pang of sadness. She knew every square inch of that place. She hated it and she also loved it, loved everything about it. It was the only home she'd ever known. She would have to learn to be okay having all her competing thoughts, because nothing would ever change, and she'd likely call the stadium home for the rest of her life.

CHAPTER FOUR

The next morning Leo woke up to the sounds of the family cleaning up after breakfast. He forgot how early they woke up there. They'd already milked the cows, made and eaten breakfast, and were heading out to do more chores. He never saw the point in being so active in a world that required very little, but it made them happy, so who was he to say otherwise?

The twins loaded two coolers with raw cow meat and ice while he ate a plate of cold eggs and hash browns Sharina put aside for him before the rest of the family devoured them. Leo thanked them for their hospitality.

The twins helped carry the coolers to his bike trailer after breakfast, each lugging opposite ends of the cooler, one at a time. One was meant for him to split with the chicken farm, the other intended for the power plant.

He wanted to say goodbye to Sarah specifically, but she was off working somewhere with Grant. He figured it was time for him to leave and he'd see her again his next time around, so he said goodbye to Sharina and the kids. The twins nodded their goodbyes and ran back inside. Dinah and Steven remained behind the inner fence while Sharina walked Leo through the middle section to the outer gate. After unlocking it, Sharina hugged Leo again. "We really are grateful for all you do." He shrugged it off and got on his bike. Before he could leave, Sharina held his elbow "Seriously. I'm relieved every time you're here, just to see you still alive, and nervous every time you ride away. That's just a mother's worry, though. It's never safe out there, even if it feels otherwise. Just do your best to stay safe, okay?"

"I will. And thank you. I mean it." Leo smiled at her. Sharina re-secured the gate and shooed the little ones back as they'd crept into the space between the fences, watching Leo ride off across the vacant, grass-filled parking lot.

Leo always felt a pang of sadness leaving the Jacksons, but it was even stronger that day. The first bit of his route was downhill, so while he didn't have to focus on pedaling, he had to be mindful of braking as the cart behind him had little interest in stopping on any schedule, especially loaded with meat and ice.

Even though he rode the same stretch he had traveled the previous day, it always seemed different going south than it did north. The previous day he had faced away from the industrial district and moved through wilting houses towards the slightly more pure nature, ending at the stadium surrounded by its large, flat lot, a reverse moat. In contrast, his return route was a quick zip past the open park and straight into a thicket of houses mired in rot and mildew. The northern faces decomposed first as the things that ate houses avoided the brighter, sunnier sides, preferring the dark and the damp. All the houses looked like they were covered with infected, rotting skin when viewed going south. That view abruptly gave way to the metal and concrete bones of the industrial area, as if Leo was traveling deeper into a corpse, a vivisection of the dying city.

Leo could see steam rising ahead as he approached the power plant, like a giant beast slumbered somewhere inside, its fiery breath warning others to keep their distance. He pulled up to the front gate and went through the process. Wait. Go through gate. Wait. Open door, drop cooler of meat. Wait. Leave through gate.

Leo had lost his curiosity about who ran the mechanics of that place. It didn't matter. Someone was there. That someone did their job so he could do his and they could all continue to enjoy the miracle of electricity, a rather novel treat in the current world. For centuries, millennia even, humans had lived without it, then in a blip it became a necessity. Everything required electricity, just as life required oxygen. People thought they couldn't go without it. Turned out most of them were right. Even Leo preferred to not go without electricity, but everyone alive in the world at one point was certain they could if they had to, because at points in their lives, they absolutely had to. There was a comfort in knowing he could do something he really hated if he had to.

Normally after his stop at the power plant he made his final delivery back at the chicken farm, but the thought of the lurker zombie he'd seen, mixed with Grant's words, had combined into strange images in his dreams the previous night that lingered in his mind. Instead of going straight to Blake and the chicken farm, he headed a couple of blocks south to where he had seen the zombie. He figured it couldn't hurt to be certain and just take it out of its misery. Nobody would complain about one less living corpse lying around.

The streets seemed quieter to him. He told himself it was because he was free of the incessant clucking, but part of his mind refused to listen. He tensed, his hairs ready to jump straight up at a moment's notice. He checked every street, but it was all clear as far as he could see. He slowed down a few blocks away from where he'd seen the lurker the day before as an added bit of precaution—partly why he was still alive. He coasted to a stop in the intersection. Nothing. *He had seen it there before, right?* In the past, something he thought he'd seen had in fact just been his mind connecting dots that weren't there. *No, I definitely saw it, it wasn't some waking dream.* He waited for a solid minute, just listening. Nothing but occasional drips from somewhere inside one of the structures. Nothing unusual.

He debated with himself for another few minutes about whether he should just finish his delivery. He could still get home with plenty of time before sunset, but would the thought he had missed something keep eating at his brain instead of allowing him to sleep that night? *Crap,* he thought, *I'm here, might as well check it out.*

Leo left his bike in the middle of the intersection. *Not like anybody will come around, anyway.* He pulled out a wooden stick secured to the down tube of his bike in case of emergencies. Another reason he was still alive. He crept, taking one step, waited, listened, then took another down the street. It nagged at him that by his assessment, the thing shouldn't have been able to walk, but somehow it had moved in the last twenty-four hours.

He'd been down that street a year or two before. One of the last few times he had explored outside his normal route. He used to do that often. That street was where he found his bike, in fact, chained and neglected inside the back end of an old restaurant, Chinese food, from what he could piece together. The tires were flat, but the frame and seat were great.

In the years since, he'd only traveled fewer, more trodden streets. Fewer every year as they'd grown too uneven for his trailer, covered in nature, hiding their secrets deeper in the shadows. He'd watched it happen to that very street. He walked down the center to give himself as many options for egress as possible. The sidewalk trees had overgrown their boundaries, uprooting the sidewalks themselves. Several had long rotted away and toppled over, providing a footing for other bushes and trees to claim their own spaces, stretching further out into the street.

Leo neared the halfway point down the block where he'd seen the thing. The only sign anything had even been nearby was a single spot where vines hung straight down, knocked from their connections when something moved through them. He couldn't tell if that had happened in the last hour, or the last month.

Leo kept glancing to both sides, checking behind him every few steps. He held his stick close and at the ready, one end sharpened to use as a spear if need be, which had been the case on several occasions.

His search brought him to the far end of the block, and still no sign. That was more disconcerting for him than finding and dispatching several lurkers. He walked into the cross street and paused again, looking all around, but nothing pinged him as out of place. His bike looked so far away through the overgrowth. *Might as well scout another block or two to be safe.* He knew his brain would cling to certain ideas, especially disappearing zombies, so it was best to shake those thoughts loose.

He walked down the cross street in the general direction of

the chicken farm. He felt better going in that direction. Even though the farm was still several blocks away, he was at the minimum heading towards something more familiar.

He wondered when he'd grown so averse to new things? He enjoyed exploring when he was younger, but then again, he was also less afraid of everything that could easily have killed him. By all rights he should've died several times, but for whatever reason, he'd lived when so many others had not. Maybe he lived alone for too long and the voices of those he lost filled his head, supplanting his own mind. Then again, Sarah seemed just as troubled as him, and she lived with other people, perhaps too many people. Maybe their voices overtook her mind just as much as the ones filling Leo's head.

A sound came from the building just to his right. Leo froze. The hairs on his neck shot straight up, making good on their earlier promise. A faint scratching, then nothing. The building looked like it used to be something upscale. Not quite an apartment. He couldn't place what it may have been half a century earlier. The glass remained mostly intact, which was impressive for such large windows. He edged towards the front door and tried peering in through the glass, but it was too coated in grime. A dim light shone deep inside, perhaps from a skylight or caved-in ceiling. He looked around him on the street, still nothing. *Might as well explore. Either that or let the vines grow over me.*

The door was locked. That wasn't an anomaly, but the fact that nobody had broken it open compelled him inside, to discover the untouched treasures that lay waiting beyond the door.

It would be a shame to just break a window. He could kick in the door, but it was solid wood, which would make the effort more difficult and far noisier than he deemed comfortable. There were no fire escape ladders to climb up, but there was a rusting light pole that had fallen over into one of the second-story windows, perhaps years before by the look of the vines clutching the fallen pole as if they were slowly pulling it down, integrating it back into the earth itself.

The pole had tipped over from the rusted-out base. Leo pushed at it with his foot, satisfied it was steady enough to climb. He slid his wood stick in the back of his pants to free his hands. He started up the top of the light pole, wrapping his hands around the underside to catch himself in case it gave way. He knew it wasn't the smartest thing he could do at that moment, but the chance to see inside a potentially untouched building overruled that voice in his head.

He wondered how he had missed the building before. He was certain he'd been down the adjacent street years ago. Perhaps there were a few zombies lurking near the front back then. They used to be numerous. He was thankful that even zombies couldn't outlast entropy, the great inevitability.

He'd never done a thorough search of the city, block by block. He remembered why he hadn't seen the building before, an older man with a lot of guns used to live nearby. He wanted his space and was very open about letting people know it. *Where did he live again? Somewhere along this street. A few blocks down? Oh well,* Leo thought, that man was surely gone, and whatever magicked the building into solitude over the years had worked well. Until that moment, anyway.

Leo was almost up to the window. He could tell the pole had rusted from the inside out and the top concerned him the most as it was much thinner. He was about fifteen feet off the ground when it occurred to him. Not high enough a fall would kill him, but he'd known others who died from smaller falls and the infections that followed injuries.

Leo took his time. He tapped on the pole to hear how hollow it sounded. He felt whatever previously held the pole in place loosen as it rocked in response to Leo's corrective leanings. The rocking concerned him. He moved forward, gripping his hands tightly around the pole the last few feet as he neared the window. He couldn't just grab the sill as broken shards of glass lined its perimeter, then he realized the pole was precariously resting on only an inch or two of rust against the brick window sill. As he moved, it slid even closer toward the edge.

"Well, crap." Leo whispered to himself, but it sounded much louder in his ears against the relative silence surrounding him. He took a deep breath. He reached his right hand to the inside of the windowsill, beyond several shorter shards of glass, like teeth waiting to dig deep into whoever dared enter its maw. The inside ledge was solid. He moved his left arm on the outside ledge, noticing the pole hasten its course to the very edge of the sill. He brought his right knee up to rest on the edge, a harder stretch than he wanted. He pushed against the pole with his left foot to get his right knee high enough. That push was the last straw for the pole, which gave a sharp metallic scrape as it let go of the ledge and fell in an arc down the front of the building, leaving Leo perched on the ledge two stories up. The pole landed with a hollow clang, bounced, and sounded again a final death clang.

Leo had enough adrenalin and experience to moderate the alarm bells in his head. He gingerly took his left leg and lifted it up over the edge, kicking in a glass shard on the bottom corner of the window to avoid the potential of cutting his leg as he got his foot through the space and into the room. He shifted his weight to his half inside the window and pushed his right knee up and over the rest of the broken glass, landing on the floor just inside. He took another deep breath and closed his eyes, focusing on his pulse. He breathed slowly and deeply, slowing his pulse to a comfortable resting rate. He wanted to be alert, but not stupid.

Leo opened his eyes and turned to assess the interior space. It looked like it had been an office of some sort. The focus of the room was a single enormous desk adorned with long dead electronics. A rolling chair sat on one side, a pair of static chairs on the other. Books and framed certificates covered most of the walls. It must have been someone's law office. *What an interesting profession,* he thought. *Fighting wars with words.* Leo wondered how the former owner of the office managed when the pandemics hit, if words were enough to help them. The owner of that office must've done well, carried whoever it had been through the last of the illnesses before the zombies hit and everything fell, otherwise someone would've looted it for sure.

It was hard for Leo to not analyze and piece together a life forensically. He'd seen a lot, and sometimes the stories he constructed in his head about people who died before he was even born were sadder than those of the people he'd known and loved. Perhaps they were just easier to let in and feel, which made them hurt more because if he let himself feel the same way about those he'd loved and lost, they could turn into vines and pull him down into the ground.

He walked to the door and pushed it open, scraping against the detritus on the floor. His eyes widened at the beauty of it all. The entire center of the building was an atrium, open three stories from the ground floor up to a domed skylight on the roof. In the center grew a glorious tree, stretching its fingers through the broken panes of glass in the ceiling. He faced the second-floor balcony which stretched around the entire atrium, a few spots blocked by branches from the overgrown tree. As he walked around the loop, he realized the tree itself was full of apples. He picked one and marveled at it.

More than the tree, the walls made Leo's heart jump. They were lined with books. An entire library of books around the second and third floors surrounded the tree-filled atrium. He wished he had discovered the place sooner. He moved a branch to the side to walk past it, then he heard rustling in the room ahead. He froze. The door was open. He reached behind him and pulled the wood stick out, ready to defend himself. A few more small sounds came from the room, followed by more silence.

Leo ducked down under a branch and moved forward. He neared the doorway the sounds came from. He wasn't the first to discover the place. He grasped the stick with both hands, sharp side out, ready to attack. He peeked around the door into part of the room but saw nothing. He brought his head back, took a moment, and pivoted on his left foot, facing the open doorway. Very little light made it through the black window slats that survived. It appeared to be another office, much like the one he'd entered.

There—he saw movement on the desk. Two small eyes looked back at him, too small to be a person, and definitely not a zombie. As his eyes adjusted, he realized it was a cat. It had jumped on the desk and was licking its own butt when he noticed Leo and lifted its head. They stared at each other.

"Hey there." Leo said, relaxing. The cat did not change its expression. "Did you get in here the same way I did?" The cat meowed at him. "Well, I have some bad news for you, then." Leo took a step forward, and the cat jumped up and hissed. "Ok, I got it. I'll leave you be." He backed out of the room. The cat relaxed the arch in its back. "You remind me of someone else who used to live around here." Leo stepped back onto the balcony. His gaze shifted to the rows and rows of books in front of him. *This would be a good day.*

He was running out of time if he wanted to finish his delivery and get back home before dark, but there were so many books to look at. He reasoned it had been extra slow zombie-wise of late, so why not peruse the library and indoor orchard? He plucked another apple off a branch near his feet, red and shiny. He rubbed it on his shirt and held it up, the color brilliant in the dim light. He took a bite. Sweet and crisp, exactly how he imagined it to be. "You don't know what you're missing." He said over his shoulder to the cat, who pretended not to hear him.

The books had strange names. "The Common Legal Past of Europe, 1000-1800". "Transgender Employment Experiences: Gendered Perceptions and the Law". "Trying Leviathan: The Nineteenth-Century New York Court Case That Put the Whale on Trial and Challenged the Order of Nature". All law books. Made sense, what with it being an attorney's office. Not exactly pertinent to Leo's world. He figured odds were low someone wanted to put a transgendered whale on trial in ancient Europe, but he hoped to find something interesting in the mix.

Leo made his way down one of the two staircases that curved around the walls, to the grand lobby on the ground floor. They must've framed the tree nicely when it was small. The architect most likely hoped to invoke a deeper meaning about an apple and a tree and knowledge, though the tree had stretched up beyond its confines through the glass domed ceiling. *There's probably an even better analogy in that,* Leo thought to himself, then froze when he saw a long since mummified corpse on the floor in front of him, lying prone under the tree.

Leo neared it for a closer look. Its legs and arms were broken. Its skull probably was too, but he didn't feel the urge to roll the skeleton over to confirm his suspicions. He looked up through the branches. One hole in the glass dome was right above him, but it didn't appear to be broken by the branches. The guy most likely fell through the dome, straight to his death. *What a crappy way to go. Unless he intended to die, then it was still a pretty crappy way to go.*

Leo looked at his half-eaten apple. His appetite had made an Irish goodbye. He put his stick back in his pants and grabbed a few more apples from the lower branches for future use, and walked towards the front door since his way in was no longer an option.

There was a lobby desk just off from the door, and on it a set of keys. He thought the odds weren't good they'd be for the door, but he grabbed them in his free hand while using his other arm as an apple basket. He unlocked the front door. It didn't budge, so he gave it a shove with his shoulder. The door opened with a sharp crack, breaking loose everything that had grown, expecting the door to never open again.

The sun was already lower than he liked, but he had some apples and somewhere to explore again soon, so he was ok. He pushed the door the rest of the way open and checked the street out front. Still clear. The sound from the light pole falling hadn't attracted unwanted visitors, so that was good. Leo pushed the door closed again. He took the key in his hand and tried to put it in the lock. It fit. It turned. "Nice!" He said to no one in particular. He found a nice little secret clubhouse, or tree-house. He hadn't felt that good in a while. He skipped down the steps and speed-walked to the side street, back to his bike.

He turned the corner, and a shot of adrenaline turned his follicles hot. Inches in front of him stood a zombie—the lurker he had forgotten he was searching for. At the moment he froze, it turned to face him, recognition of a warm body flooded into its otherwise cloudy dead eyes.

It was an affront to Leo that even when a zombie was turning into mush, it could still move and even walk. Before he could finish the thought, Leo turned in a snap, half the apples flying to the side from his left arm as he reached behind his back with his right arm. The zombie lunged at him, but it fell forward instead, its arms catching Leo's feet. Leo fell face-first to the ground, released the remaining apples, and threw the stick to catch himself with his hands. A sharp pain bolted through his right wrist as he hit the ground. He rolled over on his back to see the zombie crawling straight at his legs. He kicked at its face, dislocating its jaw, enraging it more than deterring the thing.

Leo kicked again, releasing the zombie's grasp on his pant leg. Leo scrambled away, but his right wrist gave him another shot of pain, which made his right arm recoil. He scrambled on his butt, feet, and left arm. He got just far enough away to push himself up and run to grab his stick. The zombie continued crawling at him like an angry alligator. Leo lifted the stick over his head and brought it down with all his weight, slamming the zombie's head to the ground as it slid off the top, scraping the skin from the bone. The zombie lunged forward again. Leo jumped up and came down hard on the partially de-gloved zombie skull, crushing it with a satisfying crack and disgusting squish.

It slumped to the ground in a pile.

Anger, pain, and relief chased each other throughout his body like children giddily playing tag with his emotions. He lifted his foot out of the dark, crimson slime, which clung to his shoe.

Another pang shot through his wrist. He held his arm up and worked his wrist. It wasn't broken, but he'd given it a nasty sprain. Just a fraction of whatever the guy inside had suffered, but enough to know he wasn't a fan.

Idiot. He thought to himself. *That's what happens when you rush. You get sloppy.* He looked at his wood stick. He'd have to sharpen it, but that could wait. He looked at the apples on the ground, all bruised. *What a waste,* he thought. *Best to finish the delivery and just go home.* He took his time back down the street, swiveling his head every which way. He was done with surprises for the day. Halfway down he looked ahead and noticed something, the lack of something. His bike and trailer were gone. "What the Hell?" He yelled.

He walked down the street faster than he knew he should. His body wanted to run, and his brain kept telling him to take his time. That resulted in a variable speed of run, walk, run, walk. Leo got to the intersection and looked around. Nothing. *Nothing!* His mind screamed. "Where the hell is my damn bike?"

His mind raced. Everyone in the city knew that was his bike. His trailer. They'd seen him. They'd all seen him at one point or another. Nobody would've taken it, because where would they ride it without other people knowing it was his? He kept people happy in the city. He was *the* delivery guy. *The best delivery guy around!* "What the ever living crap?" He said. "Seriously!"

He stood there perplexed for a solid minute, trying to work out what could've happened. Should he have hidden his bike or taken it down the alley with him? *Seriously, it's not like whoever took it could get away with it—literally.* Then he noticed the shadows on the ground from the buildings. It was late. He'd have to walk the entire night if he wanted to get back to his apartment. That wasn't an option. Neither was going to the chicken farmer. Every interaction he had with Blake was transactional, and he couldn't show up without the meat and ask to stay the night. He didn't even know if there was a way for him to get up to the building if he wanted.

He looked down the street behind him and shivered.

Leo shook his head. He cradled his wrist in his left arm. It was already swelling. He cursed and thought to himself, *this was supposed to be a good day.*

CHAPTER FIVE

Leo opened the door to the lawyer's office and slumped inside, locking the door behind him. The place felt different. It had been so full of promise just a few minutes earlier. Now it had a petrified corpse right in the middle, and a dead zombie just outside. Deflated, and cradling his wrist, Leo climb back upstairs, hoping to find something to keep him warm so he could sleep for the night.

Apparently individual lawyer's offices were all the same; a big impressive-looking desk, what they probably considered an impressive-looking chair behind it, and a couple of simpler, smaller chairs on the other side, a wall of books as evidence they were well read, and another wall with various pieces of framed paper showing how legitimate that person should seem. The only room that varied from that pattern was the last office on the far end of the building. It was larger than the rest, and it had a couch! The stuffing had been pulled out long ago by rats, but some cushion fabric remained. It could at least function as the bottom of a makeshift mattress, or a blanket, depending on how desperate Leo found himself in a half hour's time.

He had not yet ventured up to the third floor. The sun was almost gone, and the light with it by that point. He had to find something soon, or it would be a much colder, longer night than he wanted it to be.

He plodded up the curved stairs. Halfway, a step gave out under him, but he reacted quickly enough to jump up a step and not jank his leg in the opening. He wondered if anything was going to work in his favor. He made it up to the third floor and checked all the offices, finding them functionally identical to the ones on the floor below aside from a couple of rooms filled floor to ceiling with filing cabinets, all full of important documents that meant nothing anymore. He preferred not to attempt starting a fire inside based on the day's luck.

In the second to last office he found the desk moved aside and two rather old camping mats sitting next to each other on the floor. Someone had used the room as a home base long ago. He assumed it had been the guy on the lobby floor. *Perhaps he hadn't fallen through the skylight and just jumped off the balcony in a fit of hopelessness. Either way, he left some nice mats to sleep on.* Remnants of food and bottled water filled another corner. "Finally," Leo said, looking towards the ledge to the body on the floor below and shouted, "thank you!"

Leo checked the last office and found more supplies. From the looks of things, that guy had planned to stay there a long time, and made it about a month based on the pile of rusted, empty cans in the corner. They were hard to discern from the unused cans as most of those had exploded from botulism, or whatever happens to things decades past their expiration dates. Nothing left for Leo to eat other than apples, which he was fine with for the moment.

He spotted two suitcases against the wall. One was open, its innards torn apart by rats or birds, the other remained clasped tight. He opened it to find several shirts and pants that looked to still be in excellent condition. It was rare to find original clothes without stains and holes he needed to patch. Leo was thrilled with that surprise.

He traded out his old clothes for some new ones. They felt luxurious against his skin. He sat on the third story balcony ledge facing the tree, plucked a couple of apples, and ate his dinner in silence. The cat sat in the open doorway below, just at the edge of Leo's line of sight, watching him as he ate.

Leo went to bed early, using clothes as a blanket in preference to the mildewed cushion covers, and doubled up the mats for extra padding. He lay, staring at the ceiling and felt his pulse in his swollen wrist.

He'd heal, but it would be an annoying day or two in the meantime.

His mind kept spinning out on who might've taken his bike. It surprised him how angry, hurt, and just confused he was about the unexpected loss. He always thought of it as his bike, but now that it was gone he really knew how much his bike it had become. It's what brought him out into the world, allowed him to be useful, and keep everyone alive and the system working. *Who would take it? Could it have been that new guy Grant saw? Possibly. Though even he should've known a bike that well maintained had to belong to someone and not just sat there in good working condition for fifty years.* It occurred to him that whoever found it might've assumed its owner had been attacked by zombies. While that person would have been technically correct, he could not forgive them for taking his Schwinn.

And the cart! His father built that cart bespoke for his needs. *Man, all that time and effort, just gone.* He had left it in plain sight, but not a single person in the city he knew about would dare take his bike. He rolled over, trying to escape falling down that rabbit hole of a shame spiral. He'd have to use his older bike, or find something else before his next trip. Even more pressing and painful was the realization that before replacing it, he'd have to walk all the way home.

He lay there quietly for a few minutes, trying to push down the concerned thoughts, but his mind was very determined to cling firmly to them. *Also, why were there two mats?* Did his friend on the ground have another friend? *If so, where was that person's body, or what had that person become?* Leo struggled to get comfortable. He thought the two mats might be too soft for him to sleep on.

He got up and pulled the bottom mat from under his makeshift bed. He lay back down, piling the clothes back on top of him to keep warm through the night. He settled his mind once again. All that remained was the loudening pulse in his swollen wrist.

He drifted to sleep, reminding himself that today was supposed to be a good day. *Maybe tomorrow something will actually work right.*

Leo woke in the middle of the night to something crawling on him. He froze as the tiny steps moved up his chest. He squinted. In the little light coming through the window, he realized it was the cat. It sniffed him as it made its way toward his face. Leo just stared, unsure how to react. The cat pawed at him through the clothes, turned around, and settled down on his chest, declaring it home for the night. Leo didn't protest and welcomed the extra warmth and figured he didn't want to piss off a creature with claws inches from his face.

Somewhere between minutes or hours later, he awoke to a wet gnawing sound in his ear. He jumped and reached for his stick, which he placed right by the pad to defend against zombies, then realized in the pre-dawn light that the sound at his ear was again the cat who jumped back and hiss-screamed at the shock of Leo's sudden movement against him, then ran out of the room. Leo felt the side of his head; his ear was wet. He looked at his hand and was relieved to see it wasn't blood, but drool. The cat had been sucking on his ear. *Man,* Leo thought to himself, *that cat must be so deprived of contact.* He looked around the empty room and realized how much he and the cat had in common.

Leo's heart beat both in his chest and his wrist as he lay back down, determined to get some rest before the sun taunted him to rise and actually achieve something.

He was in the light dream state imagining himself on a roof looking across a dense forest when the cat nudged his arm, bringing him back to the cold room. Leo lifted the shirt covering that part of his body and the cat crawled under, lying its cold body next to Leo's stomach. He figured if the cat would not bring up the whole ear thing, neither would he. He drifted back to sleep into some other dream he soon forgot.

He woke up about an hour after the sun. The previous day had been long, and the night even longer. He reached down to his side to find the cat was gone. He looked around the room and saw no sign of it anywhere. He figured it was done with his warm body for the time being. He'd served his purpose.

His wrist reminded him about the previous day's mistakes when he momentarily put his weight on it while getting up. He winced and remembered his stupidity anew. His brain began rattling through every mistake he ever made, starting with rushing around the corner straight into that zombie. He'd gotten lazy. The world had been easy on him the last couple of years and he'd gotten soft. It almost killed him. *Never again.*

He rose and looked out the window. It was a marvelous view of the city, building tops mixed with vines and treetops. A strangled jungle of curves and angles.

He walked to the hallway and grabbed another apple from a nearby branch. It made little sense to him that a building like that would have a fruit-bearing tree. *Wouldn't it have made a mess back in the day and required a lot of upkeep and cleaning? Or maybe there was another tree in its place and someone planted this one after things turned, perhaps by his friend on the floor below. Or perhaps that guy had brought apples with him and just tossed a core on the soil, and the apple took advantage of the situation.* Impossible to be certain of the truth.

Leo wandered around the third floor, looking at the books and art lining the walls. It looked much better in the daylight, more regal. That, or now that he wasn't moving through it looking for a good place to sleep, he could appreciate the space. On the far end, he walked up another flight of stairs that terminated at a closed door to the roof.

The door looked bent in odd places. Not rusted, but bent. He turned the handle, and much like the front door, it didn't want to budge. Leo put his shoulder into it and pushed. It was tight. He pushed again with more force and the door screeched open. Once outside he could see why. Someone had beaten it from the outside. Maybe his friend trapped a zombie up there, possibly a zombie made of whoever shared his second sleeping mat who had been bitten and turned at some point. The marks on the door didn't look like random zombie marks, though. It had been hit near the handle, and the corners were bent from attempts at prying them open. Someone wanted desperately to get in.

Leo walked towards the dome structure. Tree branches reached up through the rusted metal frame of the huge dome skylight. He walked around it towards the far side where a significant amount of glass remained, save the missing pane he spotted from below. As he edged around the last branch to the far side of the dome, he found another surprise. A small decayed body lying at the edge of the broken glass opening. A child. The man did have a companion, his son. That explained why there were so many supplies, and who the other luggage must have belonged to. Rats had torn all the child's clothes to shreds long ago, as had nature done to the remains.

Leo peeked down through the hole in the skylight. It was right above the body on the floor. He moseyed to the edge of the building and walked the perimeter as he was accustomed to do at his apartment complex. No fire escapes, ladders, or other means to get down. The door he'd come through was the only way up or down. A gust of wind blew from the west, followed by a loud clang that shocked Leo. He turned to the roof door, realizing the breeze must've caught it, and slammed it shut. As the clang reverberated, Leo ran to the door. He turned the handle and yelled as he realized exactly what had happened to his new dead friends.

The door automatically locked when closed. The father and son had gone to the roof, much like he'd done with his own father, to watch the sunset. Then they got some terrible news. The dad probably thought the only way back inside would be through the skylight, maybe even thought he could jump to the third floor, but he missed. Leo felt light-headed and fell butt first to the roof. *How long had the child been up here after that? Had the father died on impact or did he live a while longer, knowing his son was alone on the roof yelling down to him?* The child hadn't moved far from the broken glass his dad fell through.

Leo looked at the door. Banging on it was useless, as demonstrated by the dead family. He wished he'd brought his stick with him. He might have been able to use it to pry the door open, but he left it downstairs right after telling himself he would be more cautious going forward. Leo shook his head at himself, *perfect. Just perfect.*

He lay down on his back and stared up at the clouds. *What a crap start to the day. Yesterday sucked so badly, it overflowed into today.* Leo laughed. *How ridiculous.* He'd made it almost thirty years in the zombie apocalypse, *or was it closer to forty? Hard to say.* Either way, he got trapped on the same roof those people trapped themselves on all that time ago. The child had most likely died a decade before Leo was even born, and now they shared the same fate. Leo watched a cloud above him imperceptibly shift its form over the course of a few minutes.

Leo sat up. "Unless..." He looked at the dome. "Maybe that dead guy had a good idea, just too early." Leo approached the dome. He knelt and grabbed one of the branches sticking through the hole, shaking it. It was thin, but not far below the rooftop was a larger branch that should be able to support his weight. He got up and looked through a broken pane of glass at the rotten corpse below. "I'll be down to join you one way or another."

Leo stepped back and reassessed the roof. No way down the sides, and the door was still a non-starter. *Yep, the dome's the only way back inside.* A few years ago he used to carry a length of rope with him everywhere in case of emergencies, but he never found a good use for it in the year and a half he lugged it with him, so he just stopped bringing it. Past Leo must be shaking his head at present Leo.

He edged back to the tree poking through the dome. The floor looked much farther away than he wanted. He figured he made several mistakes in the past twenty-four hours, so by that point he'd surely earned a good turn. The branches—more like twigs at his level, forked together a few feet below, but he was sure it was still too thin there to hold his weight. He'd probably have to fall a good ten feet below the roof before hitting a branch big enough to support him. The more he strategized his best approach, the worse his odds seemed.

The cat strode to the edge of the third-floor balcony and sat down, looking up at him.

"Have any better ideas?" He yelled down to it.

The cat said nothing.

"Yeah, me neither." He analyzed the tree for the best plan of attack. He swept away the fragments of broken glass on the rim with his foot and sat on the edge with his feet dangling through the skylight. He moved the tops of the branches out of his face to get a better view below. He was at the best spot he could manage. He turned around on his belly and edged his legs further into the void below him. He rested there a moment and took a breath, regretting ever going up to the roof, regretting coming back to check out the zombie in the first place. If he just let it be, he'd be home right now with his bike and trailer instead of ready to jump off a building. Curiosity might kill him *and* the cat, assuming it didn't have another way out of the building it wasn't telling him about.

Leo crawled backwards on his arms, holding his weight on his elbows as he leaned back to look down, making sure he was above the branch he wanted to hit. Not that he wanted to hit *anything*, but a branch was a much better option than what his friend three stories down landed on. He moved one hand to the edge. He slid down so his other hand could grasp the edge, leaving his entire body dangling from his hands three stories above the very hard floor. He looked down again to check the branches. The drop somehow looked farther than when he stood on the edge, just a few feet higher. *Perspective can be a funny thing.*

Leo kicked his legs forward and backwards to add a swing to his body that would theoretically allow him to fall closer to the center of the tree. He swung a few times, then he let go.

The top leaves slapped him in the face. Time and space shifted in the fall, making him feel not like he was falling as much as the tree was rushing up fast to meet him. The crotch of the top branches caught him on his left ankle first. Pain shot through his leg, but even in that state where time stretched out in front of him, he did not have a moment to consider it. He swung his arms, attempting to grasp the nearest branch. In a matter of what was actually just a second, but felt much longer, he found himself hugging the top branch with his arms and legs. He made it. That was when his ankle told him it was unhappy with his choices. His wrist agreed. They had a heated discussion back and forth, telling Leo he should make better choices. He pushed the pain out of his mind and shimmied his way to the next branch down, closer to the bottom of the tree. The floor had changed allegiance and become a friend coming to greet him rather than a threat waiting for him. He worked all the way to the lowest branch near the trunk. His heart raced, happy to be so close to the roots and soil. He lowered himself down and hopped to the floor, just feet from his ill-fated friend. Leo looked over to him. "Well, here we both are."

He panted, then hopped to the stairs to sit down and rub his ankle. He didn't dare remove his shoe since it was working as compression against the swelling, and he wasn't sure he'd be able to put it back on if his ankle swelled too much. Apples covered the floor, shaken loose from their limbs during Leo's descent. The tree itself was fine. Leo had two limbs worse for the wear, but he was otherwise healable despite his damaged pride. *All in all, could've been much worse.* He sat for several minutes, catching his breath and thinking about his next move.

He could walk on his foot, but if he tried walking the entire way home that day, it would be more harm than good. He didn't want to spend another night at the lawyer's office either, but that was probably the best option. He could visit the chicken farmer or one of the other people on his route back over the hill, but he hated owing people, plus he wasn't sure what any of them could offer him he didn't already have. *Everyone prefers their own space.*

After a long deliberation, Leo landed on staying there another night, letting his foot rest before heading back home.

He spent the day perusing books. Though they were all related to the law, he found a few that especially intrigued him. He collected them into a stack he could come back for when he had a ride again, or hopefully when he had his own ride back. That loss was still as present to him as his ankle and wrist.

He read until the fading sun made it impossible, then he fell asleep. A couple of times he woke up with a sudden shock from dreams of falling.

In the middle of the night, the cat returned and nudged Leo until he lifted the shirt covering him. The cat crawled under and curled up next to Leo's chest. In the morning he woke up again to find the cat was gone. He tested his wrist. It was still sore, but less swollen, which was a good sign. His ankle ached worse, though. He desperately wanted to get out of there. He was tired of eating just apples, especially since it gave him diarrhea, which was just adding more insult to his injuries.

He sat up and spun his legs to the side, stepping on something wet. He lifted his foot and found a dead mouse sitting beside him, the cat's way of thanking him for the warmth. He wiped off his foot and sank his head into his hands. He just couldn't go anywhere with his injuries.

He laid back down and cried as his pulse screamed with each beat in his ankle. He spent the day reading, sleeping, eating apples, and going to the bathroom. The day prior he used a trash can in the second-floor bathroom, the toilet itself had long ago dried up and the pipes below surely broken. He'd rather crap in something he could remove and clean since his original intention was to return to the building. His mounting diarrhea and no ventilation in the bathroom made for a rather unpleasant time. He gathered fallen leaves from the tree and put a layer of them down between uses, both to hide the smell and turn it into mulch he could use for the tree.

He stayed another night. Again the cat came to remind Leo

of his role—body warmth for the little furry one. In the morning Leo woke to the cat sucking on his ear. He allowed it to continue for several minutes before shooing the cat away. It eventually nuzzled back up against Leo's legs.

He spent two more days reading, eating, sleeping, and shitting water. Each night the cat slept with him, and each day it ventured a little closer, always keeping up its guard.

Five days in he'd finished reading three books and though his foot was still sore, his wrist was more or less healed. He was determined to get the hell out of there. When he first discovered the building, it seemed like a mirage, or his own personal Shangri-La, but by then it was more of a trap, a halfway house he'd been forced to recover in before reentering the danger-filled world.

He took one of the pair of pants and tied knots in the bottom of each leg. He gathered apples and put them down the legs along with several bottles of water. The water inside tasted more like the plastic bottles they'd lived in for half a century, but it was better than nothing. He hung the pants around his neck like a bulky denim scarf. That'd work well enough for transportation. He wrapped a book and more clothes in a shirt to make a bindle out of them on the end of his stick.

He limped down the staircase to the front door. He ripped out one of the wood spindles that held the banister to the stairs. It was about the right height to use as a cane. He removed one of the extra shirts and wrapped it around the spindle, tying it on the top to act as a soft handle. He called for the cat, but heard no reply. He shrugged and opened the door. Outside looked clear, but he knew he couldn't trust that sense of security. He locked the door behind him and hobbled down the steps to the street.

CHAPTER SIX

Leo's return was very slow going. He started later than he had hoped, and with his ankle continuing to swell, he didn't dare attempt making it all the way back home in one day. It felt better than when he janked it on the tree, but he figured it was still a week away from full recovery, especially considering the walk ahead of him. He knew there were remnants of a billboard roughly halfway home that still had its platform, which could make a nice high place to spend the night. It would be more drafty than he wanted, but it was safer than anywhere on the ground. He made it his goal to get there before dark, but he still had a long way to go before then.

He'd spent so much time riding his bike past all that landscape, it seemed like an entirely unknown world on foot. More full of detail, like he was looking at it through a microscope. It was beautiful up close. Elegant, even. The slow demise of a world that probably didn't belong in the first place. *How strange humanity must have seemed to the rest of the earth. What if some other animal had taken the world and transformed it to better suit them?* He vaguely remembered a film about something like that about monkeys on earth. Humans destroyed themselves in it, if he remembered correctly. In reality, nature did most of the heavy lifting on that front with the smallest things: germs, or perhaps it was microbes. That reminded him of another film—War of the Worlds. Germs got them in the end, too, though they were the heroes in that one and the humans survived.

"Planet of the Apes." Leo said the second it came to him. *That was the film about monkeys taking over the earth. What if that happened, but with bulldozing parakeets, bird-dozing nature to erect giant buildings, or would they build giant cages?* He realized the analogy might not work as well, but from the earth's perspective, it must've been weird for one species, his species, to take over the whole place for its own. All along nature was waiting, playing the long game for humans to grow so numerous they couldn't fight the tiny things that lived in and infected their own bodies.

It must've been a shock when the first few pandemics hit, Leo mused. *Goliath bested by a pebble. Achilles and his heel.* Though the last pandemic brought with it a whole new order. A deathblow to humanity where death was no longer the end. That had to be the hardest idea to grasp. Either that, or by then it was just the most logical conclusion to the whole endeavor. That, or aliens.

And then there was Leo himself, and those like him. Raised in a post-human world, though it seemed strange for him to think of it that way. Post-human. Leo's human. There are other humans, just not that many compared to what the ruins they lived in were evidence of. Films and TV were further proof, showing a world full of people, a New York City street like a stream packed with salmon. Noisy, angry, honking, salmon.

He stopped to sit on a rusted out car hood to eat an apple and sip his plastic-flavored water. His stomach ached. It yearned for something other than apples. He willed it to be patient, to wait just one day more. The afternoon was warm. He sweated from the weight of all the clothes he carried with him, but he knew he'd be thankful to have them that night. His foot ached, and he leaned on the rod-cane. His body was ready to stop, but his journey was not over.

The sun was still an hour above the horizon when he arrived at the billboard. It was a beautiful sight, that large cylinder of steel reaching up to the sky. The billboard frame disintegrated long ago, but the metal grate on top lived on. He just had to find something to step on to reach the ladder section. He spotted a nearby rusted out minivan topped with an old roof rack. He removed it from the wreck. He hoped it could function as a good enough step to get him within reach of the ladder on the side of the pole. The rack bowed under his weight, but it held, allowing him to reach the bottom rung, which was enough.

He climbed up, checking each step on his way, ensuring that they were sturdy. The grating on the top was solid. *Finally,* Leo thought, *the world is being kind to me.* He spread out a layer of clothes on the metal grating, as that would be the coldest and pointiest part. *Good enough for one night.* He read until the sun bowed over the horizon, then lay down to sleep. He was just settling in when he heard a meowing from below. He rolled over and saw the cat from the lawyer's office meowing up at him. It must've followed him. He didn't realize how valuable his body heat had been to that poor cat.

Leo hesitated, then climbed down the steps to scoop up his little friend. When he landed on the ground it ran away. He called for it, but cats were notoriously not good listeners. He waited several minutes for it to slink back, but a chill ran through him so he made his way back to his perch.

Again, Leo drifted towards sleep until the cat pulled him from his rest with incessant meowing. Leo grew more angry at the cat than sorry for it. He climbed back down "You better not run this time, or you're on your own." On the ground he stepped towards the cat and again it ran away into the darkness. "Fine, you little annoying fur-sack. If you're not gonna let me take you up there, at least be quiet, okay?"

Leo climbed back up the pole and nestled into his makeshift sky-bed. He lay there with his eyes open, just waiting for the cat to call him again. His eyelids felt heavy and pulled themselves shut. He was woken up again by meowing. He yelled, it meowed back. He cursed and threw one of the shirts down to the ground. "There! Use that to stay warm you whiny ass." He rolled over. "And how'd you get out of that building? Hiding a way out from me? You probably knew how to get off the roof, too."

The night was chilly and Leo didn't sleep much, trying to work his legs and arms closer to his torso to keep the feeling in his fingers and toes. He shivered the whole night through. In the early morning hours Leo awoke, surprised he had even fallen asleep. He heard rustling below and called down to the cat, "I told you, use the shirt and let me sleep." Something grunted back at him. It wasn't the cat.

Leo slowly rolled over and looked down through the grating. Clawing at the metal base was a zombie. "Crap." Leo said to himself. He looked newish, not as broken down as the ones he was accustomed to, plus he wore a bright red sweatshirt that looked as new as the clothes Leo carried from the lawyer's office. He heard more rustling in the distance. He thought it might be the cat, but in the low early morning light, he couldn't be certain what was out there. The red sweat shirted zombie noticed Leo looking down at him. He cocked his head, almost curiously, as his eyes darted around and his mouth worked, emitting various grunts as he tried to work out how to get at his food.

Leo lost all hope of sleep. His mind turned to devising a way down until the rustling in the distance neared and another zombie formed out of the darkness, walking straight towards Leo's perch.

Leo asked himself where he'd gone wrong. *This seemed like such a good place to sleep, too. High and protected, safer than anywhere else on the way back home.* Maybe those things would've found him eventually somewhere else too, but up in the air he was just on display.

The second zombie looked even fresher than her friend, Red Sweatshirt, below. She wore a long yellow dress, a section torn from its side. She grunted at the first zombie, sounding like a groaned, "Hey." Leo knew his ears were playing tricks on him. Red turned and grunted back at his friend Yellow as she approached. Yellow swiped her arm to the side. A moment later, Red shuffled a few feet over, giving his zombie friend a straight path to the pole.

Well, that's new, Leo thought. He'd never seen anything like conversation between those things. He was still telling himself he must be imagining things, putting pieces together that didn't fit when the new zombie made it to the base of the pillar and looked straight up at Leo. He went cold. There was something behind her eyes. Something he'd never seen from those things his entire life, and he'd grown up with them all around, survived decades worth of zombies, and killed hundreds. That was the first time one of them looked at him and really saw him. *This is bad.*

Yellow dress swiveled her head around the pole, seeing the roof rack leaning against the other side. She shifted her head awkwardly up to the ladder. She reached out and grabbed the middle bar on the sideways roof rack, grunted again, and looked up at Leo, almost smiling, hunger in her eyes. Leo wondered if those things could have figured out ladders somehow. Yellow thrashed at the rack, trying to get higher, but unable to figure out steps. Leo gave a deep sigh and relaxed, leaning against a couple cold vertical metal billboard frame remnants.

Red ambled back toward Yellow, who yelled at him and pushed him away. Red lashed his arms at Yellow. They seemed to be in a fight, even arguing with each other. Yellow lunged at Red, bringing them both to the ground. Yellow had one hand on Red's sweatshirt hood, holding his head firmly to the ground, her knees restraining Red's torso and arms, then attacked him with her mouth, gnawing at Red's throat. Red fought back hard, but as the other zombie fed on his blood, he slowly lost his energy. After a minute, Yellow got up and walked away into the dark, her dress waving behind her in the chilly morning breeze.

Leo kept still on his perch, heart beating fast. "What the hell was that?" He whispered to himself. *No zombie had ever attacked another zombie. They're supposed to eat people, not other zombies.* Leo wondered what could be going on inside those things' heads.

A moment later, the other zombie returned, holding a rock. She knelt back down on Red's chest. She lifted the rock above her head, tearing the side of her dress more, and slammed it down on Red's head, smashing it open. She then pushed the rock off the crushed skull and bent over, pulling the skull apart with an unintelligible grunt, and began eating the smashed brains. She carefully picked out the bits of skull, only feasting on the tender brain matter.

Nausea rose through Leo's chest. This was all new, and it was bad. He could only assume that this was precisely the thing Grant told him to look out for. He wanted to run. He quickly and quietly packed his things, keeping his eyes on the zombie below. He edged towards the ladder, hoping to make it down before that thing finished eating her friend and noticed him. As he edged his feet over the side, Yellow shot her gaze right at Leo. Blood and brain goo dripped from her chin as she chewed and swallowed.

Leo froze.

The thing rose and turned to face the pole, fixing her gaze on Leo, and walked towards him. She scanned down from him, following the ladder down to the roof rack below. She looked back up at Leo and reached her bloody hands out and grabbed the roof rack.

Leo thought to himself, *no. You can't figure out a ladder. You things never could.*

The zombie tested the rack, then stepped forward. She lifted her leg to step on the bottom rack rung. She overshot and her leg came down awkwardly beyond the rung. She fell forward and caught herself, recovered, and tried again. The ripped part of her yellow dress wafted under her foot and it slipped off again. She yelled and ripped the torn fabric from her dress, and tried once again to step on the rung. Her foot made contact. She looked up, then grabbed the top rack rung with her hands and lifted herself up.

Leo couldn't move. Even if he could, how could he get away? Down was not an option, and that thing was making staying up there a non-option as well.

The zombie reached for the bottom rung of the ladder and missed. She fell shoulder first into the pole with a thud. She hoisted a leg onto the top of the rack and lifted herself up within reach of the bottom ladder rung.

Just then the cat leaped into view below the zombie, hissing and screaming at the creature in the torn, yellow dress. She looked down. The cat took a step back, continuing to hiss at the zombie. Yellow looked back up at Leo. The cat leapt at her feet, biting and scratching at them. Its claws connected with her dress, which threw the zombie off-balance. She lost footing and fell backwards to the ground. The cat let go and ran out of reach from the zombie, who clamored to get the dress off from over her face and tried to get back up. She looked to the hissing cat and crawled at it with alarming speed. The cat ran away; the zombie rose and chased it, her yellow dress disappearing into the darkness.

Leo remained motionless for a few more seconds until he realized now was his chance. He climbed down the ladder as fast as he could manage with his sore ankle. He jumped to the ground, careful to put most of his weight on his good foot. He grabbed the walking stick he'd left and limped with all the speed he could muster back to the road heading north. He wanted to put distance between him and that thing. He suddenly realized that the cat was in danger, but figured it had lived in the world enough to know how to survive, he just wanted to do the same. It was time for Leo to land on his feet.

After an hour of limp-speed-walking, Leo needed a break. He sat down on a dilapidated chunk of cement divider and hunched over, catching his breath. He had heard nothing behind him and had been checking every few minutes. He appeared to be in the clear from whatever the yellow dress zombie had become. *Some sort of advanced zombie? Definitely not a normal person.* It was a new breed of terrifying.

It occurred to him that his home wouldn't even be safe anymore. If that thing could figure out ladders, his second-floor residence meant nothing. Even so, he just needed to get back there. He needed something comforting, if only for a few minutes. He read once that placebos could lead to real healing, so he bet on that if nothing else.

Leo stood and continued north. His pace was much slower than he'd been going the previous hour, but still faster than his leg preferred. A few hours later he made it to the peak of the hill. He looked back at the road, still nothing following him that he could see, just the city in the distance. It looked different. It used to be familiar, a friend, and now it was full of strangers and strange things. Something was different about the city, or different about him. He shook off the feeling and continued on.

He saw a pile of something in the road ahead. As he got closer, he recognized the pile was Anna, close to the spot he'd seen her almost a week prior. Something was wrong. She lay motionless in the road. Leo stopped. *She shouldn't be here.* He listened for anything unusual, but there was nothing, just his breathing and heartbeat thumping in his ears and ankle.

He approached her cautiously. Still no sign of anyone or anything else. He stopped about twenty feet short and called to her. "Anna?" Nothing. "Hey Anna, you okay?" No movement.

Leo just wanted to go past her and go home, pretend like he hadn't seen her like that, like she was ok, maybe just taking a nap. He knew better, though. That annoyed him. He walked towards her body, face down, sprawled on the ground. As he got close, he could see blood spattered nearby, almost in a trail away from her body, so either she'd gotten whatever attacked her and it left a trail limping away, or she'd gotten away, leaving the trail on her escape. Leo didn't really want to know which was the case because neither scenario had a happy ending.

Leo poked her lightly in the side. He heard a feint release of breath. *Was she still alive somehow? Or was it gases escaping from the movement?* He poked a little harder and heard a quiet groan.

Leo knelt down beside her. "Anna. It's me, Leo." He touched her arm. It didn't feel cold, but the sun had been shining on her for several hours, so he couldn't be certain the warmth was her own. He lifted her arm, slowly rolling her over. Her body was limp, her head hanging, following the roll of her body. He lay her on her back as softly as he could, then he saw the blood on her neck, and the hole bitten into it. Still, it seemed the only wound was on her neck. That was odd. If it had killed her, the zombie should've eaten more of her, not just left her to rot, or to turn into one of them.

That's when he saw the knife in her hand. She hadn't just been attacked, she'd fought back, so the trail of blood was from that thing as it limped off so she could die in peace. Leo looked around, he was still alone. He looked back to Anna whose eyes were half open, as happens to the dead. He lowered her eyelids. He removed the knife from her hand and readied himself to stab her head just to make sure she wouldn't come after him someday.

"I'm sorry, sweetie. Sorry you had to live in this world, sorry this happened to you. Still, in all this you brought a brilliant light to the world. Thank you for that. You gave me hope, and I know you gave your father hope too." He thought about how he was going to tell her father Arthur about what he found. That would be rough. They'd known each other most of their lives, though they'd only seen each other a handful of times, which was standard for most human interactions in a zombie-filled world. Leo had helped them rebuild after a stranger came through town ten years earlier and tried stealing from Arthur and his wife. *Or was it fifteen?* It was hard for Leo to remember as everything seemed to be locked in a pattern and he was just fulfilling his part of the plan. He had fought the guy off, and the guy had taken some explosives and taken out part of the wall surrounding their property. Leo and his dad had helped Arthur rebuild the wall. That was before Anna had been born. It seemed like so long ago and also seemed like just last week.

"No matter what happens, we rebuild." Leo said to himself.

That was another one of his father's mottos, and he'd adopted it as his own. It had gotten him thus far. He took a deep breath, readying himself to mercy-stab Anna's brain. He looked down and realized her arms had moved, curled up to her chest. Her eyes reopened, and she looked straight at Leo and groaned. It was too late.

Anna rolled and lunged at Leo. He stabbed at her, but she knocked him over. The knife plunged into her leg. He kicked her off, and she landed on her back. Leo pushed off the ground, lunging at her knife-first. He got her in the mouth, stabbing through the back of her head, but she still clawed and growled at him, coming out as a wet gargle. He stepped on her neck and pulled out the knife. He plunged it down on her skull through her left eye socket. Her body became limp. Leo felt sick. He wanted to be done with zombies. There had been so few in the recent years, he'd let his mind go to a place where he didn't have to worry about the dead trying to kill him anymore. He realized he'd never live in that world, that it would never exist again. That time had passed, ended long before he was born. That world only existed in books and movies.

Leo yelled a great yawp of frustration, his eyes teary. He rose and looked to the ground, following the trail of blood heading away from Anna's lifeless body. He noticed a hand lying there. *At least she'd gotten that off him before it got her*, Leo thought. He pulled the knife from her one more time and stumbled away, following the trail before it disappeared in his tears.

In the distance down the road he saw the thing, stuck in black-berry brambles. She must've gotten its Achilles tendons, making it almost impossible for the zombie to walk. It was ensnared in blackberry thorns growing along the side of the highway. Leo called out to it. It turned back to him and gave several grunts, trying to turn the rest of its body around to get at him. Leo stopped and watched it struggle its way through the vines. The thing that killed Anna. It looked like it must've been relatively new, turned within the last six months. It wasn't anyone Leo had seen before. He kept watching it struggle. It fell to the ground, trying desperately to catch itself on its handless stump. Leo felt it deserved to struggle, to suffer. Its legs bent so much at the knees from the sliced tendons. Anna did excellent work, just not good enough to save her own life. They'd both been raised in that world, prepared for such things, but sometimes the evil just got the better of you.

Leo yelled at the zombie, enraging it more to free itself from the briars and attack him. Leo told it how it didn't belong. The zombie struggled, nearly out of the briars, and fell to the ground as a few vines remained wrapped around its feet, tethering it to the patch. The zombie twisted its legs around backward as it struggled, rendering them useless as it crawled toward Leo, scraping flesh on the grass-strewn pavement. Leo rose and walked to the scrambling zombie. It reached out to him with the arm that still had a hand. Leo stomped on it, smashing it as hard as he could. Its other arm lunged towards him. He stomped on it as well. That gave the zombie enough leverage to pull its legs away from the vines. Leo kicked its head, knocking it at an impossible angle on the neck, breaking its spine. Though it couldn't move its body, the zombie continued gnawing the air, its torso motionless and impotent. Leo walked around to its side and stabbed it in the back. He stabbed at it again. And again and again and again. He stabbed until the tip of the knife broke off, leaving a jagged metal edge. He moved around to its face, twisted helplessly up at the sky.

Leo brought his face inches away from the snarling zombie's eyes and stared at it. His teeth hurt from clenching his jaw so tight. He grabbed the zombie's hair and pulled at the head. He took the knife and slashed at the neck, cutting the head loose. Its mouth kept opening and closing like a chicken head freshly decoupled from its body. Leo dropped the knife and held the head in both hands, squeezing it as he screamed in its face. He tried as hard as he could to crush the skull in his hands, but it was too solid. Leo lifted the head into the air and slammed it to the ground with a wet crack. The sound felt so good to Leo. When the head stopped rolling, the mouth quit pointlessly opening and closing, but the eyes still twitched. Leo ran to it and jumped, landing on it with both feet. The head splattered, leaving a red halo around Leo's bloody shoes.

Leo's ankle pulsed with pain. He stood there motionless for several minutes, just breathing and crying, letting out all the pain and anger and frustration from the last few days, from what happened to Anna, and how he'd have to tell her father. Leo crumpled to the ground, crying. After a while his tears slowed and he lay on his back, looking up at the sky. He closed his eyes.

Some time later he woke up to the sound of something sucking on his ear. The cat had somehow followed him once more. Leo reached up slowly with his hand to pet the cat. It tensed up and froze, but didn't run away. Leo rolled over and looked at it face to face. It had followed him, saved his life, and followed him again. Leo smiled, tears still in his eyes, and whispered to the cat, "Ok, let's go home."

CHAPTER SEVEN

Early evening, Leo made it back to his apartment complex. Having been gone for almost a week and so much happening, it felt like a foreign land to him. The cat allowed him to pick it up on their walk back, and Leo set it on the second floor of the complex so it could explore its new home. That was, until the cat ran off somewhere else, as Leo assumed it eventually would. Nothing was certain anymore. Leo could see that clearly. Plus, he was covered in all manner of horrible and wanted to wash that off. He removed his clothes and climbed down to the first-floor apartment where he'd rigged up a shower fed by a large tank that collected rainwater. He wanted to wash the entire world off his skin.

Leo didn't sleep much that night. His dreams kept him from feeling rested in the morning. The cat didn't seem to have any issues, though. It remained under the covers against Leo's belly all night. It woke him around sunrise and began sucking on his ear. Leo gently swatted it away. "I gotta name you." Leo said, lifting his head. The cat crawled on Leo's stomach, settling between his legs. "You already have a name?" The cat stared at him, purring. Leo dropped his head back down on the pillow. "Never really had a pet before. Not saying you are my pet or anything, but if you were, it'd be nice if you had a name."

After going through a Rolodex of possible names, Anna popped in his mind. He didn't look forward to telling her father he'd lost his only child, but it was something he had to do. Eventually.

Leo got up and opened his fridge. No eggs. No milk. No meat. He checked his sourdough culture on the counter. It had a black skin on top from not being fed for a week. Leo scraped the skin off and stirred in flour and water to bring it back to life. He'd have to wait a few days to make bread, and what he had left was already moldy. He took it outside to the mulch barrel under the carport and stirred it around. Breakfast would be oatmeal with apple and honey.

He climbed up to the roof to survey the area. Looked like every other day to him, which he gladly accepted as good news. Leo sat in a chair under an awning he'd set up to shade him from the sun. He also brought paper and charcoal with him. He sketched while birds chirped from neighboring rooftops. He spent an hour sketching a portrait of Anna with her bouncy hair and serious face that also seemed to be smiling. He was proud of the drawing he'd made of his lost friend. He lay back and took a nap. An image of Anna lunging at him with mouth wide open, jaw unhinged like a snake woke him with a jump.

Leo brought the drawing downstairs. He took a small nail and hammered her sketch on the wall next to another sketch he did a few years ago of a couple he considered friends. He drew them together after he discovered the husband had slit his own throat when his wife died during childbirth. At least that's what appeared to have happened when Leo investigated after not hearing from them for some time. He avoided that section of town ever since.

He backed up to regard the wall. A collage of sketches. Close to 150 at that point. Everyone Leo had known who was no longer in the world. A wall of lights that had gone out. He remembered their names, had mourned their losses. It seemed that all that remained was Leo, himself and that cat, who still needed a name of its own.

Leo packed snacks and water into a backpack. He went to the carport and pulled out his old bike, formerly known as his dad's bike. It was very rusty from neglect, the chain was on its last leg, several links having been replaced over the years. He put the extra chain he'd used to cannibalize pieces from in a bag and put it in his backpack. The tires were flat. He pumped them up and checked for leaks. Seemed like they could still hold air, at least for a few minutes, so that was something. He heard the cat meow at him from the balcony. Leo looked up and waved at it. "I'll be back, just gotta go deliver some bad news."

Leo pedaled down the driveway, opened the gate, and walked the bike through. As he brought the chain closed around the gate, he wondered if even that would protect him anymore from the yellow dress zombie he'd seen. An even worse question bubbled up: how many more zombies like that one were out there. They could climb ladders, but could they also figure out chains and locks? They weren't the mindless dead-heads he'd grown up dealing with. They were thinking, cognizant things. A shiver moved down his spine. *That's a thought for later*, he told himself and hopped on his bike. The ride wasn't far, but it was mostly uphill. It took him a little over an hour to navigate the street up to Anna's father's compound. An old tree had fallen across part of the road, its roots stretching into the air, confused at the situation. He moved the tree as far off the road as he could.

Arthur, Anna's father, had a simple strategy for protecting the compound: tall effing walls with sharp stuff at the top. Keep zombies and people out, let anyone who wanted to enter cut themselves up first. Leo rode past the area he and his father helped patch years ago. Most of the wall had been brick from the before-times. Arthur added a few feet of stone to the top, with a cement that still held nicely. It was quite the under-taking, and it seemed to do the trick. That was, it protected people as long as they remained inside the wall. Outside was still the outside.

Leo raised a flag on a pole by the front gate, letting Arthur know someone was there. The gate sat near the bottom of the property, with the house's large windows facing it, the flag visible from inside. The forge which Arthur constructed and used to make all manner of metal tools and devices, had its back facing the gate, but there was no smoke coming from the chimney, so Leo wasn't sure where Arthur would be or what he'd be up to. It may take some time for him to notice the flag. Leo took out the book he'd been reading and tried to forget the business at hand of how he'd tell Arthur that his daughter was dead.

That didn't work well. He found himself re-reading the same sentence for a solid two minutes while his mind worked different combinations of words to break the news.

Alternating footstep, crunch, footstep, crunch made their way toward the gate down the gravel drive. Leo turned to see Arthur hurrying down the hill to meet him, slowed by the crutches he was using.

Arthur was tall, over six feet, and thin. His hands were rough from the work he did. He was out of breath from the effort.

"Arthur!" Leo inwardly grimaced as he heard himself overcompensate and sound too happy.

"Leo. Well, that's one heck of a surprise. What are you doing here?"

Leo lost all words.

Arthur breathed heavily, slowly regaining his breath from the run. He searched Leo's face, and gradually dropped his smile. "No." He said.

Leo's heart dropped. He nodded.

Arther's legs lost all will to stand. He slumped over onto his crutches, and a moment later fell to the ground on his side. "No! No, no, no."

Leo stood there. The world dissolved as he watched Arthur weep. He had no words. He'd known people who had died. The wall in his apartment complex was evidence of that, but familiarity with death didn't make their loss any easier. He didn't cry. He wanted to, but couldn't manage it. Anna had carried the knife with her, and he carried out its task on her, the finishing blow.

Arthur worked his way to stand, apologizing to Leo. Leo shook his head, telling him it was understandable. They'd both known loss. Slumping, Arthur invited Leo into the compound and unlocked the gate, sliding it open.

Arthur's compound was a sprawling house at the top of the hill butted against the forest, making it convenient for Arthur to chop down trees and collect wood to run his forge and furnace. Some artist had lived there back when the world was full of people. Presumably a potter or sculptor based on the kiln and other supplies left behind that Arthur repurposed. The wide front terrace used to be filled with sculptures that Arthur long ago removed and melted down for his own purposes, turning the terrace into a proper functioning garden.

Arthur led Leo to the second floor of the house where they sat on rocking chairs looking out the great front window on the property below. Leo told Arthur what he deduced had happened to Anna, reassuring him that it appeared that she hadn't suffered, and done good damage before the end. Leo told him he'd taken care of the zombie that did it, not going into much detail beyond that. Arthur took the news as well as a parent could.

Leo asked about the crutches, as they were new. Arthur told him that about two months earlier he had been collecting wood, chopping branches off a fallen tree. He was working on a major branch from the trunk when it bucked suddenly into his leg. Anna was gathering and stacking wood nearby and luckily was out of harm's way. She helped him back to the house and set his leg in a splint. Thankfully, the wound hadn't become infected and was healing. He'd just been able to get back to work recently to fulfill a request from the power plant for a few parts, which was why he'd sent Anna on the delivery and not gone himself. Arthur looked out the window in silence.

Leo gave him a moment to his own thoughts. Arthur's leg still caused him some pain, and probably would the rest of his life. He thought about how he didn't cry when giving the news to Arthur. When he was young, he cried at the loss of friends. Until the loss of his mother, when his tears just stopped. He didn't remember crying about that, which felt wrong. He realized that must've been the moment he started putting up walls. They'd always been there, but like Arthur's compound, he'd added to them, building them up, protecting his heart and emotions from the inevitable. It worked. It also gave him a deeper sadness, like the walls held in all his pain. Perhaps his protection made him lose something. He found that incredibly annoying.

"I should've known." Arthur broke the silence. "I felt I should not have let her go alone. Should've sent her to have you make the delivery since I couldn't."

"It makes sense what you did, I probably would've done the same."

"Don't try to make me feel better. I knew. Felt it in my gut. When she didn't come back... I wanted to go out and look for her. I tried. I just couldn't make it far; this damn leg of mine. Pulled the splint off to make it lighter, but," Arthur winced as he tried lifting his leg to demonstrate. "I just couldn't."

"I could've brought them, too. I saw her on the road last week when she left." Leo said, shame building that he hadn't pushed harder to make the run himself. "I offered to deliver them, but--"

"She wouldn't let you." Arthur shook his head. "I raised her too headstrong."

"You did a good job." Leo said. Arthur took several deep breaths and closed his eyes, fighting back tears.

"So she didn't make it, then?"

Leo shook his head. "No, I guess not. I could—I suppose I could go back and get what she left and deliver it to the power plant. If you want."

Arthur looked him in the eyes. "Thank you."

Leo nodded.

"Oh, why were you on that old bike?" Arthur asked, wiping his eyes.

Leo groaned, not wanting to say the words aloud that his bike was stolen, not wanting it to be real. He did, though, and told Arthur about the new zombie in the yellow dress, how it scared the hell out of him.

"Maybe that's what got her. Why she didn't make it." Arthur said after a long pause.

"Yeah, maybe." Leo added, certain it wasn't, but not wanting to say that to Arthur.

It was getting late and Leo knew he should leave, but he didn't want to go out in the world, perhaps not ever again. *Was there just one of those new things, or were there more?* Then, there was the living to deal with, and whoever stole his bicycle. There was also Anna. He especially didn't want to revisit the scene of her death, but he knew he had to, eventually.

"Stay the night, will you? You can leave in the morning." Arthur said. Leo was more than happy to oblige, leaving the dangers of the outside world to wait another night until he had to face them again.

CHAPTER EIGHT

Leo left Arthur's compound after breakfast, taking a canteen of water, and a satchel of walnuts Arthur gave him. The day was overcast, which suited him well. He rode toward the spot he'd left Anna's body. He was grateful Arthur didn't request that he bring her back for a funeral. Instead, he'd been tasked with placing her body on the nearest patch of soil so she could return to the earth on the earth's terms. The closer Leo came, the heavier his legs seemed, like the entire area had grown more dense. When he neared the spot, the hairs on the back of his head stood up. She wasn't how he'd left her, she'd been rolled over. Leo stopped his bike and listened. Nothing but birds and leaves.

He slid off his bike and warily approached her body. The closer he came to the spot, the more it became clear something had broken open her skull and removed the brains. It couldn't have been a wild animal, they'd go for the easy meat first and the rest of her body was intact. Zombies didn't even do that, or at least the old zombies wouldn't, they went for whatever they could get. The thing, or person, had broken Anna's skull open and gone straight for the brain, just like he'd seen the yellow dress zombie do at the billboard.

Leo backed away from her body. He couldn't move, couldn't

touch her, not yet. She'd have to wait. He still had to find what she was sent to deliver, though. He searched, wanting to find it fast and get out. He spotted a leather pouch rolled up with a few metal parts inside close to her body. Blood stained the leather. *So Anna had been protecting it when she was attacked.* Leo wanted to be done thinking about that. He put the pouch in his backpack, hopped on his bike, and took off towards downtown as fast as he could.

The closer he came to the billboard, the more his stomach twisted. He pedaled fast and kept his eyes circling around to make sure the thing that knew how to climb wasn't still hanging around waiting for him. He hoped he hadn't inadvertently led it to Anna's body. He shivered at the thought. It had to be dealt with. Leo hoped the yellow dress zombie was an anomaly, but something inside told him there were more, since the world seemed to be telling a joke, and he was the butt.

His ankle ached. When he was a good two miles from the billboard, he slowed and took his time as he pedaled through old downtown. He took a route that brought him past a few buildings he knew that housed people. He avoided those areas to keep things simple, but he had checked in on them in the past and even done a few supply runs for a couple. *Always a good idea to be valuable and respected when these are the people who might save your life one day.* It was quiet, and nothing seemed out of place. *At least that area didn't seem to be affected yet,* which was enough for Leo to relax as he neared the power plant.

He heard the parts in his pack clanking around as he pedaled, wondering if they'd been doing that the whole time or if the noise had just started. His focus had been on the road and his surroundings, and ignoring the pain in his ankle, so it was possible he'd missed the sound. He hadn't seen a soul peering out any windows in the occupied section he passed through that he was aware of, leading him to believe the rattling was a recent development. He debated stopping to shift around the package on the off-chance the parts were getting damaged, but he was just a few minutes from the power plant at that point, so he figured he might as well stay on course. *If there was damage, it was already done.*

He turned down the street to the entrance. Still clear, a breath of calm. At the gate, he rang the bell and waited.

He waited quite a while. He wanted to ring again, but also didn't want to annoy whoever was inside. He waited twenty minutes before relaxing and sitting down to eat. Before he could get the first walnut in his mouth, the gate began rattling open. He jumped back up to his feet and wheeled his bike inside. He put away his food and pulled out the metal parts he was delivering.

The inner door opened, and he entered the room. The cooler he'd left last week was sitting there empty. "Oh, I'm not doing that run today." He held up the pouch and set it on the floor. "This is from Arthur. I think you know what it is." No response. "He was hurt. His leg, so that's why I brought it." Could whoever was working the doors even hear him? "Oh, and his daughter… she was… she didn't make it." Leo waited an extra moment hoping for something, but there was a reason the master of the power plant distanced themselves from the outside, protected from all news, good or bad.

Leo turned and left the room, leaving the cooler in the dark between space. When he closed the outer door, it locked with a click. By the time his eyes adjusted to the sunlight, the outer gate opened. Leo walked his bike back out to the street, unsure of his next move.

Arthur could use more time. Sarah and her family wouldn't be expecting him for another two weeks. He didn't want to go home since it meant going past the billboard and Anna's body. He could go to his new downtown lawyer's office. *Or was it a tree-house, since it housed a tree?* He wondered what he should call the place full of books where he found the cat. *The cat!* That decided things. He had to go home to take care of the cat. One more thing without a name. *One problem with naming things*, he thought, *is that you just end up missing them more when they're gone.* Though he'd never named his old bike and trailer, and that didn't stop him from missing them.

It had been years since he'd traveled other routes back to his apartment. Odds were high that nature had grown over a good portion of them. He stopped going those ways because they made him feel like he had to go uphill more than the highway route. He knew that couldn't be right, but it seemed true. The fact he did not frequent the other routes only made him want to travel them less with the trailer in tow. More nature growing in the cracks quickly turned the roads into small jagged teeth that wanted to swallow his tires. Since he was without a trailer and wasn't in a huge hurry (and again wanted to avoid anywhere the yellow-dressed new zombie might be) he'd go the back way home.

The first part brought him up towards the stadium, again he thought about making a pit stop. He knew Sarah's mother wouldn't mind, or at least she'd be so polite he'd never know if it bugged her, but he'd rather not put them out. Family was important to them, and he wasn't actually family.

It was early afternoon, and as he turned northwest away from the stadium, the world seemed both greener and darker. The trees in that area hadn't faced resistance. Perhaps somewhere within them hid a survivor or a family who wanted to stay far off grid and leave no trace. Leo had never done runs for anybody in that part of the city. It was a strange, almost suburban section in between downtown and the rows of apartment complexes where he lived.

He knew the route would take longer than his normal one, which was the hypotenuse to the whatever you call the other two sides that add up to his current route being longer. Plus, he already had to go around one tree that had fallen across the road, cutting through knee high grass and undergrowth.

He considered he'd made the wrong choice, but it was too late to turn back. The bridge that connected that section of the city to the center of town had collapsed a couple decades earlier, so he'd have to go almost all the way back to the power plant to get to his normal route, and he would not do that.

That part of the city was just a stone's throw from the rest. The former bridge spanned across a stretch of railroad tracks, lost beneath a thick swath of trees, a linear forest cutting through the former city. It must have carried supplies on train cars back and forth, though the first trees that grew there had ripped the tracks apart, the section was now onto the second or third generation, creating a legitimate forest. It confined some segments of the forest between its cement barriers, others flowed seamlessly into the rest of the streets. Just like the tortoise, the forest would ultimately win.

The only way out is through, someone had told him. Or had he read it? Some memories grew over others like grass on the sidewalk. It was getting more difficult to distinguish the two halves of the world apart.

They were becoming one, but in the past, they were kept very distinct. Leo wanted to know where he heard the saying. As he searched his memory, he entered deeper into the wooded section of road.

His stomach groaned. He needed to stop and eat even though it was getting late into the afternoon and he would likely not be home until after dark. He didn't want to sit still on the ground, he never fully trusted the forest. He climbed a tree with a decent branch to sit on, opened his pack, and ate. His ankle ached. The long active days so soon after his injury just weren't giving it time to heal. He rubbed his ankle, leaning back against the tree trunk. He asked himself if his father would've gotten into the same situation. *What would he have done?*

A twig snapped near Leo's perch. He froze, looking in the sound's direction, waiting for what would come next. There was movement in the underbrush. Something was coming—no, somethings. Out of the brush emerged antlers, followed by the rest of the creature—an elk. A couple of fawns bounded out, one tripping over a bush. *They must be fairly young.* Several deer followed. They gathered in the open part of the road, the herd numbering about twenty-five in total. He thought deer only traveled in the early morning and evening. *Maybe it was later than he thought.* After a brief deliberation, the herd turned south down the road past Leo.

He wondered whether he had spooked them on his journey north and made them pause until they felt it safe since he no longer seemed like a threat, or if they had been traveling and just didn't notice him at all. The fawns bounded into each other as they passed, looking young and silly. Leo wondered what the root word for fawn might be, if it had some connection to looking silly and foolish like he assumed the word foal might. Watching them hop and stumble, a smile crept over his face along with the hope that the word fawn was connected to happiness and excitement somehow. Language tended to have strange circuitous paths of meaning sometimes.

Leo watched the herd disappear around foliage down the road. *It was nice to know deer continued to exist as they had for centuries.* He wondered if they were the same herd he'd hunted with his father years before, and attempted hunting himself a few years prior, or if it was a different herd altogether. Then the birds ceased chirping and Leo's arms tingled with goosebumps. *Something wicked this way comes.*

He remained frozen on his perch, wondering what else the forest concealed. *Another one of those new zombies? An entire herd of them?* A small tan thing emerged up the road from under a bush—a mountain lion. It entered the clearing and started straight down the trail from the deer. *It must be hunting them.* Perhaps that's what led the herd to move when they did. Leo hoped it wouldn't notice him. He breathed as quietly as he could while his heart raced. Ten feet away and ten feet below him it stopped and looked straight at Leo, looking right through him. A chill started in his neck and traveled through his entire body. He could see the creature do the math in its head for its next move.

After a long moment, it turned its attention back to the road and continued on the path toward the deer. Leo wondered what factors led to it moving on. *Had it attacked a human in the past and that not gone well? Or perhaps it ate a zombie and thought all humans tasted that bad. Perhaps fawn just tastes delectable.* Whatever the calculus, Leo would not be on the menu that day. Which Leo appreciated, since he wasn't certain how to fight off a cougar (or mountain lion, or was there a third name for the animal? He'd heard several).

After waiting a few more minutes for the animals to pass further into the distance, Leo carefully climbed down from the tree and mounted his bike, continuing north.

The path would have been impossible with his trailer in tow. Not that he would've gone that way if he still had it, but he felt vindicated for not traveling that way before.

Leo followed a ramp to a larger highway that traveled north. He'd take that for a stretch, hoping it was a more open route, then catch another one west towards home.

The highway was noticeably more open. It still had pockets of trees and bushes, but not as dense as his previous route. Little chance for wildlife to surprise him there.

"Stop!" A voice yelled out. Wildlife couldn't sneak up on him, but humanity was another story. Leo pressed the breaks on his handlebars. He made a mental note that it wasn't as reactive as his old bike and took several more feet to stop than he liked.

"Offdabike." The man's voice called at him from ahead, low and scratchy, the words almost mumbled despite being yelled.

A man walked out from behind a bush that sprouted from the

cement divider. His skin was leathery, grey wisps of hair floating just above his scalp. He pointed a gun at Leo as he slowly stepped closer. Leo had seen something like the man before. Road-sickness was the colloquial term. People who hadn't settled in one place, but traveled on the road, or through the wilds. Most of them died. They either found a group or another person and established a home somewhere, were turned to zombies, or were driven mad from their solitude in the wild. The man ahead of Leo seemed to be on the verge of the last one.

Leo hoped to humanize himself, the best strategy he knew to deal with road-sick individuals. "My name's Leo, what's yours?"

"Shuddup." The man said holding the gun firm. *Well, there goes that option.* "Whatdoyagot?"

Leo deflated as he removed his backpack. Luckily, the important stuff was already delivered. He just had some water and food he hadn't finished before the mountain lion took the rest of his appetite. "Just a little water, food, and change of clothes. You're welcome to them if you want." *Keep it cordial,* he told himself.

The man narrowed his eyes, doing the same calculus the mountain lion had done on Leo just an hour earlier. Leo set his backpack on the ground and taken several steps back. The man continued his approach.

Most road wanderers long ago learned that type of behavior was only a short-term solution, and a crap plan in the long run that would only lead to death. People had to work together to survive. Even separated by walls or never officially interacting, they had to work together. It was the only way. Something had happened to that man and twisted him.

"Where you from?" Leo asked.

The man flinched. He hadn't expected questions, that gave Leo hope.

"Nowhere." He grunted as he picked up the pack and opened it up.

"I know the feeling." Leo said.

"My dick you do."

"No offense, I just mean even though I live here, who can say what here is anymore, right?"

The man grunted and took the water from the pack, drinking

like he hadn't seen any in days. "You're one—uh them."

"One of who?"

"Them!" He pointed in no direction in particular.

"I've never been out of the city."

"No different. All the same." He emptied the bottle in his mouth and carefully put the lid back on, returning it to the pack, placing the strap over his shoulder. He noted the confusion on Leo's face. "The great reclamation. Free City! Reclamation City, what they call it now. There's where I'm from." He relaxed his gun arm. "Live outside it, long time. They rebuild. Made walls ta keep tha—things out." He meant zombies. "Walls got bigger, closer. Wanted me in the new city. I say no! They don't care. Build the wall anyway. Tried to keep me inside. I leave."

"Wait," Leo said. "they're building a wall around an entire city, making it what it used to be?"

The man nodded. "Make it bigger, too. Stupid, all dem. No future in da past." The man stared blankly at Leo for a long time before backing away. "Don't you follow."

Before he could stop himself, Leo began talking. "Actually, I'm sorry to ask, but... I need to go that way to get home. You want to be left alone, I respect that. If it's no trouble, maybe I ride past you in peace, then you go wherever you want. Looks like it's gonna rain tonight, I'd like to be home first, if it's no trouble."

The man reworked his calculus. After a few moments, he stepped toward the edge of the road and nodded for Leo to pass. Leo nodded his thanks and rode on slowly, feeling the barrel of the gun following him as he pedaled. He did not look back, knowing he'd pushed his luck already.

Leo rode north another mile, then turned west. It would be a few more miles of riding, but the sun was already setting. His shoulders were tense, so he relaxed them, thinking how lucky he was to have a place. Not just a place, but a home, and a network of people. He couldn't imagine being like that road warrior, always traveling, slowly going mad from the solitude and sun.

Life must have been tough the first decade after the fall. He'd heard stories of people just like that man, everywhere. Bands of people, even. Gangs traveling from place to place, stealing and killing to stay alive. He was thankful they'd mostly grown up or died out before he was born. It still felt strange for Leo to have seen one last vestige of that type in the world. That man and his mindset seemed more out of place than the zombies. He was lucky that the stranger had been fairly reasonable.

Leo was annoyed he'd have to use one of his other packs for future runs. None of them were as comfortable as that one, but that was life. It appeared the world was trying to teach him to let go of possessions. That, or value them more. The world could be fickle and confusing.

The road ahead was easier, though that side of the hill always seemed hotter. Whatever the temperature, that valley was always warmer than downtown. The slight temperature discrepancy discouraged smaller plants from rooting in the road, which gave less opportunity for larger bushes and plants to find room and still less chance of larger trees making their homes there, roots further cleaving the pavement. The moon was close to full, but covered by clouds. Some light shone through, but avoiding the bumps in the road was difficult, especially since he didn't normally go that way and hadn't memorized the obstacles along his path.

About fifteen minutes from home, Leo felt the first drops of rain on his arms. He pedaled harder, not wanting to be outside when the clouds got more serious. It was a slow build. One drop, then a few, then a regular smattering. By the time he got to the front gate of the complex, his clothes were sufficiently damp, just wet enough to be uncomfortable. He rode through the gate, closed it behind him, and ditched the bike under the carport where his old one used to live.

In the building he called for the cat, but it didn't come. Not that he expected it to, but he still had hope. He couldn't blame the thing, he had left it alone for a couple of days. Then he stepped on a cat turd. *Yep, that's life.*

Leo cleaned off his foot and heard the rain begin in earnest. The normal quiet turned into a roar, thousands of tiny drops adding up to something far more impressive. Leo quickly moved through the apartments, checking for leaks. A couple of the usual ones he hadn't gotten around to fixing yet dripped, plus a few new ones for good measure. He set pots and buckets under them to collect the water.

When he entered the room with his sketches, he jumped at the sound of the cat hissing at him.

"Oops, didn't mean to scare you." The cat didn't accept Leo's apology. "And sorry for leaving you here all alone. I hope you got on all right. Other than the poop, anyway, we'll have to figure that one out." The cat calmed, but ran off when Leo tried to pet it. *Fair enough.*

Leo checked the rain collection barrels to make sure the hoses were still in place and connected properly. All seemed right. "Right as rain" he said to himself. Something his father used to say after checking the rain barrels. He mused at how funny it was being confronted with the moments he missed a person. *Most of the time you don't see it coming, then suddenly the hole they left in your life is so present you can see the dark shape where they used to be with disturbing clarity.* That void ached and felt more real than his sore ankle.

Leo strode back to the bedroom area. He wished he still had the book he'd been reading, but it was still in his backpack, long gone. It made the law seem interesting, like a discussion in balancing polemics, like math if numbers were words. He'd have to return downtown and collect the pile of books he made of the ones that most interested him. He turned the light off and slipped under the blankets, listening to the rain. A great white noise. One of the loudest things in the world, as far as he knew. Waterfalls were noisy, as was the teapot whistle. He wondered if all the loudest sounds were water-based. With those thoughts, he fell asleep.

Leo woke up to the sound of the cat hissing from another room. Leo grew tense as the cat continued its high pitch whine. He arose and grabbed a baseball bat. He slowly made his way through the sawed out door-holes to the room where the cat had raised the alarm. He peeked his head in and saw the cat on a windowsill looking outside. Leo approached it. It turned to him with a surprised screech and leapt off to the floor, bounding to another room.

Leo slowly leaned next to the window and peeked out. Nothing but rain and darkness. He leaned to both sides of the window, trying to see as far in both directions as he could, but there was nothing outside that didn't belong. He wasn't sure what the cat had seen.

He went back to bed, finding the cat had already taken his spot, attracted by the warmth. Leo cleared his throat, but the cat pretended not to notice. Leo eased under the covers. He lay on the very edge, careful not to disturb the cat. He remembered just a couple of weeks before when it timidly approached him, and now just weeks later it laid claim to his bed, making Leo the one gingerly approaching it. Leo figured life could be worse, and he still needed to give the cat a name. He made a list in his head of possibilities, trying them out in different scenarios as he drifted back to sleep.

CHAPTER NINE

By the time Leo woke, the rain had stopped, and the sun was out. He tried rolling over, but felt a warm furry thing in the way and remembered the cat. He realized that this was the first time it had stayed with him the whole night and not run off early or sucked on his ear. His little furry sidekick remained. "Sidekick." He whispered. *That's as good a name as any,* he thought, *Sidekick. Yep, that's the cat's name.*

Leo got out of bed. The cat—Sidekick—yawned at the movement, then curled back in a ball. Maybe it had stayed up when Leo was away, not sure what to make of the new location and the perceived loss of the only other non-zombie it had known. That, or it was just a sleepy cat. Animals as pets was all new to Leo. His family had tried having a dog when he was little. Dogs were great guards, alerting humans when a zombie or other threat was near, but that same perk was exactly what had ended his pet's life—it was too noisy and had attracted a small herd of zombies that eventually surrounded it. He remembered his father embraced Leo and held him close, turning his head away as they devoured his dog. That was the last time Leo considered being responsible for a life other than his own.

Leo ate some food and left bits of meat in a bowl for Sidekick, hoping the cat would like them. He put on clothes and trudged to the roof to survey the area. The carport was alright, just a puddle in the corner that always bloomed after a rain. South side was ok. East—the front of the building—had a lot of standing water, but shouldn't be too muddy. He walked along the north wall and saw a curious line of tracks. Not animal, but unmistakably human... or zombie. *Must've happened last night based on how deep each foot step had sunk into the grass, leaving a clear muddy line.* The trail had a larger muddy spot halfway down the wall below the window Sidekick had been meowing at. It occurred to Leo that Sidekick might be a good guard cat, letting him know there was danger outside.

Leo was impressed with his cat, thinking it might be worth putting up with the added responsibility and cat poop. The tracks disappeared in both directions, leaving it unclear which way the thing had gone or come from. If it were a zombie, it would've stayed in the same general area, clawing at the wall, trying to get up to the sound. The fact it hadn't, was strange and disconcerting to Leo. *Could it've been the man from the road? Could he have followed Leo on foot? Not likely.* Either way, Leo made a mental note to double check the fence around the complex to make sure there were no attempts to break or jump it, or any other signs of something nefarious. But first, chores. He had to dump all the containers of rainwater. He brought them to the rain barrels and poured them in. *Senseless to waste it all.* By then, Sidekick was up and finished the meat, licking its paws.

The exterior fence looked good. Nothing had tried to test it, or if they had, they hid it well. Leo grabbed his bat and raced out to see where the tracks led. Going east to the street side, they seemed to disappear toward the road. Leo couldn't get any specific lead beyond that, so either it left with no clear direction, or it specifically wanted to see his building up close. Leo concluded it had to be the work of a person and not a zombie, which made things more complicated.

Leo rested the bat on his shoulder and followed the path along the side of the building. His feet squished in the water-logged earth. The drainage on that section was never great. The tracks veered away from the fence near the carport section, towards the adjacent apartment complex. Leo followed the tracks until they ended at the edge of the pavement behind that building where the residents used to park their cars. Nothing but piles of rusted metal and plastic bumpers remained between the dim line segments on the cracked pavement. There were a couple of small puddles of muddy water on the cement leading away from the tracks in the dirt, so whoever it had been, had retreated that way. Leo walked around the perimeter of the pavement but couldn't find any more tracks leading away. After walking the perimeter twice, he returned to the front of his complex and wandered back inside, unsatisfied.

Who had stalked his place? Or was it just someone passing through, surprised to see a cat and signs of life from his building? Too many questions. He stayed inside the rest of the day, making sure the windows and doors were sealed, ruminating on the possibilities.

He didn't sleep much that night. Images of the man from the road and the new zombie he'd seen merged into one specter that followed him through every dream that night. When the sun came up, he stayed in bed lying on his stomach, staring off. The cat had been up for hours. It sucked on Leo's ear lobe until it tired of that and ran off. At that moment it meowed by the kitchen, probably wanting more food. Leo sat up, the meowing forcing him to face the day.

After eating and then feeding the cat, he figured his garden was past due for a good weeding. He grabbed his spike and stepped outside. He stood at the edge of the balcony that stretched across the entire complex interior. He'd have to remove the ladders, and probably the planks too. He'd just keep the pole to slide down and climb up. *That had to be harder for those new things if they ever showed up.* That meant more of a workout for future Leo, which was probably good for him. His legs were sturdy from all the bike riding, but he'd gotten complacent in the last few years. Sidekick mewed from inside the window. Leo looked at him and sighed. He opened the door a crack, and the cat shot out to join him, living up to his new name.

Sidekick watched as Leo pulled up the ladders and set them down on the balcony, then did the same with the wood planks. He'd tested them on zombies years before. They were just too dumb to stay balanced on the thin beam and couldn't make it a quarter of the way up. *All bets were off now. The inconvenience and annoyance of change.* Leo figured it would be nice to leave one as a way for Sidekick to go up and down if he wanted, but prudence held him back, and he removed the last one.

As he left toward the carport, the cat meowed from the balcony. Leo stopped and looked back. Sidekick stared at him. He walked to the pole and climbed up, lifting the cat in his arm, and slid down the pole. Its claws dug into his arm on the way down. It wasn't a pleasant moment for either of them. Leo set the cat on the ground. They were both happy about that.

Leo grabbed a hoe and strolled around to a patch of soil behind the building to the south of his complex. The cinderblock wall had been partially knocked down years before, and Leo hopped over it, keeping a cautious eye out for anything strange. He remembered when he used to carry caution with him every day. *That was a long time ago.*

Leo hoed the weeds, glad everything in his garden was coming along nicely. Another six weeks and he could start harvesting zucchini and corn. He finished his work several hours later.

Leo could feel the muscles in his back telling him he wouldn't be able to ignore them the following day. He stretched his back and looked around. *No Sidekick.* He called for the cat, but didn't hear a response. *Where'd he go?* Leo tried to figure out how long it had been since he lost track of the cat. He figured it was somewhere around the green beans an hour ago. He called again, searching around the perimeter of the garden. At the back edge, he found Sidekick sleeping in the sun. Leo took a deep breath, just realizing how much he'd worked himself up about not finding this cat. He knelt down to pet it. As he did, he noticed footprints in the grassy soil that weren't his. *They could be from the same person who left the tracks the night it rained.*

Leo followed the trail. The garden had better drainage, so the tracks weren't as clear. They led Leo to the far side of the property, ending at the cinderblock wall. There was mud on two of the blocks, as if someone had climbed over the wall. That meant it really had been a person with intention and not a zombie, and it knew exactly where he lived. Leo's mind raced, wondering how long it had stalked him. He returned to Sidekick, picked him up, and hurried back to his apartment complex. He wanted to go to the roof and survey the surroundings, but he also didn't want to reveal he suspected anything. Instead, he ran to every window and scanned the area, but nothing stood out. Eventually he had an idea on how to trap his stalker.

He slid down to the ground and tied strings across the walk-ways connected to bells. He'd done that years prior, shortly after his father passed, to alert him to zombies. Eventually he deemed them not useful and stored them. He was glad he hadn't turned his alarm system into something else in the intervening years. He connected the strings even further, going inside the apartment to light switches, so if anyone tripped the strings, they would turn on the lights.

Leo packed supplies for a couple of days in one of his older packs, including two blankets. He got a long sleeve shirt and tied it around his waist, making a pouch. He Picked up Sidekick, testing how he'd react to riding in the pouch. Sidekick squirmed at first, but soon settled in, using it as a hammock with his head sticking out one side, tail the other. He was content enough not to whine, which was enough for the moment.

Leo mounted his bike and rode to the front of the building, making a loud show of opening the gate, taking his time with the chain. He walked his bike out front all the way to the street, not looking behind him or re-locking the gate. "Well kitty, time for us to go downtown. Say goodbye to home, we won't be back here for another two days." He waved at the complex and took off down the street. He knew his performance had been unbelievably big, but that increased the odds that whoever left the footprints could hear him.

He rode a few blocks, then turned left for a block and left again on the street next to his own. He rode as quietly as he could and stopped two blocks before his street. He coasted on his bike and stashed it behind a large bush. He continued on foot, hunched down. Sidekick fell asleep, much preferring life on foot than the bike.

Leo counted the apartment buildings up the block and stopped in front of the one in line with his building the next block over. The building in front of him had collapsed about a decade earlier, the one directly across from his building stood behind the debris. He walked along the rubble, searching for secure footing, so as to avoid making a sound. At the back, he climbed over the wall dividing that property from the back of the building facing his. That one was still in one piece aside from the roof, which had been slowly caving in over the past ten years. The back door was wide open, so Leo entered without a sound. Mold and moss coated the walls, the air thick and musty. He climbed the staircase. The steps were slightly loose and creaky, so he climbed slowly, taking his time. On the second floor, he walked down the hallway to an apartment at the front of the building. Sunlight shone down on him through the collapsing roof and ceiling. The apartment door was stuck. The wood and locks had all expanded from rot and rust and water damage. He tried another door down the hall. The ceiling in that section had held on a little better, though the floor was still squishy from the rain. *It was amazing that building hadn't completely collapsed in on itself like the one behind it. Anything not actively cared for, slowly gave up the ghost over time.* Leo's building was going in that direction as well, but he did his best to slow the process.

He tried the door. It was sticky, but had some give. He took off his pack and pulled out a screwdriver. He pried at the doorjamb. The wood rotted enough around the handle that it almost melted away. He pushed the door open with some effort as the old carpeting had become a base for a thick layer of moss. He entered the dark apartment, making his way to the front of the building. A few vertical blinds still clung above the windows like strange teeth in a ruined mouth, giving a clear enough view of Leo's building. *It may not be a fun stakeout, but it was necessary.* Leo removed Sidekick from his shirt-cradle. The cat wasn't enthused to leave the warmth, but he stretched and smelled out the place.

Leo searched the apartment to find a piece of floor that wouldn't soak him through that night. The only option was the kitchen floor. The linoleum there curled up at the seams, but it would hold enough of the moisture out to be worthwhile. He found some old moldy towels in a drawer and wiped up the floor as best he could, happy for his luck that there was another window by the kitchen near an old dining table that had lost its integrity and collapsed. Leo slid the moist, rotting mess of a table against the wall. That patch of linoleum would be home until he had more answers about whoever wanted to know more about him.

He waited. The smell wasn't too strong at first, but it slowly grated on him. The mold and rot and decay entered his nostrils, filling his lungs. The odor made him feel heavier, like the air was thicker, textured. A miasma of despair. Sidekick didn't seem too interested in the new digs. The cat looked out the window, then sat on the floor facing Leo as if asking, "Can we go now, or what?" Leo sighed and picked him up.

"Sorry bud, but I need some answers first." He fed the cat and ate a little himself, but the thick air had a dampening effect on his appetite. He figured night would be the most likely time whoever it was would make their move, so he leaned against the wall and let his eyes shut.

It was almost evening when Leo woke with a pounding head-ache. He urged Sidekick off his lap and got up to stretch his legs. The musty air was almost attacking him, but he didn't want to leave before nightfall.

He slowly crept back out of the apartment into the hallway to get some fresh air. It was incrementally better, as the holes in the roof and ceiling allowed a bit of slightly less stale air to vent in. He walked back downstairs and out the back door into the afternoon shade of the rotting building. He sat on the back step to empty his lungs of the damp air. Sidekick joined him, exploring into the taller grass and bushes that grew from the soil and detritus that filled what used to be a swimming pool half a century earlier. *Some stakeout,* Leo thought. He regretted not bringing one of the old face-masks with him. He'd seen a few people wearing them when he was young. His father said everyone had masks in the time before the fall. There had been a severe sickness, or flu that shocked the world, waking some people up to the eventual dangers nature would unleash on humanity. Things cleared up for a while after that one, then another one hit, even more contagious than the first. For a while, every few years brought a new strain of something novel that crossed the globe until the final one turned its victims into what could only be called zombies.

Survivors wore masks for years after that until the way the virus spread became obvious. The zombie virus (or whatever it was) was not airborne, but spread through saliva or bodily fluids from those already infected. Some people still wore masks just to be safe, those being the few people Leo had seen as a young child. He still had his parents' old masks somewhere. He felt stupid he hadn't dug them out, figuring the place was full of mold spores. *Oh well,* he thought. Going back now would kind of ruin the ruse he'd set up, though he wasn't certain it was even a good plan to begin with.

That's when he noticed a dark patch of cloud rising into the air—smoke. Somewhere in the distance near downtown, something was burning. Leo suddenly worried it was his newly discovered library, or one of the other inhabited buildings. It was rare, but sometimes buildings, or even entire city blocks, just erupted in flames. Most of them were disconnected from the live electric lines except for those wired up on purpose. Leo knew he should probably check that out, but it was too late in the afternoon to travel that far. Plus, he wanted to finish his stakeout mission, though with his headache dissipating, he was certain spending the night in the mold building was not a great idea. He whistled for Sidekick, knowing he wouldn't respond, but figured it was still worth a try.

Leo trudged back inside to get his pack and abort the plan. Going up the stairway, one step mushed through. The wood underneath a rotten mess. Leo caught himself, angry he'd let his mind wander, almost injuring himself again. In the apartment, he grabbed his things and took one last look outside across the street.

In the front window of his building, a light shone. He suddenly questioned if he'd somehow left it on, however unlikely it seemed. *Was it on before he'd gone out for air? Possibly. That or it had just been triggered and who or whatever triggered it was still there.* It was his chance. Leo zipped down the stairs and ran around the side of the building, ducking under a section of fence that had fallen under the weight of the adjacent building's partially collapsed hulk. He squeezed through and made it to the street, heading as quickly and quietly as he could to his building. He moved through the open gate and paused. He closed it and chained it, so anyone who tried leaving that way would have to make a sound. He grasped his sharp stick tightly and made his way to the back of the complex.

He peeked his head around the corner, making sure it was clear. The back entrance gate between the inner courtyard and the carport area within the complex was open. He knew he closed it before he left. He ducked lower to the ground, knowing full well he'd still be in plain sight, but hoped it would help somehow. The first tripwire was intact, so either the person hadn't seen it and walked over it, or they were paying attention. He continued. The second one had been tripped just before the pole. *Was it triggered on the way in, or the way out?*

Leo set his pack down gently on the ground at the base of the pole. He put his stick-weapon in the back of his pants and climbed up the pole to the balcony. He knew it would squeak on his way up, but it was his only option. He'd secured it as well as he could, but through the years it just kept making noise. He stood up and gripped his stick. All the doors were closed. That probably meant the trip wire had spooked the person who ran away, leaving the gate open, not even making it to the second floor. Leo still had to check to be certain. He carefully opened the main door inside the second floor at the back end of the complex. Everything looked normal. He checked all the nooks and closets in the room, then moved on through the wall to the next apartment, the one he slept in. Nothing out of place. The next one was where he cooked. Still good. He continued through all the rooms. The entire apartment complex looked good as far as his second-floor living quarters were concerned.

Leo stepped back outside and slid down the pole to check the first floor doors. They all remained barricaded and locked. He walked through the interior of the complex one more time to make sure nothing was out of place. He checked the carports. Still nothing odd. Leo again questioned if he had accidentally left the light on and not realized it. He hoped that was the case, because if it weren't, he did not understand who or what could've tripped the wire. He wandered back to the central courtyard to think. Sidekick was sitting there waiting for him, meowing when it saw Leo.

Leo brought the cat up the pole with him to the second floor. He climbed up to the roof to watch the sunset and think. The entire day had been a bust. There was still smoke rising from downtown. It must've been from at least a block's worth of buildings going up. He'd have to wait until the morning to investigate, hoping the next day would turn out better than today's investigation. He stroked Sidekick. Then it hit him—Sidekick. *Could he have been the one to trigger the light?* The cat *had* left Leo before he noticed the light, and he knew how to get to the complex, and been waiting for him there. Leo leaned back in his chair. *Crap*, he thought to himself. *All that rotten air in my lungs wasted because of this cat.* Sidekick purred on his lap. "Ah well," Leo said "At least now I know."

The next morning Leo woke with the sun and gathered his

things. He ate some food and left a meal for Sidekick in his dish, hoping he wouldn't come back to find it left as crap on the floor for him to step on. He was ready to leave when he realized Sidekick hadn't eaten yet. Normally he went straight for the food. He called for the cat but heard nothing. He walked through to the next room to check. A few rooms later, where he kept his drawings, he found the cat sitting by the window looking out. "Stop scaring me like that." Leo said, going to the window and looking out. A bird on the roof of the neighboring building had taken the cat's full attention. Leo picked him up and walked back into the room. "I need to find a way of making you come when I call, especially if food won't do it." He held Sidekick close. "Ok, I gotta go again, you be safe here, okay?"

Leo set Sidekick down, who immediately started rubbing himself against Leo's legs. Leo looked up and noticed a blank spot on the wall. One of his sketches was missing. He scanned around and realized it was the sketch of Anna. It hadn't fallen on the floor, and it never got windy enough in that room to blow it elsewhere. It had definitely been taken.

Sidekick wasn't the one who triggered the light after all, or if he did, someone had come there, gone through the entire complex and only taken a sketch of the little girl who died a week before. Leo's mind raced. *Who the hell would've done that? Had they known where to look? The last person he had had over was Sarah, and that was a decade before.* Sidekick continued rubbing up against Leo's leg. He picked the cat up and walked out of the room "You're coming with me. I can't trust this place anymore. Can't trust anything about this world."

Leo put the cat in his waist pouch and raced back across the street to get his bike. He pedaled towards downtown, mind and heart racing, trying to piece together who would've been to his place. In the meantime, he was off to figure out the source of the smoke from the previous day. *One mystery at a time.*

CHAPTER TEN

A wisp of smoke still rose from downtown, which meant the fire had burned throughout the night. It had been a big one, and it was close to the lawyer's office. The closer to downtown Leo got, the more nervous he was that his new discovery had gone up in flames. He wondered if the light-pole that fell might have been attached to the new power grid when it fell down and the stripped wires just started throwing sparks. His heart sunk at what a waste that would be. Then it hit him: it was the chicken farm that burned down.

The entire building had burned and collapsed in on itself. His brain turned from his own building to the inhabitants of the high-rise farm. *Had the people gotten out? How many lived there?* Leo only knew about the man and the boy, but there had to have been at least one other person to make the boy possible. Leo saw a couple of chickens wandering aimlessly down the street. *At least a few of them got out alive.* He wondered if they somehow jumped or were thrown and flapped their way to safety. He wished the people could've done that.

The buildings on the surrounding blocks were all scorched on the sides facing the smoldering heap. It seemed like the fire had been contained in the main chicken high-rise and another building that had an umbilical rope bridge connecting it to the main chicken farm. The other buildings used for farming crops looked like they were still mostly intact, if not severely singed. Several blocks away, the smell was already horrendous. All that chicken poop had gone up, combined with the smell of burned feathers from hundreds of chickens, led to an unholy stench. Scorched excrement and a half century old corpse of a building created a thick layer of sadness, more than the smoke in the air. It definitely wasn't good to breathe, but Leo figured it was better than the mold from the previous day. Leo turned the corner a block away and saw three zombies standing outside the burning wreckage, staring up at one of the adjacent buildings.

Leo looked up, but the glare of the sunshine off the remaining glass panes got in the way. He looked back at the zombies. It wasn't like them to just wait like that. Had they seen something up there—a survivor from the fire, maybe? They should be scrambling uselessly to get up to them. Then it struck Leo. They were not the usual zombies—they must be more of the new ones. Even worse news than the fire. *Fire at least followed natural logic. Those things—who knew?*

Leo backtracked and rode around to the next block over to avoid those things as much as he could while surveying for survivors. A few more chickens clucked their way down the street, pecking at the soil gathered around the smaller plants.

The chicken farm had fallen more to the south, the still smoking skeleton of the building collapsed, blocking the street. Leo rode another block over and back towards the far side of the building the zombies seemed fixated on. There used to be wood and rope walkways connecting the tops of those buildings to the main farm. If Blake and the boy were lucky and acted fast, they could've made it across to safety before the flames devoured the bridges.

Leo got as close as he could, but it was still too hot and smoky for him to get close to the wreckage. He stopped and blocked the bright sun with his hand to see if there was any sign of life on the roof. He thought he saw something poke out above the edge, but it could've just been his eyes playing tricks. He saw it again—there was definitely something up there. It was hard to make out, then it popped up one more time. The silhouette of the boy. He looked down at Leo for a good ten seconds, probably trying to place his shape as Leo and not a zombie, though he'd only seen Leo on his old bike, not the new (though even older) one he currently rode. The boy's head dipped back out of view. The boy had survived, combined with the fact the fire hadn't spread further, meant the day wasn't all bad news.

The boy's behavior confused Leo. *Why is he being so cautious,* he wondered. *The boy surely needed help.* Leo did not want to wait any longer. "Caw caw!" He yelled up, hoping the kid would recognize the call. His head peaked over the edge, so it worked well enough. "It's me, Leo! I did the deliveries. Picked up the chickens every couple of weeks?" The kid stared back, motionless. "Are you alright? Do you need anything?" Still nothing. "Is your...is Blake ok?" The kid's head dropped down.

After a long moment, another head popped up beside the boy. Leo's heart almost beat through his chest. "Mom?"

He knew that couldn't be right; he had watched his mother die years ago, buried her, but the woman on top of the building in front of him looked so much like her it scared him, her golden hair almost glowed in the late morning sun, a halo blowing with the breeze, obscuring her face. Unsure what to do, Leo waved at them. A moment later, the woman waved back. He knew it couldn't be his mother, but something inside him stirred. She may not be his mother, couldn't be her, she was a stranger, but he had to help. He couldn't save his mother years ago, but he'd do everything he could to save those two.

"Hi," Leo said, his voice cracking. "We've never met, but like I said, I'm Leo. Do you need help?" She stared blankly, just like the boy. Leo wondered if he was stirring in her some vision from her past as she was causing in him. The kid tapped her shoulder and started moving his hands for her to see. It took Leo longer to recognize what the kid was doing than he was happy to admit. Sign language.

The two conversed back and forth on the rooftop. They stood up, and the kid yelled down in a high pitched, shaky voice, "We're ok. Daddy was saving the chickens, but the building fell." Leo didn't know how to respond, but knew he needed to.

"I'm sorry to hear that. Your daddy was a good man." Leo said. The boy might've nodded, but it was hard to discern. The woman looked to the boy, he signed to her. Her head drooped. She signed back. The boy looked down to Leo. "Mommy says we need to go, but the things won't go away. We're scared of them."

"The—the zombies?" Leo asked. The boy nodded. "Yeah, these

ones are different." He had to think. "Do you know how to get down from the building? I mean, if I could get those things away, could you two find your way down from there?"

They boy and mother signed back and forth. "You mean to the street?" The boy asked, more confused than before. Leo told him yes. They continued their flurry of sign language.

After a minute the boy said, "Yeah, I think we can."

Sidekick squirmed in his pouch. Leo considered leaving him behind, but didn't trust how he'd react and didn't want to risk losing him. Leo would feel much better with Sidekick against his body. That was new for him. Leo was accustomed to doing everything alone, and his new attachment surprised him. He wondered if the momentary vision of his mother stirred something in him, had broken something loose. He pushed the thought down. He had more pressing matters.

"Okay, wait half an hour for me to lead them away, then come down. There's a building three blocks that way, two blocks east from where you are. There's a fallen lamppost out front. The door's locked." He pulled the key from his pocket and held it up. "This is the key. Unlock the door and stay inside. I'll join you later. Can you repeat what you need to do?"

"Um. Get the key. Go two—no, three blocks straight and left two blocks. The fallen light post out front."

"Exactly! See you later!" Leo took off around the building opposite the smoldering wreckage. He rounded the corner and saw one of the zombies heading in his direction. Its shirt was completely torn off, revealing a large scratch of long dried blood across the pallid skin of its chest. The thing must have heard him yelling and went to investigate. *Of course they followed our noise*, Leo thought, then he wondered why only one of them came and not all three. "Oh yeah, these guys are thinkers. Crap."

The moment the zombie saw Leo, it took off running towards him. Leo pedaled hard, backtracking and heading around another block. He still needed the other two to join in behind him. Luckily, he could still pedal faster than the thing could run, but if he hit the wrong piece of buckled sidewalk, he doubted he'd be able to recover in time to escape.

He checked behind him to make sure the zombie was chasing

him. The crimson slash almost appeared like it wore a red ribbon across its chest. "Come on, Red Stripe!" He called back at the zombie.

Leo made it back to the street where he'd seen the zombies earlier, just three blocks away. The other two were still there, looking up at the roof. He just needed to get closer and grab their attention. He kept a little less than a block ahead of the zombie following him. He was two blocks from their original position and closing. He'd have to turn up a block before them to have any chance of escape, but the other two kept their focus on the building top where they must've seen the boy some time before. He needed to get their attention, and soon. He slowed down on his approach to the next block—his last chance to veer away. "Hey! Uglies!" He yelled. The two zombies turned. Leo checked behind him, the third one was gaining on him. "Hey! You wanna eat me?"

The other two zombies moved toward Leo. *Good,* he thought to himself. *At least they follow some of the old rules.* He took off north down the parallel street, peddling hard. Close to the far end he looked back to check—Red Stripe and the other two were in pursuit. He turned east. He'd take them deeper downtown. He figured he'd start the chase with as much of a straight shot as the overgrown streets allowed, checking behind him as he traveled. He knew he was coming up to a dead end in half a mile where all the streets butted against the railway. He slowed down to let the zombies get closer before he turned down a different street, then he'd begin the dance of weaving around blocks to lose them. He didn't know how to kill them, or if they still died the old ways, but he knew he didn't want to discover if they didn't die normally amid all three of them.

Sidekick grew stiff and gave a low, annoyed growl-moan. Leo felt the same way.

The zombies were closing in on Leo. *Perfect.* He turned down a larger street. He wanted to stay on open streets for a few more blocks. He looked back. One rounded the corner, then the second one. Then—no third one. He kept going straight, checking and adjusting his path. Still no Red Stripe. He hoped he hadn't lost him with the turn. He knew he'd have to go back west eventually, but he wanted to bring them all over one of the few remaining bridges to the east side of the city first.

He wondered if his plan was still worth trying if Red Stripe was MIA. The only thing worse than knowing where zombies were was not knowing. He continued straight for another block as the two tailed him. He figured he'd be better off circling back. He made a right, heading west a block to backtrack, maybe even circle a few blocks to find the third one. The two trailing zombies remained in tow. The next street over, he had to make a wide turn around a large blackberry vine filling half the intersection. He wanted to head back north a block or two and see where he'd lost the other zombie.

That's when the answer appeared a few feet in front of him. Red Stripe was coming up that block, running straight at him. Leo quickly hit the brakes on his bike and dropped a foot to the ground to turn 180 degrees and take off. He ran a few steps on the ground, straddling his bike to pick up speed and pedaled as hard as he could heading south. Sidekick's claws dug into his belly. It was not a fun ride for either of them. The other two zombies were in arm's length as he zipped by them, swerving to avoid their outstretched fingers. He pedaled hard for most of the next block before daring to look behind him. He needed all the distance he could get. Thankfully, all three were there. He continued for several blocks before getting to one of the few streets with a crossable path over the railway. He turned east and was happy to see all three still in pursuit. "Attaboy, Stripey!" He called behind him.

His relief at knowing all three zombies followed him was soon tempered by the realization that they'd figured out how to outflank him. Plus, they didn't seem to tire, whereas Leo's legs burned as he pedaled over the bridge. He steered towards the center of the road as trees had grown up from below, encroaching further on both sides of the bridge.

Leo originally intended to take the zombies on a wild goose chase around a few buildings then head back over the same bridge, but with Red Stripe's surprise flanking maneuver, he thought it best to make the return trip on a different bridge entirely, since he didn't know what kind of memory those things had. He wondered if they were even zombies at all. They looked like the old zombies, but they did not act like them.

Leo spent the next hour zig zagging down streets he'd barely ever traveled to try to lose them. After about ten blocks with no sight of Red Stripe or his merry band of ghouls, he decided it was clear enough to head towards the bridge back. He looked behind him to the east as he neared the far end of the bridge. No sign of the zombies. He made a quick right down the next block and left on the following one, continuing that pattern most of the route to his downtown office. "Downtown office" sounded funny to him, like he was just going to his office to get some work down before traffic got bad.

His legs ached. He hoped the other two had made it out of the building and found the right door to his office to hide in, and stayed on the ground floor. He kicked himself for not mentioning they should avoid the roof.

He arrived in front of his office and got off his bike slowly, legs aching. He checked the door—it was locked. He gave a "Caw caw" and waited. Sidekick squirmed uncomfortably in his sling pouch. Leo removed him and set him on the ground to stretch his legs and work out his annoyance at the long, rough ride they just had.

A moment later Leo heard a slight movement from inside. He cawed again. He heard the lock on the door turn, and the door itself moved slightly, but did not open. Assuming it was still sticky, Leo grabbed the handle and jerked the door open. The boy almost fell out of the doorway as he had tried to hit the door with his shoulder at the same moment. Leo caught him. They steadied themselves and stepped inside. Leo held out his hand. The boy stared at it for a moment, then handed him the key. Sidekick bounded in the building, recognizing it as home. Leo re-locked the door, and they all made their way to the central atrium.

The boy's mother leaned into the light ahead of them. She had been leaning against the wall in the shadows, watching her son at the door. She sighed and held her arms out. The boy ran and hugged her. Leo wanted to tell them about his escape from the zombies, but before he spoke he stopped himself. He wished he knew sign language. He'd seen it once before when he was young. A family used it. They were passing through town. They wanted to live on the coast. Figured it would be better than Arizona where they were escaping from. Leo's dad had met them on one of his runs and brought them home, back when his mother was still alive. He smiled at the memory. It had been a good night. The family had a son a year younger than Leo; he was the one who was deaf. Leo remembered showing the boy his rock collection. He couldn't remember the boy's name. He tried describing the rocks, explaining why each one was special. The boy watched his mouth intently, but couldn't quite understand him. It frustrated Leo that he couldn't fully communicate with the boy. He'd enjoyed watching the boy feel the rocks, though, exploring the different textures. He never saw the family again. He imagined they made it to the coast and settled in a beautiful spot. Perhaps they were eating crab or clams at that very moment, still a happy family.

The mother stood and looked at Leo. She signed "Thank you" (one of the handful of signs Leo actually remembered). He didn't know how to say "you're welcome," so he gave a double thumbs up and immediately felt embarrassed at how inadequate it was. He added, "Let's get some apples and rest for a bit, shall we?"

The boy nodded and grabbed his mother's hand, leading her further inside. Seeing her up close, Leo could see the similarities the woman had with his own mother, what exactly reminded him of her, but he could also pick out the differences. That woman's face was thinner than his mother's, her features stood out a little further from her face. They had the same hair, though. From the back, he could imagine he was showing off his apple tree and scholarly library to his mother. He let himself smile at the thought, indulging in the fantasy if only momentarily.

They sat on the edge of the second-floor balcony eating apples. Leo was drained after his intense ride, and the other two were still in varying stages of shock at the loss of Blake and their home.

"You know, I never got your name." Leo said. "I've seen you peek down at me once or twice before." Leo thought about the last time he'd gotten chickens and eggs from Blake. It hit him in the gut that that really had been the last time he'd ever do that. He wished he had said something, anything, rather than nothing of importance when he left.

"Adam." The boy said, "and my mom. Esther."

"Esther and Adam. Good names. Well, it's nice to meet you in person." Leo held out his hand and the boy tentatively grabbed it, confused when Leo shook it up and down. *The boy had never taken part in a handshake before.*

Sidekick rubbed up against Leo, feeling more comfortable around the new people, but not enough to approach them yet. "This is Sidekick." Leo said. The boy reached out to pet the cat, but Sidekick back away behind Leo.

Being with people was hard. At least being with strangers was, much less strangers that shouldn't be strange. He'd known the principal person in their life for years, at least cursorily, but the people beside him were still very much a mystery. He wanted to ask about Blake, but on the other hand, he didn't want to know more. They sat, silently ruminating in their own thoughts, staring off into space as they munched on apples.

"So," Leo said after a long pause. "What next? Where do you want to go, I guess?"

Adam shrugged. Leo looked to Esther, who gave a faint "hmm?" She and Adam went back and forth talking it over. After a while Adam looked to Leo and said, "We want to get to my aunties. Can you help us?"

Aunties. More new people. "Sure. Where are they?"

"In the country."

"Oh, how far?"

More talking between Adam and Esther. Leo noticed how intently Esther listened with her eyes, more than he usually did. He trusted his ears and let them do most of the work. He realized how difficult being deaf must be. On the other hand, she never had to hear the cacophony of a thousand chickens, which probably improved her life beyond measure, calling the farm her home. She had a nice setup before it all burned down. *How had it gone up in the first place?* Another question he wanted to ask, but didn't necessarily want the answer. With the world full of zombies new and old, why did it also have to keep fire on the payroll?

"Just a few miles west." The boy said, eventually.

"On the coast?"

Adam asked his mother. "No, not that far."

They'd have to travel on foot, which would slow them down, and they'd be more susceptible to attack, having two people that seemed unaccustomed to life on the ground, one of them being a child. "Ok," Leo said. "I think we better stay the night and leave in the morning. It'll be safer that way." That also meant more awkward time for Leo to be with people.

Leo gave them a tour, pointed out the room and bucket he used as a toilet, explaining the use of leaves between rounds. They understood, probably used something similar in their building, though he did not want to imagine what exactly that might've been. Esther fell in love with the books. Over the remaining afternoon hours she grabbed many, reading through a few pages of each, setting a couple aside that piqued her interest. Leo told them not to go up to the roof for safety reasons, leaving out the part where a child's long desiccated corpse sat on the roof right above them. He figured neither of them would benefit from that knowledge.

Adam dug through the forgotten luggage and found a couple of games and toys which occupied his attention. That allowed Leo to escape up to the roof himself and survey the area to make sure there were no new surprise zombies gathering outside. He brought a large bookend with him to prop the door open, a bust of a lion, sitting regally with its right paw on a sphere. He left its rear half holding up the other end of books on the shelf.

The sun was low, his favorite time to be on the roof. He felt the world closest to being right when he was on the roof watching the sunset. It was a good end to his day.

He was thankful the night was warmer than it had been the last time he was there. He let the other two have the sleeping pads and clothes he'd left behind. He used the worn out sofa material. It didn't give him a good night's sleep, but at least kept him from having a terrible one, which was enough. They all slept in the same room with Leo closest to the door just in case anything happened. Sidekick curled up next to Leo, both giving each other warmth through the cold night.

CHAPTER ELEVEN

Leo woke before the sun peeked over the horizon. He nudged Esther and Adam, waking them up.

Esther gazed at the bookshelves as she strode downstairs. Leo let her know she could take a few books if she wanted. Her spirits lifted at the news. She found an old plastic crate filled with rotting files in moldy folders. They dumped the papers and filled the crate with books, apples, and water. Esther carried it outside to the street, revitalized if only for the moment.

Leo locked the door behind them. He and Esther carried the crate between them, each holding one side, while Adam held Esther's other hand. They walked in silence through downtown. Shadows stretched far ahead of them and slowly shrank with the sunrise.

Leo figured it best they travel on foot and leave the bike inside the office building to secure it, as having one person ride didn't seem right. That, and Leo wasn't prepared to teach the boy how to ride a bike, assuming he had spent little time on the ground. Sidekick rode in the crate for most of the day in silence. Eventually he whined until Leo put him in the sling pouch. Sidekick wasn't enamored with the change, but he stopped meowing, which was enough for the group.

Leo kept an eye behind them as they traveled. It was unlikely the three zombies tracked him, but anything was possible in this new world. He asked Adam if he knew the way to their auntie's. Adam asked Esther, and she nodded, pointing straight ahead. They made their way up to an old raised highway stretching out into the distance above the surface streets.

Leo hadn't been that way before, which both scared and excited him. A couple of miles later, a section of highway had collapsed ahead of them a few years earlier based on the growth. They sat down and ate their lunch a short distance from the collapsed end of the road. They talked it over and backtracked to the previous offramp and traveled the lower streets to the next ramp up on the other side.

The surface streets were much more like a jungle than Leo had seen near the main civic area. All the houses and buildings there had been shorter, and a fire had swept through that stretch long before, clearing the way for nature to reclaim the land much more swiftly. They had to weave around various trees and undergrowth, which slowed their progress significantly. Leo wasn't sure how far they'd traveled on the ground and was concerned they had missed the nearest way back up to the raised highway. He wanted to get back up there. He didn't recognize half of the many animal sounds around him, which made him uncomfortable and nervous. It was also hard to keep the highway in sight. The area directly below and next to it was the most lush, so they had to veer away from it to find a more open path through the undergrowth, which meant the trees blocked their view of the raised highway. Sidekick seemed keenly alert in his pouch, holding his head above the rim, keeping a watch out for danger.

"There" Leo said, pointing to their left. They'd gone just a little past the ramp, as it was buried in blackberry vines. He climbed a tree right next to the ramp, held on to a higher branch, and jumped on the lowest, thinnest one. He jumped several times until the branch finally snapped, dropping onto the vines. It covered just enough of the briars for them to walk over the prickly vines. Leo picked up Adam and carried him over, his pant legs catching several sections of vine. Esther followed. Once past the worst section, Leo clambered back for the box of supplies.

They were all thankful to be back up on the raised highway.

Leo and Esther both had minor scratches on their ankles. They rinsed them with water, hoping they would not get infected.

A few miles later, Esther led them down another ramp to the world below. The fire had not made it that far, so there were still patches of buildings and open areas where parking lots had been that hadn't yet been completely consumed by nature. Leo's arms were tired. He and Esther had switched sides, carrying the bin the whole day, and both arms protested. She didn't seem to mind, though. He wondered if she was more accustomed to lifting heavy things on the chicken farm. Leo missed his bike, though he knew it wouldn't have been possible to get it through the jungle section. *Still would've been nice to have for the morning section,* he thought.

Esther led the way. "When's the last time you were here?" Leo asked. Adam asked his mother. She tried to respond, but it was hard with just one hand. She tried saying aloud.

"Four years?" Leo asked. "Four—oh, fourteen years?" Adam clarified the question and Esther nodded. "You still remember the way?"

Esther nodded. "I grew up here."

Leo looked to Adam. "So you've never even met your aunt?"

"No, I have! They visit sometimes."

"They? I thought you said your auntie's place. Who does she live with?"

"They're both my aunts. They live together."

"Ah. I see." Leo said, too tired to ask for further clarification.

They arrived at a tall wooden fence, roughly eight feet high, vertical beams hewn from tree trunks split into beams set eight to ten feet apart. Horizontal planks spanned the gaps between them, nailed all the way to the top with gaps large enough to look through, but small enough to keep out any zombie threat. Any *old* zombie threat, anyway, saying nothing about the new ones. It reminded Leo a lot of Arthur and Anna's place, just much lower tech, though the fact it was still there was evidence enough of its efficacy.

Twine wrapped around the outside of the fence about two feet off the ground, and again towards the top. Esther and Adam climbed, using the horizontal boards as a ladder near one of the vertical support beams. Leo followed suit near the next closest beam. They couldn't help but disturb the string, which gave off reverberant metal dings. Leo realized they were attached to wind chimes on the inside of the fence, spread out on roughly every fifth beam. *A decent method of triangulating where the sound—and thus the threat—may be coming from.*

The grounds were almost entirely garden and orchard. In the middle of the area, which covered a sprawling chunk of land bigger than Leo's apartment complex, was a modest one-story house with an ample deck wrapped around three sides. Whoever lived there loved to be outside.

A cha-chunk of a shotgun being primed echoed from the direction of the house, followed by a serious "Who's there?"

"It's us, Auntie Ray!" Adam yelled.

"Oh child, what are you doing here?" The voice came softer and a full octave higher. Its source walked out from behind a shed not too far from the house, a woman slightly older and more amply built than Leo. She was stocky and wore a large-brimmed hat that shaded her neck and shoulders.

When Esther saw Ray, they ran to each other and embraced. Ray let the shotgun hang in her hand. "So this isn't good news, then." Ray said to the world in general. Adam shook his head. Ray saw Leo, her grip on the shotgun tightened, her voice lowered an octave. "Who's this, then?"

"He saved us. Got rid of the bad things and gave us apples and helped us get here." Adam said.

"I'm Leo. I used to deliver chickens and whatnot for Blake and them."

"I see," Ray relaxed, pulling away from Esther's embrace. "and Blake—didn't make it?" Nobody responded. "I see. Well, let's go inside, your auntie Sam will be thrilled to see you."

Adam ran to the house and called for his aunt Sam. Ray wrapped her arm around Esther and walked them toward the house. She glanced at Leo, sizing him up. He pretended not to notice as he followed them. A muffled yelp of surprise and happiness came from inside as Adam found his aunt.

"He friendly?" Ray asked.

Leo looked at Ray, wondering why she asked that question about him, then realized she was talking to him about Sidekick. "Oh, yes. Well, he takes time to warm up to you, but I've never had an issue."

"That's good. You might want to hang on to him at first, though. Our cats are mostly friendly, but they're not fans of four-legged interlopers, we've found."

They sat around a large dining table inside the house. Sam had quickly made dough and baked some small, crunchy, lightly sweet cookies. They nibbled on those and drank water as Esther and Adam updated the others on the events of the last two days. Maybe longer, Leo wasn't sure. Their conversation was silent aside from Ray's occasional reactions to the news. Leo assumed what point in the story they were at based on her responses.

While the rest of the group talked in sign language, Leo focused on Sidekick, who hunkered down in his lap. The three other cats took turns inspecting Leo's legs and the new strange cat in their home. The friendliest of the three was bright orange and almost jumped onto Leo's lap, which startled Sidekick, who swatted at the orange cat. It just dodged the swat undeterred and stuck its face back towards Sidekick. The other two mostly circled and meowed curiously. Sidekick eventually relaxed enough for Leo to lower him to the floor. The cats all sniffed each other except for a young black and white spotted one that stayed in the adjacent room by the open door, judging.

"Oh, sorry," Ray said to Leo, snapping him back into the conversation. "Didn't mean to leave you out, we forget some people don't speak the language."

"Oh, no problem. I was just making sure Sidekick was getting along with the locals."

"Well, we're going to start getting ready for dinner. Would you mind helping me pick some pole beans? Unless you want to rest. Nobody would blame you if you did, based on the day you've had."

"Oh no, I'd love to help. Probably be a good cool-down for my muscles. They started tightening up just sitting here."

"Great!" said Sam. "While you two are out playing in the garden the rest of us will get things started in here." She smiled sincerely and slid her chair out from the table.

Leo got up and followed Ray to the door. He stopped and looked back to Sidekick, who sat frozen on the floor, overwhelmed by the new company and location.

Ray opened the door, and while putting her boots back on told Leo "He'll adjust fine. As long as he doesn't bother Sadie, but looks like she's keeping her distance, anyway. No need to worry about that one. C'mon."

Leo followed her outside. The sun seemed warmer and more pleasant. He wasn't that far from his home, but being on the south side of the hill and away from the tall downtown buildings, he somehow felt closer to the good parts of nature. At first he liked it, then it just felt odd.

"You pick beans before?" Ray asked, handing Leo a bucket.

"Kinda. I mean yes, but it's just been a few years. I lost my seed stock to mold when one of my water tanks sprung a leak. Learned my lesson. I store them high and dry now, and check the tanks regularly."

"Sorry to hear that. We can give you some of ours if you like."

"Oh, I couldn't ask you to do that. Don't want to mess up your setup out here."

"No trouble. Plus, I owe you for saving my only nephew and his mother."

"I didn't save them, just helped them get away when they needed it."

"Yeah, so... what happened exactly? With the fire, I mean?"

"I dunno, really. I saw the smoke rising from over the hill. What, two days ago now?" He shook his head. "Seems like longer. Anyway, I rode down to investigate yesterday and saw the aftermath. Would've gone sooner, but I was dealing with—another thing at home."

"I see. What do you think started it?"

"No clue. I mean fires happen, but usually the cause is pretty clear. Their building was wired, so maybe could've been something with that, but... who knows. Either way, whatever started it, the old chicken shit made a substantial meal for the flames."

"Yeah. That's one way to put it." Ray stood and stretched her back. "What I'm gettin' at is, anybody have reason to start it?"

"Oh, I doubt it. They provided eggs and chickens to a good portion of the area. Nobody had reason to hate Blake. Other than the smell, depending on the wind direction, but even then most people lived far enough away to not have that be an issue. Nah, people aren't what worry me out there."

Ray cocked her head at Leo. "How d'ya mean?"

Leo stood up, the muscles in his back protesting. "They told you about the zombies outside their place, right?"

"Yeah. Said they seemed spooky."

"More than spooky. Downright creepy. Those new ones—they're different."

"Darn it. I was hoping they were exaggerating out of fear or confusion from—everything, you know?"

"I wish." Leo shook his head. "These things are different. Smarter, somehow. I saw one—not one of the ones outside their place, mind you, but same type—it knew how to climb a ladder."

Ray took a long pause, considering the news. "Riiiight."

"I swear. It climbed a ladder. That cat in there is the only thing that saved me, distracted it. Also, it attacked another zombie."

"You mean--"

"Ate its damn brains right there in front of me."

"Sure it wasn't a *person* it ate and not--"

"100%."

"Maybe that's good news. They can get rid of each other for us."

"No. The more I think about it, the more I realize these new things—they must get smarter after feeding somehow. It was only after it ate the other one that it figured out how to climb."

Ray walked a few feet away to the shade of a pear tree. She looked across the garden toward the fence. "How good a climber?"

Leo followed her gaze. "Good enough to make it over that, I'm sure."

"Well, that *is* bad news."

Leo and Ray brought the beans inside and started slicing the ends.

Sam sent Adam to the root cellar to get potatoes for dinner. When he left, she made sure Leo and Ray had their backs turned. She stopped Esther in the middle of setting the table and signed, "Are you certain Blake is...you know?"

Esther nodded, her eyes turning glassy.

"And the farm, everything?"

"We have the roof gardens, and some loose chickens running the streets that Blake saved. Maybe we could gather them, but it can never be what it used to, not without a lot more work than we could put in."

"We can help, you know."

"I don't want to go back there."

Adam returned with a half dozen potatoes in the crooks of his arms. Sam set him up in the sink to wash the potatoes.

They all finished preparing dinner in silence.

After dinner, Adam asked to play outside. Ray told him to stay close to the house. Leo thought how much of a novelty it must be for the boy to be in that place, not confined to the chicken farm. The farm itself comprised many floors and the rooftop gardens on several buildings, technically making it more spacious than the ranch they were currently at, but the farm had an openness about it that buildings simply lacked.

Esther excused herself to sit on the porch outside. Ray motioned her head at Sam. They held hands for a moment, and Sam stepped out to join her sister, leaving Ray and Leo at the table. Ray leaned back and said, "Well..." and grabbed a few plates.

Leo rose and helped her gather and wash the dishes.

Ray said in a quiet voice, "So what's the plan now?"

"Uh. Well I guess I stay the night if that's ok, kind of assumed it, then I leave in the morning."

"Right. I mean fine, but.. I meant what's the plan for those new zombies? How many of them you think there are?"

"Can't say. Might be coming from the east, as far as I can tell. As for stopping them? Haven't tried yet. I imagine the basics are still true—no head, they're dead. Beyond that, your guess is as good as mine."

"And here we are surrounded by useless fencing. More of a cage than protection."

"Yep," Leo said, sadness in his voice. "We're all back to the days of worrying. Don't know where might be safe now."

They finished washing the dishes in silence, listening to the sounds of Adam playing outside.

Sidekick stayed close to Leo all night, neither of them too comfortable in the new surroundings. Leo thought the whole setup was too comfortable for their situation. It felt safe, probably just as safe as the chicken farm or his own apartment complex had. Even Sarah and her family couldn't be safe, and they were closer to harm's way. That realization raised his pulse. The Jacksons were the closest thing he had to family, and he couldn't imagine losing any of them. Sarah's face floated through his mind as he drifted to sleep, morphing into unfamiliar faces through each dream, but he recognized them all as Sarah.

Leo woke up early and quietly organized himself. He wanted to leave right away and warn Sarah's family. *Who knew how many of those things were coming their way. It seemed like they were increasing in number every day. Maybe something bad really had happened back east, and those things were spreading in all directions, making more smart zombies on their way.* The thought sent a sudden shiver down his spine. *Hadn't the world been strange enough already?*

Leo put Sidekick in his waist pouch and wandered outside.

"Morning," Ray said. Leo jumped, surprised he wasn't the only one up so early. She sat on a chair, drinking something warm and steaming from a metal cup. "You off?"

"That's the plan. How long you been up?"

Ray sighed. "A few hours, I think. Couldn't sleep. Thinking about how to bolster the wall. Make this safer now that it looks like our population's doubled."

"Yeah, I hear you." Leo looked out to the wall. "Wish I could help, but I have a few other people I need to warn, and I feel time slipping away, somehow."

"I get it. I'm just glad everyone I love is here now. I'd hate to have them out there, not knowing if they were in danger. I'd never tell her, but I worried about Esther every day. So yeah, I'm good to take care of my people here, you go take care of yours."

Leo smiled. He hadn't thought about the Jacksons as *his people* before, but in that moment he realized they really were his people. More than that, the notion was congealing in his mind that Sarah might be his person in particular. She popped into his mind so often through the years, he'd grown accustomed to having her around, and the thought she might be in grave danger brought things into focus. He wondered if what he felt inside was love. That scared and excited him.

"Anyways, there we are." Ray took a sip of her drink. After a moment she squinted at Leo. "Wait, you're the de facto delivery guy, right?"

"Yep. At least I used to be. Still could be once I have decent wheels again."

"Did you know the old delivery guy?"

A tingly wave moved through Leo's hair follicles. "You mean... Dave?"

"Yeah. It was a long time ago, didn't know if his name was still out there. You take the job after he died?"

"Yeah, you could say I inherited it." Leo had a million questions, but figured they had to wait, though he doubted he'd ever make his way back there again. "Did you know him well?"

"Met him a couple times. That was before Esther and Blake were a thing. We visited the city every year or so, bartered with some locals. We have great honey here. Anyway, he seemed nice. You just made me think about him is all. Out here, we kinda miss out on all the doings over there. How'd you know him?"

"Well, he was my dad."

Ray reacted as if she'd been hit in the forehead with an errant pebble. "Oh, my gosh! Well, that makes sense, then." She shook her head. "Wow, okay. Well, glad to see he raised a good one."

Leo felt warmth flush over his face. "Thank you. Well, I better go."

"Yeah, get a start at it. You have enough food?"

"I've been enough of a burden already."

"Leo. You saved my family. Shut up and grab some food before you go. Who knows when our paths will cross again, I better treat you well enough for a lifetime."

She got up and filled his pack with items.

"Stay safe out there." Ray said, walking Leo to the fence.

"Thanks. Oh, I don't suppose you know a better way to get

past the fallen highway section? We came down the ramps on the north side, and it was a heck of a time."

"Oh yeah, that can be tricky. The south side is your better bet. Shorter, too. Going east, you can go to the collapsed edge and climb down the rubble if it isn't too overgrown yet. Last time we went was about a year ago. Then head to the south on-ramp, it's closer than the north route. That was a real inconvenience when it collapsed."

"Thank you again. For everything."

"Thank you."

"If it's any consolation, I think you're far enough off the regular path, you're likely to be safe out here. Safer than anyone in the city, I'm afraid. Wish I had a solution for your fence, but I think the chime alarms are a good touch. Just don't make a lot of noise if you don't have to."

"Not a problem here. Don't really get visitors either, so..." She shrugged.

"Tell them bye for me, ok?"

"Will do."

Leo climbed over the wall and hopped back to the ground. It was a bit of a trek back to the highway. After a few minutes, he was afraid he'd been going the wrong direction. Then he finally saw the cement stretch sitting above the trees ahead in the distance. He made his way toward the cement beacon slicing through the sky. He was still a way off from the ramp up and had to slog through the underbrush. The morning dew made his pants and sleeves wet.

He was happy to make it back up to the highway. Sidekick had been squirming in his pouch the whole time, so Leo set him down to walk alongside and burn off that energy. He wished again he'd brought his bike. The sun warmed everything up, which was good to help dry his clothes.

The collapsed section was much closer than he remembered on the trip out. He walked to the right edge as instructed and found there were enough chunks of cement piled below for him to find a decent path down. He picked up Sidekick and hopped his way down to the forest floor. He walked alongside the collapsed road, which made a terrace beside him. The older trees were crushed under the collapsed section, and not enough time had passed for more to take their place. It made their previous route to the north seem silly in comparison.

He spotted the ramp ahead. As he got closer, something stood out to him—handlebars. He rushed over to them and found his bike buried in a bush. Whoever stole it had come that way, deeming it too much effort to lug the bike through the forest. He was happy to see his old Schwinn, but his trailer was nowhere in sight. As he lifted his bike out of the foliage and brought it up the ramp ahead, he realized the front tire was flat. Most likely popped from the careless rider, bringing it over the rough cracks in the road. *You had to be careful.* Whoever stole his bike was not. It had to have been that guy Sarah's father told him about. If not him, then someone else looking for a quick route west, away from whatever hell was making its way toward Leo's city. He walked the bike—or rather dragged it—up the ramp out of the forest to the unnatural cement canopy.

He was happy to find his bike, even if he couldn't ride it yet. He'd have to get to his place and patch the inner-tube before it was usable again. *A fortunate discovery to start the day.* He walked faster towards the city. He could see the buildings in the distance, like an amorphous grey mirage in the sky, the sun just peeking over the tops, casting lines of light and shadow through the high-rises.

"What a strange world," he told himself. "Not that it's more strange now than it had been at any other time." He wondered what it would be like to take someone from another time and place them there at that moment. *What would a Roman soldier think of this world?* Then he wondered how he'd fare if he were suddenly placed in other times in the past. That occupied his thoughts for a good portion of the day.

Leo stopped for a drink, and to rework his plan. Originally he was going to head straight for the stadium to warn Sarah and her family—his people—about the new threat to their survival. He could still do that, or he could walk home first and fix his bike, then ride to the stadium. He figured he'd still be able to make it before dark, assuming no other obstacles jumped in his path. He had to choose soon as the best route north forked off the highway not far ahead of him. He remembered that he had left the other bike downtown so he could just go there instead. It would be a shorter trip, and he could leave his Schwinn there for safekeeping. He looked down to Sidekick, who lounged on his back with his head leaned out of the pouch, eyes closed. "What do you think, buddy? Go home first?" Sidekick half opened his eyes groggily and closed them again. "Good point. Might as well get my wheels back in order first."

Leo took the butterfly ramp headed north. One of the ramp edges was broken off, either from someone running into it after taking the turn too fast back when the world was winding down, or from a tree falling, smashing the edge. It was hard to tell the difference at this point. On the road north, Leo walked fast, pushing through his tiredness. He'd given his legs quite a workout the last few days, but that stretch put him in almost direct sunlight, and he felt the heat.

He made it home mid afternoon. It felt good to walk his bike through the fence and into the carport again, even without his trailer. He wondered when he'd have a chance to ride around the downtown streets between the office and highway west, to see where the person who stole his bike had ditched his trailer. It might take him some time to cover all the streets, but the manner in which his bike had been left, he figured he'd just find his trailer discarded randomly with a flat tire or two. He worried they might've bent the wheels from the careless thief taking it over uprooted pavement. Either way, that was future Leo's concern. Present Leo had to patch up the tire on his Schwinn.

He set Sidekick on the ground, who groggily stretched and bounded off, chasing a butterfly, clearly living his best life. Leo strolled to the complex to fill a bucket with water to locate the leak in the inner tube. On his way, he noticed a door on the second floor was open. He froze. He'd made sure they were all locked before he left. After discovering his drawing of Anna was stolen, he'd been on high alert. Whoever had been in his home before had returned.

CHAPTER TWELVE

L eo slowly set the bucket on the ground. He quietly stepped to where he kept his water tanks and unlocked the door, holding the keys tightly in his fist to keep them from jangling. He grabbed the large wrench he kept just inside to work the pipe connections if they came loose and moved to the pole. He wished he'd left at least one ramp up, but that wish came a few days too late. He'd have to climb the pole, which would put him at risk if someone were waiting and rushed him from the open door. Leo reassessed his stance on firearms, regretted not having a gun. He figured the need for them was long gone, after the road warriors and bandits had all retired either at the business end of a gun, or through the march of time and age. Guns weren't too useful against zombies since the noise alone attracted more of them, plus bullets were rarer than ever.

He put the wrench through a loop in his pants and climbed up the pole as quietly as he could muster. He stepped onto the second floor and readied the wrench for attack. There were two closed doors between him and the open one, a door he rarely used, as it opened to what he referred to as "the library," which would be an odd choice for someone who might be robbing him to open. He ducked below the window and edged to the door. He paused and took a few deep breaths, bringing his heart rate down and focusing himself. He peeked into the room. A few books were strewn on the floor. So someone had definitely been there, if they weren't there still. Leo rose and pivoted into the doorway. It took a moment for his eyes to adjust.

It looked like someone had pulled books at random and tossed them on the floor, like they were looking for something, or just curious about Leo's things. He remained still and trained his ears on the silence, but after several minutes nothing stood out. He stepped inside. He searched through the entire complex again, room by room. Most rooms looked undisturbed, but a few had signs that someone other than Leo had been there. A table lamp near one of the wall openings lay on the floor. He wondered if the bulb was okay. Those were harder and harder to come by, and he hoped whoever had knocked it over was gentle enough to leave the bulb intact. He barely used the lights and only had a precious few left. He needed them to last for unknown future emergencies when he'd absolutely need their electric light.

Leo entered the room with his drawings and scanned the walls. Anna was still missing, but another blank spot on the wall stole his focus.

He had sketched several images of his father through the years, and after he'd passed, Leo put two of them up. The portrait of his dad he made right after he passed was still on the wall, but the earliest sketches he did of his father as a younger man, was gone. A corner of the paper still clung to the wall, thanks to a push pin bearing witness to the torn, missing image. Leo's mind screamed for answers. *Who the hell would take that sketch? Who was screwing with him?* His head grew hot and his heart beat loudly in his chest. He spun around and marched his way through the rest of the rooms in the complex. Other than a few other minor oddities, they were clear. Whoever had been there wanted him to know they'd been there.

Leo packed a few pairs of clothes, watered the indoor plants, and locked all the doors. He wouldn't be returning to his apartments for a while, couldn't trust his own home any longer. His home, his whole life, even, wasn't safe from anything, not from people, not from zombies.

He quickly filled the bucket with water, inflated the inner-tube and found the hole. He patched it with a cannibalized section from another inner-tube and a small dollop from the last tube of glue that remained from the old world. *That too would run out soon.* He sealed the tube and put it in his backpack. By then, Sidekick was nearby, lounging in the sun. Leo picked him up and took off on the bike on his way to the Jacksons's stadium.

The idea that someone was screwing with him wrapped around his brain like a python, and tightened, cutting off circulation to everything else. He pedaled mindlessly, knowing the way by heart. Before realizing it, he was almost at the stadium as the sun just started to set. He had no memory of traveling the last few hours.

He heard a gunshot and squeezed the brakes on his bike. It screeched to a stop. Another gunshot rang out from the stadium. Leo took off full speed toward the fence. The gates remained locked shut. More gunshots rang out, mixed with yelling from inside. Leo begged whatever tugged his life strings that Sarah was okay, adding Sharina and the rest of the Jacksons to the list.

Leo unwrapped the cat sling from his waist and draped it on the handlebars. Sidekick protested, but Leo had no time to comfort him, and didn't want something with sharp claws right next to his belly if he encountered something bad inside.

Most of the razor wire at the top of the fence had rusted away through the years, allowing Leo to climb over the outer fence. He landed on the other side a little too hard, giving his heels a short, sharp shock. He didn't have time to feel the pain and ran to the inner fence, climbing over it, and leapt to the ground inside. The cows bellered, and the ground rumbled from the herd. Leo's stomach braced itself for bad news.

He ran through the entrance into the center of the stadium. There was a small fire on the far side, close to the family's main living quarters. More gunshots rang out up the bleachers ahead of him. It was Grant, shooting at five figures who chased him up the stands toward the top of the stadium where they drank beer days earlier. Grant shot at them again, hitting one in the arm, but the figures continued, unfazed. "Zombies." Leo whispered to himself.

The ground rumbled with the sound of the cows stampeding back and forth across the field below. Another figure chased them. It looked like it could be one of the Jackson children, but it was too hard to make out in the moonlight, and the light from the fire across the stadium didn't stretch that far, but it was definitely growing.

Grant headed for the stairs up to the roof, scrambling up the ladder just inches ahead of the five zombies in pursuit. "Save the children!" Grant yelled to whoever could hear him. Leo almost responded, but stopped himself. He knew Grant's best chance at getting headshots on the group would be when they tried to climb the ladder after him. If Leo yelled, he'd only distract them, giving them someone else to chase, and Grant couldn't shoot them if Leo stood in the line of fire.

Leo jumped down to the field and ran to the far end of the stadium, ducking just out of sight of the zombies chasing Grant. He hoped Grant had enough bullets, and certain he'd realize really quickly that those weren't normal zombies chasing him, that they could climb the ladder up after him. Leo couldn't yell out a warning without risking everything else.

At the rate the fire was consuming the mostly wooden structure, it was only a matter of minutes away from reaching the entrance ramp below the stands to the family's main inhabitance. The cows were going crazy behind him, running against fences and each other. He was sure some had injured themselves beyond repair. He couldn't see the figure in the field anymore, but hoped if it was Dinah, she was ok. Leo ran into the tunnel leading under the stands, feeling the surrounding warmth from the advancing flames. Screams echoed around the walls inside the quarters.

He saw the body of one of the twins on the ground against the wall, bloody and lifeless. She was so torn up he couldn't tell which one it had been. He continued ahead, deeper inside. Steven, the Jackson's only boy, zipped down the hall to the right in front of him.

Leo stopped at the junction and saw the rest of the family to the left. Sarah swung a baseball bat, fending off a zombie while Sharina hunched behind her, holding whichever twin wasn't in the hallway outside. The zombie's jaw hung by a shred of bloody gristle, swinging back and forth under its face as it lunged. Sarah swung low, breaking its leg. On its way down, the zombie reached out and grabbed Sarah's leg, jerking her off balance. She fell, tossing the bat to free her hands so she could catch herself. Leo ran in and leapt on the zombie feet first, crushing in several of its ribs. It seemed to give a gargled yell and let go of Sarah, semi-confused, and looking around to see what hit it.

Sarah looked up in surprise, assuming the form that sped into the room was another one of those things, relieved at recognizing it was Leo and not an additional threat.

The zombie swiped at Leo's legs. He kicked it away and helped Sarah back up. She grabbed the bat and swung at the thing's head, smashing it. Bits of brain and blood splattered around the room. The zombie went limp on the floor. Without catching her breath, Sarah ran to her mother. Leo joined them.

"Tina?" Sarah asked, already knowing the answer.

Sharina shook her head and tears fell from the corner of her eyes as she held the lifeless body of her second youngest daughter in her arms.

"We gotta go." Leo said "the whole place is going up in flames. We have to leave now."

From another room they heard Steven yell, followed by several gunshots.

Sharina yelled, "No! My babies!"

Leo grabbed the bat off the floor and ran back down the hall toward the noise. Another two gunshots echoed through the halls ahead, accompanied by a pained scream from Steven.

Leo neared Grant and Sharina's bedroom, a part of the stadium Leo had never been in before. He ran inside, getting his bearings. Another zombie lay prone, unmoving and lifeless on the bed. Leo called for Steven. A few seconds of silence that felt like several minutes passed. Leo's heart sank. He could hear breathing across the room. He slowly edged toward the far side of the bed. On the floor, against the wall, on the other side of the mattress, he saw Steven hunched over. The boy breathed shallow, pained breaths.

"Steven?" Leo asked, hoping it was still Steven he was talking to and not a Steven-shaped zombie. The boy slowly looked up towards Leo, groggy.

"Wh—what are you—oh!" Steven winced and grabbed his right arm. Steven had been firing a rifle at the zombie. He must've known it was hidden in the room for just such an occasion, though he'd either fallen, or tried pushing his body against the wall in his effort to get away from the zombie as it ran towards him, and when he fired the last shot, the rifle kicked back into his shoulder smashing it hard against the wall. "I hurt my arm."

"I can see," Leo said. "Are you ok? You know, otherwise?"

"It hurts real bad." The boy said, fear and shame mixed with pain in his voice.

"I see that. Can you walk?"

Steven nodded. Leo realized the boy had grown up faster than he should have, but just as fast as the world had forced him to. Leo helped him up. The boy's shoulder hung low and appeared to be shattered. Leo ripped part of the sheet off the bed and made a makeshift sling for the boy's limp arm. Steven was in more shock than pain at the moment, so Leo picked him up and carried him as gently as he could out of the room and down the hall.

Sarah led a limping Sharina toward the exit. The heat and smoke from the flames had already started making the whole place unbearable. They saw each other in the hallway and wordlessly made their way out of the tunnel together. Sharina gave a brief wail as they rushed past her other daughter's body. Flames had already began licking the outside edges of the tunnel entrance, almost overwhelming the exit with heat. Leo's scalp singed as he ran the injured boy out into the open field, away from the flames.

Leo set Steven down "you're gonna have to walk now, okay?" The boy nodded. Sarah grabbed his good hand with her free arm, the other wrapped around her mother's shoulder. "You all get to the parking lot. I'll check on Grant."

"Wait, where's Dinah?" Sharina said.

"I think she's with the cows. I'll look for her too, but you need to get out of here now!"

Sarah nodded and urged the other two to move. "Don't worry mama, I'll come back too after we get you out of harm's way, ok?" They made their way towards the fence at the far side of the field. Leo could see Sharina had a severe limp, but they could tend to that later. Sarah was qualified enough to handle both her mother and brother.

Leo bounded up the stands towards the ladder to the roof. He could see several dead zombies piled up at the base, which he took as a good sign. "Grant!" Leo yelled. He could hear movement on the tin roof above. He climbed over the bodies, counting four, and climbed up the ladder as fast as he could. "Grant! Sir, are you ok?"

"Not great," he heard from the far side of the roof.

Good, Leo thought, *at least he's still alive.* Leo popped his head through the opening and saw one of the zombies running at Grant. Grant backed farther away, holding the pistol as a club, out of bullets.

Grant yelled to Leo, "Is everyone ok?"

Leo climbed onto the roof "Sharina, Sarah, and Steven are, yes. Dinah too, I think." Leo's yelling made the zombie spin around and look to where the new voice was coming from. Grant took the opportunity and ran full speed at the zombie, rearing back his hand to strike with the butt of the pistol. "Grant! These things—they're different!"

The zombie turned, seeing Grant flying at him. Grant's arm came down fast, and just as fast the zombie spun out of the way, striking Grant's arm. They both lost their balance and fell to the roof with a hard metallic slam.

Grant stood up. "I see that." The zombie rose, glanced at Leo, then back at Grant. It hunched down in a starter's position and rushed Grant. Grant threw the pistol at the zombie, hitting it in the face, but it didn't slow down one bit. Grant swung wide again, but the zombie was faster. It made contact with Grant's stomach, its momentum propelling both of them backwards. In a second they flew off the roof. Leo watched as time slowed and realization washed over Grant's face and they disappeared over the edge. Leo's stomach fell with them. A moment later he heard them hit the pavement. Leo stepped to the edge of the roof and saw their two bodies limp on the hard ground below.

Leo's knees gave out, and he fell backwards onto the roof. He felt like nothing in the world was fair, but he'd have to even out that score later. He had to find Dinah. He couldn't let any more of the Jacksons die that night. He slid down the stairs and almost tripped on his way down the stands as he rushed to the field at the stampeding cattle. The flames had already consumed a full third of the stadium, and were quickly making their way towards Leo and the front entrance.

"Help me!" He heard a child's voice from the field. Dinah was close to the stadium entrance, but the herd was chasing her towards the flames.

"Where are you going?" Leo yelled.

"I have to get the cows out. They can't die like this." Leo thought of Blake, how he must have felt trying to save his family and the chickens before sacrificing himself in the fire. "Get down here and help me herd them out! I opened the fences already!" Leo saw the fences towards the entrance were wide open. "I'll drive them towards you out the fence. You push them towards the front gate!"

Leo leapt over the barrier between the stands and the field and ran towards the part of the stadium already on fire to get on the other side of the fence opening. The cows rushed at the open section. They were going mad and crowding each other, pushing a few in the herd against the fence, scraping up their bodies. Leo did his best to keep them as organized as one could when a group of beasts go wild. They overwhelmed the opening, crushing the fence. The flames neared. The last few ran through, and Dinah followed, out of breath. She tried to yell at Leo to follow, but he didn't need the words to understand. They ran behind the herd, chasing them to the entrance, hoping Sarah had opened the gates enough and was out of the way not to get crushed by the impending stampede.

Sarah helped her mother and little brother hobble to the fence. As she neared the chain securing it shut, she realized she didn't have the key to the lock. She asked Steven to help their mother the rest of the way to the gate as more of a motivation for him to be strong and go on than a real help to their mom as they were both in severe pain. Sarah hadn't seen exactly what happened and how her mother hurt her leg, but she knew Sharina was the first one to fight back against the zombies when they invaded their home. She wondered how they'd gotten in and set the question aside in her mind for another time.

Sarah rushed back to the stadium. They kept the key just out of sight around the grandstands; Close enough to the gate to be helpful, but not so close any passerby would know where it was.

Sarah fumbled, searching for the box with the hook that held the key, finally finding it. As she grabbed it, she glanced back at the field and paused. "The cows are out!" She yelled, then realized the cows weren't out as much as they were being herded—straight towards her.

Her heart pounded as she sprinted to the fence.

"Move back! Move back!" Sarah yelled to her mother and Steven. "I'm gonna open the gate all the way! Get behind it, now!"

Sharina was confused and tried to ask what was going on, but Sarah cut her off with "Stampede!"

Sharina took a moment to take in the meaning, and a second later she moved as if her leg were in perfect shape. She picked up Steven, who yelled at the pain shooting through his arm. At the same moment, Sarah struggled to get the key in the lock. On normal days it was a little sticky from all the rust gathered through the years. When she finally got the key in and opened the lock, the ground shook as the herd closed in. She ripped the chain off, throwing it behind her. She lifted a corner of the fence and ran with it in an arc towards the stadium wall. The cows rounded the corner, looking for any open space to run towards.

Sarah slammed the fence against the stadium wall, putting it between her and the herd. She jerked it tight against the wall, hoping it would withstand the onslaught. The cows ran straight towards her. Sharina tucked behind Sarah, still holding a wildly screaming Steven tight in her arms.

The first of the herd saw the opening between the outer and inner fences, stretching as far as it could see. It recognized the fence as a friend and rushed straight for the opening. As cattle do, the herd followed their leader into the fenced-in chute. The space between the two fences was big enough for barely four cows at a time, but the herd had no interest in counting. They swarmed, slamming the end of the fence Sarah held against the wall. She blocked her face with her arm. Sharina screamed in terror. Sarah put all her weight into the fence, trying to keep it from falling over on them, risking being trampled by the herd.

Sharina set Steven down by the wall. He was in tears from the pain shooting through his arm and the rumbling threat breaking upon the fence like an angry wave. Sharina joined Sarah, pushing her back hard against the fence. It shook violently as dozens of one ton animal bodies slammed against it, inching it closer to collapse. They yelled at the cows, confusing them enough to slow the ones nearest them down. The rumbling continued, but the fence shook less as most of the herd was already through, running down the long stretch between fences. Sarah wondered if the front of the herd was heading straight into the flames or was the fencing far enough away from the building, making them safe. If not, the herd would panic and start trampling itself as the front end resisted being pushed headfirst into a wall of flames.

The last few cows made their way around the corner of the stadium and between the fences. Sarah yelled for Sharina and Steven to follow her to the outer gate. She knew either the herd would make their lap around the perimeter in a minute or they'd head back the way they'd gone with renewed vigor. Either way, she did not want to be at the business end of the stampede a second time. She pushed the gate back enough to leave room for her family to squeeze through, and ran to the chain locking the outer fence, but remembered she left the keys in the other lock in her panic to open the inner gate. She heard footsteps and was happy to see an out of breath Leo come around the corner, followed a moment later by Dinah.

"Oh, thank God!" Sarah said. "The chain! We need the lock in the chain!" They scrambled, searching the ground for the errant chain. Dinah accidentally tripped on it. Sarah grabbed it and sighed in relief, finding the keys still inside. She pulled them out and ran down the trough between the fences and quickly unlocked the chain on the outer fence and swung it wide open. Leo and Dinah helped Sharina and Steven make their way to the world outside the fence, beyond their formerly safe home within the stadium walls. They limped further into the parking lot and turned around to watch everything they'd known and loved burn.

"Wait," Sarah blurted, "where's my dad?" The family looked to Leo. He shook his head and looked at the ground. Sharina wailed. The family hugged each other, Steven yelped and turned to the side with his broken shoulder away from the huddle.

The herd returned from the direction they'd stampeded, much thinner than before. Those would be just the first that had turned around. The ones leading the charge most likely perished in the flames, pushed to their doom by those behind them.

The cows paused at the opening in the outer gate. The first one sniffed and pushed its nose in the space, like it didn't believe there was no fence. It took one cautious step forward. Other cows ventured to the opening out of curiosity and pushed against the first one, giving it the last motivation it needed to walk the rest of the way out into the open parking lot. Several more followed. A few errant cows continued straight down the other side between the fences, unsure of what exactly to do next. The bulk of the herd rushed into the parking lot, though, and ran full bore out the opening to freedom, incapable of understanding the cost of their freedom.

The outer fence toppled to the ground, lacking the people and wall to support the onslaught of the herd. Some confused cows took advantage of the wider gap, running over the downed metal fence, but two of them caught their hooves in the fencing and broke or sprained their legs in the struggle.

The far end of the stadium collapsed in on itself. Their home was officially gone, up in smoke. Leo looked to the family and sighed. "I hate to be the one to say this, but we have to move now."

Sarah looked at Leo with anger and sadness in her eyes. She knew he was just the messenger, but the pain from everything she'd lost was overwhelming.

"Please," Sharina said in a feint whisper, "just a little while longer." Leo nodded.

Sarah saw the few cows on the ground struggle and bellow with their hurt legs "We have to help them." She let go of her family and took a step toward the struggling creatures.

"No." Leo said, much more firmly than he intended.

"Excuse me?" Sarah said, Leo's words sounding alien to her.

"We have to move, I'm sorry."

"But--" Sarah pointed to the animals "They're in pain. We're responsible for them."

"They're on their own now. We all are." The remaining Jacksons all looked at Leo with disbelief. After a moment he said, "The flames, they're going to attract things we don't want to deal with."

Sharina gave a deep, angry sigh. "We've dealt with zombies before."

"Not these ones! The ones that just destroyed your home—they weren't normal, were they?"

Sarah and Sharina exchanged looks. Steven looked up and said, "they were fast."

Sarah looked at Leo, lost in a sea of thought. "You saw the fire downtown a few days ago, right?" He said.

Sarah had, knew nobody in the city could have missed it.

Leo continued. "That was the chicken farm. It burned down too, and a few zombies stuck around, but they were different. They were fast, yes, but they were also—I don't know—smarter, somehow."

Sarah shook her head, not wanting to believe any of it.

"They chased me, one of them separated from the pack. There were three of them at first, then two. I thought it must've gotten lost, but then I turned a corner and found it was there—it knew where I was going and tried cutting me off. These things—they're getting clever. They learn and think."

"The fire." Sharina said. "How'd it start?"

Leo shrugged. "They didn't know. It happened in the middle of the night."

"And those things—they were there when it happened?"

"I—I guess. I don't know. They were there when it was over, just waiting for the survivors to come down." They were silent for a moment. "How'd this fire start?"

"I don't know." Sarah said, and looked to her mother, deep in thought, shaking her head.

"They have to be connected." Leo looked to the ground "It's just too close together for both these fires to be coincidence."

"Then you're right, we have to go." Sharina said. "Those damned things—I don't want them waiting for us. They can't get all of my family."

"But mom-" Sarah started, her mother cutting her off.

"No buts. You're not taking more chances. We're not giving those things another opportunity. Where can we go?" She looked to Leo. "Where can we be safe from them?"

CHAPTER THIRTEEN

Leo walked to his bike. He stopped dead when he saw the sling draped over the handlebars was empty. "Sidekick!" He yelled, spun around, and began searching the ground wildly.

The Jacksons were confused. Sarah walked to Leo and asked, "What?"

"Sidekick!" Leo said, panic growing in his chest. "I have a cat. Sidekick. I left him here." They all looked around. The moon gave everything a general glow, and the stadium-sized fire illuminated the open lot nearest the flames. Cattle meandered around the parking lot, mooing randomly and eating the grass and weeds that sprouted from the cracks. Leo suddenly realized how he must seem. Sarah lost her father, two sisters, her home. Her mother and only brother were injured, and Leo was freaking out about a cat. It seemed selfish, and he knew it, but he couldn't help it, and the fear and loss overtook him.

Leo pointed to the cows struggling in the fallen fencing. "I'll find him. You can take care of them." He walked away from the group through the meandering herd that slowly spread across the lot. He called Sidekick's name, unsure if the cat even knew it had a name, much less that it was Sidekick. When he was far enough away from the Jacksons that the stray cows blocked their view of each other, in the shadow of the last section of stadium that wasn't yet on fire, he collapsed to the ground and wept.

Leo sat there for a while, letting the tears flow out of him. He hated that he'd never cried like that for his mother. He felt stupid for crying that passionately for a cat he just met a couple of weeks earlier. He wondered if it was the loss of everything combined that brought him to that point of emotional collapse. The Jacksons had lost their home and too many members of their family for the world to be fair. Leo lost his home to some unknown force, and Esther and Adam had just lost Blake and their home. So many displaced people, and the city would soon suffer even more. With the loss of both the chicken and beef farms, the city had also lost their primary source of meat, eggs, milk, cheese, soap, leather, and whatever else he couldn't think of at the moment.

The most reliable sources of protein for a good portion of the city were up in smoke, the last remnants wandering the streets until mountain lions, wild dogs, or some other predator took advantage of the opportunity for a free meal. More than just his apartment, Leo realized he'd lost his job, and possibly the city itself. Even if only parts of it were on fire, the whole place was up in smoke one way or another. He wondered if the city had been declining for years and he was just lying, telling himself that life would always go on as it had. *Maybe it did, just not for everyone.* He wished nature weren't so heartless.

Leo wiped his face with the bottom of his shirt. Even if the Jacksons were justifiably deep in their own sorrows, he did not want them to see evidence of his tears. He sat there another moment, collecting himself, emotionally preparing to lead the Jacksons out into the vast, dark night.

Somewhere at the edge of the herd farther out in the darkness, Leo heard a feint meow. He perked up and froze, listening, scanning the darkness for another sign. He heard it again. He jumped up and walked in the sound's direction towards the far edge of the parking lot. There, only small streaks of light danced across the ground in patches of pavement and grass. He saw the silhouette of a lone cow eating. Near its face he heard the meow again. As he got closer, he realized rather than eating grass, the cow was licking a small creature. "Sidekick!" Leo yelled, feeling the pressure behind his eyes return as tears pushed their way out.

Sidekick looked to Leo, and the cow gave another long lick at the cat's fur, making that side of Sidekicks fur stand straight up, like half its body was frozen in a heavy wind. Leo picked up his cat and squeezed him in his arms. His hands and shirt wet with cow saliva. Leo didn't mind, he had his Sidekick back. In a long night of sadness, standing deep in the darkness of a parking lot, Leo found the bright spot of the evening.

Sidekick seemed more confused than anything. Leo figured he'd never seen cows before and must have been scared at first and ran away, but eventually gotten curious enough to explore what they were all about. The cows must have been similarly confused, being out in the world beyond their fence for the first time, and finding a new little creature.

Leo collected himself and walked back towards the Jacksons. Their silhouettes lit by the flames tearing their home to the ground. Entropy once again showing just how vicious and inexorable it can be. *Or is it nature showing humans who's really in charge?* Leo mused. No matter who or what was saying it, the message was clear—humans were small and finite, so they better appreciate what they have while they have it, because sooner than anyone realizes, it would all be gone.

Leo approached the Jacksons. They held each other close, watching the flames, listening to the message loud and clear.

Leo came up beside Sarah. She looked at him and saw Sidekick in his arms. They could tell they both had been crying. She leaned in slowly towards Leo, his heart suddenly racing, and kissed him. The warmth in her lips belied the sorrow they held back. She felt so warm and alive against him, his body tingled like an electric wave rolled through it, lighting it up from the inside out. It lasted for just a moment before Sarah slowly pulled away. They stared into each other's eyes for a long moment. Leo put his arm around Sarah and pulled in close next to her. They looked back to the burning stadium. With great loss comes sadness. Sometimes it brings with it despair. Other times, great loss brings clarity. Leo didn't need places or things, he just needed people. He needed Sarah, and maybe a Sidekick.

It was Sarah who eventually said, "we should go now." Feeling the coldness creeping in behind them, knowing it no longer helped to witness their loss so closely.

Leo squeezed Sarah's shoulder, and she leaned into him. "I'll get my bike. Sharina, you can ride it if you're able."

"But my leg, I can't pedal, Dinah should have it. Or Steven." Sharina said, always the giver.

"We have several miles to go," Leo said, taking a step closer to get a better look. "Your leg can't take that walk. We'll steady you, no need to pedal, and Steven's arm won't be able to take the constant bouncing you'll get on the bike. We can all walk, right?" He said, looking right at Steven. He could see the boy look around, realization on his face he was the sole man of the family now, whatever that meant anymore, but Leo knew Grant would've raised him, his only son, to be responsible for the entire family's wellbeing. Steven nodded and lifted his head, standing taller to carry the unfamiliar weight on his shoulders. Even if one of them was shattered.

"I'll walk too. Mama can ride the bike." Dinah said proudly.

"Good." Sidekick squirmed in Leo's arm, his fur stiff from the drying cow lick. "Oh, and this is Sidekick. He saved my life."

Dinah smiled and looked to Leo, pleading with her eyes.

Leo smiled back and asked, "I don't suppose you'd be able to carry him for a bit?"

Dinah jumped. "Yes, please!"

Leo grabbed the sling and wrapped it around Dinah, shortening the loop with an extra knot to make it a more ideal length for the child to carry. Sidekick was unsure of the whole situation, but quickly turned to purring as Dinah petted him, ignoring his cow-licked fur.

Sarah and Leo steadied the bicycle and helped Sharina lift her hurt leg over the center bar. Her stockings stretched up above the bottom of her dress and Leo could see blood staining her hurt leg. He asked her what exactly happened.

"Oh, it's nothing, just silly."

"It would help to know, even if it's silly." Leo said, concerned.

"I got scratched when the thing attacked."

Sarah chimed in, "It knocked her to the floor trying to get her. She kicked it off."

"Yep. Just a scratch, that's all." Sharina said, "How far are we going again? And where are we going, exactly?"

Leo turned the question over in his head. His home was no longer an option, plus it was much farther than he'd be comfortable taking the Jackson family, anyway, and Arthur's compound was even farther from the stadium than his apartment complex. He even questioned how safe his downtown escape would be at that point. Sure, it had a door that locked, but doors and windows were breakable, plus whoever was going around starting fires could easily burn the whole building down with them inside. No. As far as Leo could guess, there was one option. "The power plant."

The family registered their own surprised reaction to the news.

"It's fortified with fencing and walls. It's the safest place in the city." Leo said confidently, uncertain if they'd even be allowed in, but it was worth a shot. He added, "Plus, it's mostly downhill from here." Leo nodded ahead, and they all began the journey toward the power plant.

"That'll be neat!" Dinah said. Steven grunted in agreement, the pain growing in his arm. "Who lives there?"

Leo thought about that for a while. "Well, hopefully we'll all find that out in a few hours."

They went back and forth discussing who might be inside the facility, providing the remaining people in wire's length with electricity in exchange for food and supplies. It was a city-wide mystery. Leo figured the discussion was a pleasant distraction from all the evening's events. It was also a distraction from the threats lurking in the darkness ahead of and around them. Old zombies, new zombies, animals, people, they were all equal and omnipresent threats. Leo looked at Sarah who held the handlebars opposite him, working together to steady Sharina on the bike. Steven and Dinah walked just ahead of them. Leo called out at them to stay close. He didn't want the smallest of the group to get so far ahead they'd look like easy targets for a mountain lion or zombie.

After a mile, Dinah's tiny legs grew tired. They stopped for a minute, allowing Sidekick and his sling to go back to Leo, who steadied the bike alone while Sarah picked up her little sister to carry her a while.

When they ran out of theories about who could have kept a power plant running through the years, they continued on in silence. The sky was the smallest shade lighter, signaling they were closer to the morning hours than the middle of the night. The fear chemicals that surged through their veins had worn off, and they were all tired from the combined lack of sleep and physical exertion in the chilly night air. Leo stopped the bike. "Wait." He said. Everyone paused, slightly confused. "Did you hear that?" They all listened.

"I didn't hear anything." Sarah said.

Leo hoped he hadn't heard anything either. "There was rustling from over there, somewhere in the forest." Leo pointed to their right. They stood in silence for a while longer. Sharina leaned the bike over, resting on her good foot. She seemed more tired than the rest of them. "I heard it a while back, thought it was nothing, but I heard it again."

"Is something following us?" Steven asked, more excited than scared.

Leo didn't want to scare the boy, but he would not lie, either. "Maybe." He said.

"Or some*one*." said Dinah.

"Or nothing, just birds or squirrels rustling around." Sarah added.

"Let's hope." Leo said, more of an encouragement to himself than any of the others.

Leo went over the options in his mind, should he go into the woods to explore the sound or should they move on? Or perhaps he should stay behind while the rest moved on to give him a chance to listen for whether who or whatever was stalking them continued its pursuit. As he weighed the options, Sharina slowly slumped over and fell to the ground. The bike tipped, pushing Leo's legs like a domino, and he fell along with her.

Leo reached his arms out to soften both their blows. He hit the ground hard on his side. His vision went white for a moment and he couldn't breathe. A few moments later, he caught his breath. Steven dropped Sidekick, who leapt to the ground. Sarah, Dinah, and Steven ran to their mother. Leo moved his body one part at a time, Sarah asked how he was. Between pained inhalations he said he was fine, he just had the wind knocked out of him, luckily. He didn't think anything was broken, but he was sure he'd bruised a couple of ribs. *Just one thing after another.*

Sharina was a different case. She was passed out. Leo sat up and helped Sarah carefully lift the bike off them while Leo lifted Sharina's hurt leg, setting it down on the ground. Sharina woke, groggy. Leo felt the blood from her leg on his hands, still wet. She'd been bleeding slowly the whole time they traveled. He hadn't noticed because the night was so dark. He started pulling her long stocking sock down to take a better look at the wound. Sharina winced.

"No, don't." Sharina said faintly. "Please."

"I'm sorry, we have to look." Leo said, pulling the stocking down, doing his best to hold it away from the wound. Sharina gave another pained plea to stop. Leo uncovered her ankle just below the wound. The reason her blood hadn't congealed enough to stop the bleeding was instantly clear to Leo and Sarah.

"You're bit." Leo said. Sarah shook her head and held her hands to her mouth, not wanting to show her family the fear and sadness coursing through her body. She was unsuccessful.

"I tried..." Sharina said, already growing distant and weak from blood loss and the zombie infection moving through her body, slowly hijacking it as its own. "It just—I'm sorry."

Steven and Sarah sat their mother up, embracing her, Dinah laid down on her mother's lap and curled up, not wanting to accept the reality that they'd lose both their parents in the same night.

"Why didn't you say something?" Sarah pled.

Sharina shook her head and kissed Sarah on the forehead. "I didn't want to scare anyone. I hoped that maybe if I didn't look, it might not be true."

"Momma," Dinah said, "Are you gonna be—one of those things?" Sarah held back a yawp of sadness.

"No, honey," Sharina said, a small smile forced on her face to mask the truth. "No, my child." She looked at Sarah "we're not gonna let that happen."

Sarah pulled away. "No. Mom, no."

"It's okay, my sweetie." Sharina moved Sarah closer.

Sarah pulled away and looked to Leo. "Do something. Say something!"

Leo wanted to make it all better, but not since the zombie plague began had anyone he'd known reversed the inexorable course of the infection. It was too late to try a Hail Mary move and amputate her leg, hoping the infection hadn't spread to the rest of her body. She was already in the late stages of turning. Even if that weren't the case, the amount of blood loss she suffered was a death sentence. He had to say something. "Maybe we can keep going together, and your mom could recover."

"Don't." Sharina said "Don't give them false hope. I'm bitten, that's all there is to it."

Sarah stood, walking away from the group to get air and collecting herself while her siblings cried. Leo knelt down beside Sharina. "Just so we know, the one that bit you—I'm sorry to ask this, but—was it one of the new ones? The fast, thinking ones? Or--"

Sharina shook her head. The color leaving her face. "No. I ran from my room to the twin's room, came around a corner, and it was just there. Knocked me over and got me. I kicked it, got away. It just crawled at me. Not like the others. I smashed its head in, but the girls—one of those other ones was in there. I couldn't get it quickly enough. I couldn't help."

"Mother, you saved us, you did all you could." Dinah whimpered.

Sharina wept "Why couldn't I do more?" She held her hands over her eyes.

"Mom." Sarah joined her family on the ground, crying.

Leo heard rustling in the forest again. Whatever they decided, they'd have to do it soon. They couldn't risk being out unprotected at night with so many vulnerable in their party. He looked at the family. So much loss, and more still to come. He knelt down to get closer to Sharina and spoke in a soft voice next to her ear. "What would you like us to do?"

Sharina uncovered her eyes, her voice only thinly veiling the tears she held back. "I don't want to be one of those things. Please. My children can't see me like that." A wave of sadness spread across the group. Dinah protested.

Sidekick stood a few feet behind everyone facing the forest. He hissed toward the same spot Leo had heard the noise earlier.

Leo nodded, tears putting pressure behind his own eyes. "I understand. However you'd like us to do it, we'll do it, but we have to move soon, we're not safe here."

Sarah put her hand just below Leo's elbow. He looked to her and took her hand in his. They breathed together in sadness.

"I—I'm cold. End it now, please." Sharina said. She looked to her children. "I'm sorry I couldn't do more."

They all comforted Sharina, telling her it wasn't her fault, she was the best mother; they loved her, but nobody protested the action. They had all come to the same conclusion, even little Steven and Dinah. It was no longer time for them to be children, their world was no longer safe enough for such ideas as childhood.

Leo tried to remember when he'd grown up so suddenly. It had happened not as a slow process, but all at once. *It was when his mother died.* The world before then was dangerous in a general way. At that exact point it became dangerous in a very specific way, and it had been ever since. Losing his mother was also the loss of his childhood, as it would be for the Jackson children.

"Ok," Leo whispered. He pulled out a small wooden spike from a pouch on his bike. "You should all step away, I don't think you want to see this." Dinah and Steven rose and took a few steps back, holding hands.

"No." said Sarah.

"Sarah, it has to be done." Leo said.

"I know." She put her hand on the spike. "I'll do it."

"Are you sure?"

Sarah nodded. "We take care of our own."

Leo wanted to stop her, didn't want her to carry the image of the last moment of her mother's life in her brain. He wanted to say that Sharina felt like one of his own too, but no words came out. He just squeezed her hand and gave her a gentle nod, letting her take the spike from his hand. He looked to Sharina, whose eyes were already drifting, eyelids half-mast and twitching. He reached down to hold her hand. It was cold, a sign she was close to the end. He whispered, "Thank you. For everything. You—you were my second mom... I love you" She gently squeezed his hand back, letting him know she was still in there somewhere. Leo stood and looked around for a sizable rock. He picked one up and handed it to Sarah.

Sidekick gave a low warning meow. Leo wasn't certain if it was aimed at the sound in the woods or at Sharina. It just occurred to him that perhaps cats could sense when a person was becoming one of those things. He heard the rustling again in the woods and picked up

Sidekick, who swatted at his hand.

Leo held his cat close to his chest. It dug its claws into Leo's shirt and twisted its head around, still focusing toward Sharina and the woods past her. Leo went to the children. He turned them to face away from their mother while he watched as Sarah whispered her final words in her mother's ear. She wiped her eyes with her sleeve and took a deep breath that brought no comfort. She gently turned her mother's head to her side. Sharina's body began to shake with palsied tremors in her limbs. She was turning. Sarah had to work fast. She held the spike to Sharina's ear like an arrowhead with her left hand. She gripped the rock in her right hand, holding the flattest side away from her palm. She slowly lifted the rock above her head. Leo pulled the children close against him. Sarah brought the rock down hard, slamming the spike into her mother's brain. Sharina's body convulsed once, then lay limp. Sarah fell back onto the ground and shrank into a ball.

Dinah and Steven wept. The sound of the stone against the spike echoed in their memories. Leo gave them a moment, then bent down and asked if they'd help him get the bike. They nodded. He squeezed them again, wishing, like Sharina, that there was more he could do.

Leo handed Sidekick to the children and joined Sarah. He knelt down and held her tight. Her body bounced with each silent cry, paroxysms of sorrow washing through her. "I'm sorry." Leo said, unable to think of anything more useful.

A while later Sarah uncurled. Leo helped her up and carried her over to her siblings, who balanced the bike upright. Leo asked them if Sarah could ride on the bike for a bit. They both nodded silently. Leo sat Sarah down on the seat. She held on to him for an extra moment and took a few deep breaths before letting go, pulling her head away from his shoulder. She reached down and held the handlebars with her hands, her little siblings on each side of the bike like human training wheels. That is what remained of the Jacksons, the closest thing to what families had looked like in the world before everything changed. Much like everything else from the old world, they'd been broken. "We should move." Leo said. They continued on in silence.

CHAPTER FOURTEEN

The sky grew lighter as they approached the power plant, its soft hum filling the air, the sun starting its journey over the horizon. They had not spoken a word since leaving Sharina. Leo was content that whatever made the sound in the forest hadn't followed them. He wondered if maybe it stayed behind for a closer look at Sharina's body, but he dared not speak the thought aloud. The Jacksons did not need that idea needling its way into their brains.

A while back, Dinah had taken Sarah's place on the bike. Since her legs were too short to reach the pedals, Sarah and Leo each held a handlebar and guided her forward. Steven had been slowing his pace through the journey. The trip was longer than he had ever walked in a day at the farm, and he had stumbled a few times in the course of the previous hour. Leo wasn't sure if it was just from his lack of sleep and the family's many losses, or how much it had to do with his shattered shoulder and the accompanying pain, and hidden threats under his skin. That was a growing concern in Leo's mind, yet another he didn't want to speak aloud. Still, he needed to break the silence and distract them all from their thought spirals. "Do you hear it?"

They listened for a moment. Dinah turned to Leo "The cch-hhhh sound?"

Leo ran his fingers through the hair atop her head. "Yep. That's where we're going."

"They'll let us in?" Sarah asked.

"That's the hope." Leo said. He wasn't lying, he only had hope that he'd accrued enough good will to warrant passage inside those high walls. Either way, he had a lot of bad news to deliver to whoever was running the place, which turned knots in his empty stomach. He'd never even heard a word from the people or person inside, except for a few distorted words like "enter" through the old faded speaker out front. He grew more nervous. He'd brought with him the worst news possible, and he'd be asking for more than he'd ever known someone to ask of the one who brought power to the city. He began to see how bad an idea it was to put all his hopes into the power plant.

If his plan didn't work, Leo figured they could just continue on to his downtown sanctuary and hope for the best, but looking at how Steven swayed side to side every few steps, he knew they could not make it past the power plant unless either he or Sarah carried the boy. Either way, Steven would be in great pain. It was a minor miracle he was still conscious. Leo's ankle had ached so much just from the sprain he got when he landed on the tree branch, he couldn't imagine what the child felt while his whole shoulder was shattered. In a sad way, Leo thought it was working in Steven's favor as a distraction from his emotional pain.

They walked up the street to the north of the plant, following the wall around to the main gate on the west. The sun had just crested over the hills to the east, giving the sky a myriad of reds, oranges, and pinks, but the Jacksons peered up at the walls beyond the fence. Steam rose from somewhere amid the complex, a white trail dissipating into the rainbow sky, pointing the way to their best hope of survival.

Sarah spoke quietly to Leo, noting it was the smoothest stretch of street she'd ever seen. She asked him how many people must there be to maintain both the plant and the surroundings. Leo shrugged and said he'd seen no one inside or outside the complex. They stopped in front of the outer gate and Leo rang the buzzer as he normally would.

He heard the buzzer somewhere inside the complex. They waited while the sun finished rising over the horizon. Leo knew it was possible, even likely, that whoever ran the place was still asleep, but he was reticent to buzz again. He'd only buzzed more than once a handful of times in his years, and even then only after waiting a long time in the blistering sun. He figured it was best to keep the mystery person (or people) happy. His current situation, however, was outside normal operation. He ran the possibilities through his head several times of different reactions he'd get for ringing the buzzer multiple times. After a few minutes, and fear mounting on the back of his neck with pressure from the three Jacksons behind him, he reached out and gave the buzzer one more quick jab.

They waited. Concern grew in his mind. He turned around, looking at the others, trying to find words. Sidekick stirred in his sling around Leo's waist, the only relaxed member of the group. The gate motor whirred to life, and the gate creaked open, saving Leo from his thoughts, bringing a whole new set with it. He ushered the others into the twenty by twenty-foot enclosure and waited for the outer gate to close behind them. He walked to the metal door, assuming it would click unlocked for them.

There was no click.

They stood there another minute in silence, wondering what was going on. The outer gate closed behind them, trapping them in the cage. Leo knew whoever was inside must be confused at the unscheduled visit. He was afraid it spooked whoever stood on the other side of the steel doors.

Leo looked up to the camera above the door. He always assumed they stopped working years before, as most unmaintained pieces of technology had. He wondered if it had a microphone, or if his voice would travel through the cement and metal to the ears inside. "Hello?" Leo yelled. "It's me, Leo. I normally bring you the meat. Chickens, eggs, and beef. I'm here with--" Leo turned around waving his arm at the Jacksons "With the people who provided the meat. Their family was attacked. These are all that—these are the survivors." Leo shook his head. "Look, a lot of odd things have happened over the last few days. Their farm was burned, same with the chicken farm. I'm sure you saw those flames a few days ago. We don't know all the details, but we thought we could discuss all that with you, and be safe in there for a bit until we figure out what to do next. So, could you let us in? We don't have weapons or anything. Please."

They waited. Leo thought he heard footsteps inside, but it was equally possible he imagined it.

A metallic clang came from the outer door. Leo nodded at the family to enter the dark room between the two doors. Leo entered last, closing the door behind him. He'd never been in that space with both doors closed before. It was unnerving and disorientingly dark. The only light was a sliver thin beam coming from the bottom of the outer door. He reached out for Sarah and they held each other close. The outer door clicked its mechanical lock, sealing them all in the dark void.

He heard footsteps again from inside, certain his brain wasn't conjuring them. They approached the inner door. A small peephole slid open, and the family unconsciously leaned away from its beam of light. A head popped into the space, blocking the light behind it, leaving just a silhouette of the person whose eyes scanned them all. Their voice echoed inside the metal chamber. "Why here?" It was a female voice, filled with caution.

"Hi." Leo leaned forward. "The stadium burned, as did the chicken farm. Those places have been safe and functioning for—well, for decades. Now they're both gone, and in a matter of a week. Also..." He hadn't wanted to give this information until he was safely inside, but knew he couldn't hide it any longer. "The uh—the zombies—they're different. Smarter. Faster. They almost—it's like they can think now. They climb ladders, they plot. Nowhere out there is safe. I can tell you more, but I want to make sure everyone here is safe inside your walls first. I hope you understand."

The eyes in the slot glinted in the bit of light coming around their owner's head. They blinked a couple times, then vanished as the door peephole clanked shut. Everyone stood still in the dark silence.

The familiar metal click of the inner door lock sounded more like a gunshot in the confined space. After another pause, the inner door moved, letting a sliver of light into the black box, causing all inside to close their eyes and readjust to the light. Leo stepped past the children and pressed on the door, slowly opening it with a metallic whine on its rusty hinges.

He always thought the complex was one giant building spanning the entire city block as the outside wall was one solid stretch of concrete. As his eyes adjusted, he realized the wall was just that—a wall. The whole inner area was open on top, filled with an intricate maze of pipes and metal tanks throughout. He pushed the door all the way open, then finally saw the mystery person he'd spent so many hours trying to imagine, and it fit absolutely none of his expectations.

A double-barrel shotgun pointed at Leo and the others. They held their hands in the air. At the other end of the shotgun was a girl Leo figured was somewhere around twelve years old. Bright red hair frizzed out around her head, her face covered in the darkest freckles Leo had ever seen. The only part of her that matched his expectations was the stern look fixed on her face.

"Lie down on the ground, all of you!" The girl barked. Leo helped Dinah.

Sarah said, "I'm sorry, but my little brother broke his shoulder. It would be too painful for him to do that. Is it ok for him not to?"

Leo watched the girl for her reaction. She gestured the shotgun for them to lie down. "He can stand. You all on the ground. Face down. Hands behind your heads. Now!"

They all complied. Dinah whimpered. Sarah laid down next to her face to face, calming her. Leo carefully slipped Sidekick to his side when he lay down. The cat wasn't happy with the change.

The girl stepped toward Steven. "Turn around," she said, then patted him down. He winced as she patted his sling. When she finished, she told him to stand facing the wall. Steven followed the command. The girl patted down Sarah, then Dinah. Leo thought she was thorough in checking all pockets and hiding places, figuring the rest of the people who ran the plant must have trained her well to cover all her bases, which is what kept their identities secret all those years.

The girl patted down Leo, starting at his head. When she got to his waist Sidekick hissed loud and swatted at the girl's hand. She jumped back, swinging her shotgun into a ready stance in an instant. Leo yelled, "No wait, please! That's my cat. I forgot to mention him, I swear he's friendly. Just maybe not to strangers at first. I'm sorry!"

The girl took two steps back, shotgun still at the ready. Sidekick relaxed the arch in his back, still on edge and confused. The girl gave a sharp laugh. "Holy shit, you tamed one of those?"

Confused, Leo responded, "Uhh... Yeah?"

The girl cocked her head, then backed away from the group. She slung the shotgun up, resting it on her shoulder, hand still near the trigger, ready to fire on a moment's notice, adding "Get up."

They all rose. Steven held his good arm over his head, holding back tears.

"Leo." The girl said, then hacked something up and spat it on the ground, looking back up at him. "You shittin' me?"

Leo cocked his head. "About the cat?"

"What? No. The fires. New zombies. That's for real?"

Leo scrunched his forehead. "Yeah. Wouldn't have bothered you if it weren't."

She stared at him for a long moment. "Well, hell. You got any *good* news?"

Nothing came to his mind.

"Ya'll can put your hands down now," the girl said, relaxing into a slouch, and gave a deep sigh. "If it's that FUBAR out there, then we're all fucked, right?"

Dinah and Steven's eyes grew wide. They'd never heard anyone curse so much in their lives, much less heard those words come from another kid's mouth. If they cursed, they got soap in their mouths, a soap their mother made from rendered fat from butchered cows. Dinah turned to Sarah, giving her a look to see if she was going to do anything. Sarah pressed Dinah closer to her body and shook her head. Dinah looked back at the girl with astonishment.

"Alright, well grab your crap and come with me. I need breakfast to clean the taste of this shitty news out of my mouth." She walked away. After a moment, the rest of them followed.

CHAPTER FIFTEEN

They all sat on chairs around a large metal table in a room not much larger than the table itself, situated a quarter of the way down the wall south of the entrance. Dinah scratched at the rust forming on one of the corners. The girl told them her name was Scout. She cracked three eggs, tossing them in a skillet heating up on a small electric hotplate on the wall-length counter surrounding the room.

"So let me get this straight," Scout said, turning from the eggs as they sizzled. "Your place went up in smoke, so now cows are just dinkin' around wherever?" Sarah nodded. "And you guys come here thinking, what, I can put you up?"

"Not exactly." Leo said.

"Yeah," Sarah added. "We'll find something eventually, but right now our farm isn't the issue. The big problem is these new zombies."

Leo nodded. "I've seen them. We all have." He gestured to the Jacksons. The younger two wilted at Leo's casual reminder of all they'd lost. "They climb, they think; who knows what else they can do."

Scout slid the eggs onto a plate and set it on the table. "Maybe they started the fires too."

Leo and Sarah looked to each other. The idea would've seemed impossible a week earlier. Scout picked up an egg with her hand and took a bite. The soft yolk oozed out, and she licked it off her fingers. She chewed while speaking. "And shit, with the chicken place burned, these could be my last eggs, like ever! Damn. That's depressing." She swallowed and looked at the plate longingly.

Leo sighed. "Yeah, the whole city just lost its main sources for protein. Most people have their own gardens, but the livestock was important for everyone. Not just the meat, but the eggs, milk, cheese, soap, leather. We relied on them and those families for a lot." Leo put a hand on Sarah's shoulder. "And we need to make sure this place keeps running too, or the entire city might officially be over, swallowed up by nature."

Scout nodded slowly, still staring at the plate with her last two eggs cooling in front of her. She looked up. "Wait, I still have a live chicken! So I can—dammit, I need a male one too, so they can screw more chickens into the world. You think one survived somehow?"

Leo shrugged "I really can't say. I just know that anywhere outside these walls isn't safe anymore, and we need to stop these zombies, or at least defend ourselves against them."

Scout nodded more seriously. "Yeah... Yeah."

Sarah cleared her throat "And Steven—we need to get his arm fixed, and soon." She looked at Leo, letting him know with her eyes the fear that it may already be too late.

"Oh," Scout said, looking to the boy, weak and pale in his chair. She slid the plate on the table towards him. He gave Scout a look, asking if it was okay to eat one. Scout nodded. "Why don't we just ask the doctor?"

Everyone perked up. Leo struggled to form the words. "You—have a doctor?"

Scout looked to Leo and laughed. "Hell no, he's on the radio."

The group's excitement turned to a collective confusion. Leo added "You—have a working radio?"

Scout scanned the room. "What, you don't?"

They all shook their heads. Dinah whispered to her brother, "What's a radio?"

Steven shook his head at her and spoke sharply with his mouth full of egg. "Not now."

Steven and Dinah remained in the room, slowly falling asleep at the table while Scout led Leo and Sarah across the compound, gravel crunching under each footstep. The ground within the walls was cement or white gravel, aside from a dozen raised planter boxes spread around the more open spaces, various crops growing happily in their soil beds. The corn grew much taller than Leo thought it should've been that time of year. When he walked past, he realized the series of pipes surrounding the corn gave off a lot of heat. Corn loves hot weather, and they apparently didn't discriminate between natural and artificial heat. Leo found pleasure in learning that bit of information, even if he didn't know when, or if, he'd see his own garden again.

Sarah asked Scout, "So, how can this work when all the transmitters are useless without power, and isn't radio a one-way thing?"

Scout gave a pfft noise and waved her hand. "CB works just fine, especially on a clear day like this. Don't go too far, but we boosted it a while back, found a doctor with his own radio out there. Two of 'em, actually, but only one of 'em's a medical doctor. The other's more of an experimental type, I guess. Odd pair. They helped diagnose my mom when she got sick. Diabetes. Couldn't do much more than diagnose it over the radio. They don't make house-calls, apparently, or ever leave their lab, I guess. Not that I'm one to talk, bein' in this place." Scout spat in a bed of kale. "Also weren't much help when my dad died. Heart attack, we think. Man, not to sound depressing, but I wonder if they can tell us how to ease the kid's pain to the end like they did with my mom. I mean, assuming...you know."

They entered a small room filled with monitors and control panels, all dark. Scout walked over to a small box on a shelf and flipped a switch, and grabbed the handset tethered to the device. She turned a dial and spoke into the handset "This is Power Scout calling for Dr. Clark. Power Scout for Dr. Clark. Got a doctor question for you if you can hear me. Over" She lowered the microphone and looked to the other two. "May be awhile. They aren't always near the radio and they miss it sometimes."

They stood for a long moment before Sarah spoke. "This Dr. Clark, is he—good?"

"Good as he can be, considering." Scout said. She sat down on a rolling chair whose cushions and padding had long since fallen away, leaving not much but its metal skeleton. Scout rotated back and forth in the chair with her legs. "We don't talk much, and never about them, really. I just know he and his wife experiment with the zombies. Guess they're trying to figure out how to stop them. Or fix them. Or whatever."

A long silence followed. Leo broke the still air. "Should they... be responding yet, or...?"

Scout shrugged and spun around in the chair again.

Leo frowned. "Is it possible—you say they work on zombies—is it possible they've seen these new ones?"

Scout stopped spinning "The hell should I know? You can ask *them*, or whatever. Look, most likely that kid isn't gonna make it—sorry to say—so don't expect a miracle here. These people know their stuff, sure, but there's only so much they can do not in person, and as I said, they don't leave their lab, like ever. Okay?"

"We have to help Steven. They have to do something!" Sarah pleaded.

"Take him and go there if you feel so strongly about it. I don't know what else to tell you." Scout said, slouching over in the chair.

Sarah took a step towards her. "Maybe we will. It's clear you want us gone. How far is this Doctor?" Leo put his hand on Sarah's should. She shrugged it off.

Scout remained slouched, looking bored. "I dunno. He's east somewhere, that's all I know."

"Is he on this side of wherever those new zombies came from?"

Scout sat up. "Again, I don't fucking know. He's east, alright? Can't be over a hundred miles or I wouldn't be able to reach him on the CB, okay?" Scout got up, pushed past Sarah, and opened the door. She stopped and looked back at them. She threw her arms up and let them drop "Sorry. I really am, but I already have enough shit going on here with the plant, I really can't deal with another person dying in these walls right now, okay?" She left and slammed the door.

Sarah cried. Leo held her close in his arms. He could feel the warmth of her tears as they flowed into his shirt.

Sarah and Leo remained in the room for a while longer. After the tears stopped, they discussed their options, which boiled down to two: either they remain there and hope the doctor answered and could talk them through the steps to heal Steven's arm, or they could risk meeting more new zombies head on and travel east to get to him in person. Either way, Steven would need surgery. Sarah had experience helping her parents with first aid on her siblings and the cows when one came down with illness, but nothing like cutting into a human being who was wide awake.

After landing on a solution, they walked back across the complex, their gravelly footsteps echoing loudly through the hum and hiss from the labyrinth of pipes.

They entered the room with the children. They found Dinah standing up with a worried look on her face, holding Steven. The boy's face was white, and his breathing strained as he winced and cried. The shock from the injury had fully worn off, and he was now suffering through the full brunt of shattered bones slowly slicing him up from the inside. Sarah told Leo to get Scout and ran to her brother.

Leo ran out of the room and around the tanks and pipes in the complex, looking for Scout. His footsteps echoed loud in his ears off the large metal tanks.

He found her on a platform with her head against the largest metal tank apparatus in the complex. It hummed and hissed the loudest amidst the machinery. Scout's eyes were closed as she listened to the machine, divining its state. Leo called for her. Her eyes shot open in surprise and she hopped off the platform onto the gravel. "What is it now?" she said.

Leo ran to her, and between deep breaths, he said, "Steven—he's in a lot of pain. We need to get him help fast."

"Yeah, I know." Scout said, crossing her arms.

"If you can tell us how to get to the doctor, we'll take him there."

Scout exhaled sharply "I know they're on the main highway out of town. Not certain how far, but I doubt the kid'll make it anyway, and if the road is full of those new zombies you're talking about, I'm not sure how far the rest of ya'll make it either."

Leo bowed his head. He hated those impossible decisions. He liked his world how it used to be, wished deeply they could somehow go back, but as his father told him so many years before, the only way out is through.

Scout leaned on one leg. "Shit. You know what? I have something that could help. Won't save him, but it could help manage the pain." She took off across the complex to another room against the northern wall. Leo followed, still weighing exactly how they'd make it to the doctor, and whether they should leave Dinah behind to be safe in case they didn't make it.

Scout opened the door to a dark room with a bed against the corner. Scout grabbed a lantern and struck flint to the wick, lighting it. They climbed down a flight of stairs to a room underneath the complex, several degrees cooler than the air above. Shelving spanned the walls floor to ceiling, each covered with vegetables and fruits, some fresh, some dried, some looked to be pickled in jars, but most of the shelves were piled with potatoes.

Leo said, "This is the biggest larder I've ever seen."

"Yeah, smaller than we needed when all five of us were still here, but now it seems too big for just me." She pulled a wood crate off a shelf.

It hadn't struck Leo until that moment what it meant that there was just a girl of Scout's age running the power plant. *There used to be five people there.* He assumed two were her parents, but didn't want to ask who the others might've been. *Everyone in the world has lost someone close, and sometimes there's little use in dredging up those memories.*

Scout grabbed a couple of bottles from the crate and handed them to Leo. They were full of a clear liquid. Leo cocked his head at Scout, wondering what was inside.

"Open one up and take a whiff." Scout said with a smile.

Leo popped the wire and gasket swing top lid off one of the bottles and brought the open bottle to his nose, inhaling. He reflexively jerked it away from his face as the fumes burned his nostrils like hot knives. Scout laughed uncontrollably for a solid minute. Leo's face burned red in embarrassment. After regaining composure, he asked her what was inside the bottles.

Scout tilted her head quizzically. "Seriously? It's vodka. Potato vodka, the good shit."

Leo looked at the bottle more closely. "Vodka? I've only heard of it. How'd you get it?"

"How does anyone get anything? I made it!" Scout shook her head and climbed back upstairs. Leo followed. "Potatoes frickin' love the raised beds. They grow so much you have to find something to do with them, so my mom built a still. I mean, we have unlimited hot gas coming up from the ground, so might as well have fun with it, is what she would say. Or at least she did until the stuff killed her." Leo stopped. Scout paused at the door and looked back at him. "Oh, I don't mean it's poison—well, in a way it is if you get addicted—I just mean… screw it, just, it's fine for people to drink. It'll help the kid numb some of the pain, anyway." She waved her hand to usher Leo back outside.

"I've only heard of the stuff, is all." Leo said, holding the two bottles against his chest. "The only alcohol I've ever had was some bad beer Grant made." The image of Grant falling off the roof with a zombie played in slow motion in his head. "Or used to make, I guess."

Scout snorted, "well I promise you this stuff'll kick the boots right off that."

They made it back to the room with the Jacksons. Steven cried out, tears wetted his face. Leo could only imagine the pain that boy was going through. Scout yanked a bottle from Leo's arm and grabbed a glass, pouring deeply, and handed it to the boy. "Take a deep breath first and drink it fast, don't sip. It'll burn like hell either way, might as well make it quick."

Sarah looked to Leo, who shrugged. Steven took the glass and tried to smell it. Scout stopped him "ah ah ah, smelling first only makes it worse. Suck it down. I'll join you." Scout grabbed another glass and poured a bit for herself. She clinked her glass against Steven's. "Bottoms up!" She jerked her head back, sending the liquid down her throat. Steven watched, then followed suit. He tilted his head and poured the liquid in. He choked and coughed, the vodka fought and burned its way down his throat. Steven tried to talk, but struggled to catch his breath.

Scout laughed. "Yeah, that first time's a real bitch. Congrats kid, you're gonna feel a lot better real quick." She turned to Sarah "Now in a while he's gonna feel good and maybe want to move around like he's all fine. Don't let him, he'll only screw up his shoulder more. This stuff only numbs pain, tries to convince you it got rid of the problem all together, but if you believe it, you'll only end up making things worse. Trust me on that one." She set the bottle on the table and sat down in a chair facing the Jacksons. She took a deep sigh. "Now. Brass tacks. You want to go to the doctor's, that'll be a heck of a stretch making it there on foot with the kid in his condition." She looked to Leo "I noticed you didn't bring your trailer thing. What happened there, more bad news?"

Leo nodded. "Yeah. It was stolen, I don't know where exactly it is."

"Sounds about right how everything else has been going." Scout put her feet up on the table, stretching her legs. "Well then, maybe you wait and leave in the A.M. Gives you more daylight and less opportunity for a night ambush."

Sarah leaned in "Is that likely?"

Scout looked to her. "Girl, what ain't likely? If something *could* go bad, bet that it will, then you'll never be disappointed."

An enormous boom shook the room from somewhere in the complex. They all jumped and Scout let off a string of obscenities. Dinah and Sarah still had no way of processing all of those words coming from a little girl. Scout jumped up and ran out, leaving the door swinging open. Leo told the rest to stay there, and he followed Scout. An immense cloud of steam shot up at an angle from the middle of the complex. He ran after Scout towards the growing cloud of boiling hot gas.

CHAPTER SIXTEEN

S cout stopped and squinted through the cloud, divining which pipe was belching liquid fire. She shot off at a right angle towards a series of interwoven pipes, stopping in front of a bank of what looked to Leo to be steering wheels. She turned one of them with all her might. The super heated steam continued billowing out from the center of the complex. She tried turning another wheel, but it wouldn't budge. Leo jumped to her side and helped her turn the valve. It seemed like the thing itself vibrated with the heavy flow passing through, fighting against their efforts to close the pipeline's throat. They turned it all the way and the steam spout stopped with a high pitch sigh. They stood for a moment catching their breaths. Scout slid down and sat on the metal grate below the bank of knobs, leaning against the metal base.

Leo wondered if they should venture closer to the problem pipe and see what exactly had gone wrong, but the look on Scout's face said they'd need to wait. She explained that the super-heated steam super-heated the ground, and it would be best to let it cool unless they wanted their shoes to melt right under them. Leo sat down next to her.

Scout leaned her head back and looked up at the sky. "Can't anything go right today?"

Leo nodded. "I'm sorry I complicated things." Scout gave him a look of *WTF.* He continued, "For bringing the Jacksons, for seeking shelter here."

"Shut up. It was probably best anyway. You know where that pipe burst? It was right by my tomatoes. Know what I was gonna do today? Weed the plant beds. I probably would've been cooked in the middle of that cloud, knowing my luck lately."

"Oh wow, I didn't--"

"Just—shut up. Please." Scout said. "You're here. That's fine. Probably good, actually, you can help me fix this mess."

"These things happen often?"

"Pipes are gettin' old. Would've replaced 'em if I could. There used to be two main lines leading to two separate turbines. My parents had to cannibalize one to keep the other working. Now I'm all out of options as far as scrap is concerned. Pretty well humped with old stuff. I need new solutions." They sat in silence for a while longer. "Sorry about the kid. I do hope you guys make it to the doctor, I just don't think we can help him here with what we got, you know?"

"I understand."

"Well, might as well see how screwed we are." Scout rose and helped Leo up. They walked across the warm gravel to the pipe, the surrounding air raised several degrees as they neared ground zero. The former tomato vines lay cooked in a wilted mush on their raised bed below the culprit pipe that sat a few feet above their heads. It looked like someone peeled it open from the inside. A ribbon of steam continued to rise from the hole, residual heat from inside the length of pipe.

"Yep. Screwed." Scout said. "Must've been a tiny crack in there, and the gas found it and just exploded it wide open. Luckily it didn't happen near the turbine, that's my real nightmare. This—this would be easy to fix with a new fitting." She looked to Leo "Which, of course, I don't have."

"What do we do? Can Arthur make you parts? He's done it before, right?"

"Yeah, parts. This is a tad more involved than that." They looked up at the exploded pipe, as if interrogating it. "Unless—no, he might be able to do it, but he'd have to be here to adjust the fit just right..."

Steven's head rested against the back of his chair. Sarah stood by him, rubbing his good arm. He said he was warm and complained the room was spinning before passing out. Sarah finally felt okay enough to take a few steps away. She walked over to the sink and moved the nozzle on the tap. She was surprised to find that water not only came out, but it was under pressure. She'd only ever known gravity-fed faucets. She marveled at the pressure, presuming it was from an old pumped water system to have that level of pressure. She grabbed the glass Steven drank the vodka from and filled it with water. It tasted good. She filled it again and gave it to Dinah, who was licking the last bit of egg off the plate on the table.

Leo entered the room. Sarah put a finger to her lips and pointed to Steven. Leo nodded and motioned for her to join him outside. She gave Dinah a questioning look who responded with a thumbs up and leaned back in her chair next to her brother.

Once Sarah closed the door behind her, Leo quickly said "I have to go now."

Sarah knew her confusion showed on her face. "For why?"

"Just for a bit. I have to get Arthur."

Sarah scrunched her forehead. She'd only been outside the stadium a handful of times her entire life, and a third of those times were to visit Leo when his father was still alive. She searched her mind for the name Arthur and came up blank.

"The guy who—what's it called? He has a forge—the blacksmith!" Leo blurted.

"Oh! I see." The pieces connecting in her mind. "And what, you want us to stay here? While you're out facing those things?"

"It's safer here, but that means we'll have to push back our trip to the doctor."

The news was like a focused punch to the gut for Sarah. She'd just seen Steven pass out and felt how sick he was getting. "Waiting isn't an option, he's in a bad way, and we can't just amputate the arm, either. I think his whole shoulder..." The pressure returned behind Sarah's eyes.

"I know. We can leave tomorrow--"

"No!" Sarah took a step back, lowering her voice. "I'm not losing Steven, too. We go today."

"Sarah, I can't. I have to help Scout or the city might lose power for good."

"Then let it! This city is dead already, but Steven isn't!"

Leo looked away, avoiding Sarah. "Look, you have to protect your family, I get that..."

"But?" Sarah asked.

"*But* I have a responsibility to the city. Lots of people depend on this plant, and it can't produce power unless I get Arthur here to help, and Scout's never been outside this place aside from literally the street on the other side of this wall. She wouldn't know how to get to Arthur's even if I drew her a map. I do this and then I go with you, I promise. Please don't leave without me. I need you to stay safe."

"And I need you to help my family." Sarah said in the calmest firm voice she could muster before Scout's footsteps interrupted them.

She came between them and asked Leo, "You going now, or what?"

Leo looked to Sarah, who maintained her position. He looked back to Scout. "Talk to the doctor."

Sarah saw her confusion echoed in Scout.

Leo continued. "Take Sarah and keep trying the doctor. You have to reach him. Do what you can here, because the second I'm back with Arthur, we leave." He looked into Sarah's eyes. "Please."

"But—if there's no power, how can we use the radio?" Sarah asked.

"Dammit you're right." Scout said. After a moment a smile slowly formed on her face, then she burst out laughing. "Just kidding, I got some solar cells. I can wire them wherever for small stuff like that. Ha! The look on your faces." She kept laughing to herself and walked toward the radio room.

Leo touched Sarah's arm. "I want to help. This is the only way I know how. Go with her. Steven's fine, and if something happens, Dinah's with him. I'll be back soon."

Scout spun around in the gravel back towards them. "Guess I should open the gate for you first."

Sarah let Leo squeeze her arm, but made no move to approve of his plan. She told him plainly to hurry.

Leo nodded and entered the dark room as Scout closed the door with a clang.

Scout jumped to the door and slid the eyehole open. "Oh yeah, the photocell is powering the doors right now, but the outer gate is out of juice. You can just open it up on your own, but make sure you close it tight. I don't want anyone thinkin' no-man's-land is open for business, know what I mean?" Leo nodded. "Cool, cool. Don't die, okay?" She slammed the metal peephole shut and stepped to the panel, opening the outer door. She waited to hear Leo close the door behind him and heard it lock automatically.

Leo rode hard through downtown. He took a new route to avoid having to see the rubble from the chicken farm. He couldn't believe that it had just been a few days earlier. It seemed like a lifetime ago, so much loss in such a short time. The thought pushed him to ride harder. He was happy to make it to the highway and be off the narrow streets. He used to prefer their shade, but the last two weeks turned them into a minefield of dangers hiding around every corner. In actuality, he was much more vulnerable on the highway with fewer directions to evade danger, but the potential dangers were just as exposed as him, which evened things out in his mind.

He felt tired, the events of the previous night weighed heavily on his mind and body. Pedaling up the hill, he ran into a mental wall. His legs were weak, disconnected from his body. His head heavy, and his back soft, like his skeleton was about to slip right out of his skin. He pedaled on, focusing on each foot pressing down on the pedals. *Right down, left down, right down.* He breathed deeply with each push. After a few minutes of the world slimming down into the narrow focus of his feet on the pedals and the foot of pavement immediately in front of him, he hit a second wind. The world opened back wide again as he pedaled over the hill.

Leo exited the highway after enjoying a short downhill stretch on the other side of the peak and returned to an uphill climb. He wasn't far from Arthur's compound, just a few curvy stretches of road, then he'd be there. Being back in the shade made him feel much better. He laughed at how important the sun was for life, and how much it could wilt a person if they spent too much time in its rays.

Leo stopped at the gate and raised the flag. He figured it would be some time before Arthur came, as his visit was unscheduled. Leo sat on the ground, leaning against the front gate. The fatigue he'd pushed away on his ride caught up with him. His body felt heavy.

INTERLUDE TWO: ARTHUR

Arthur lay motionless on the couch, looking out the great window on the grey sky.

An hour later he rolled onto his back, looking up at the wood ceiling beams stretching across the void above him, holding up the roof, large timbers hewn from larger trees back before the world ended. Long before his own world ended days earlier.

"Why?" He said aloud, continuing the one-sided conversation he'd been having in his head. "Why!?" Arthur demanded of the room. He listened for a response. His breath echoed loud in his ears, the only sound left in the house other than his own sorrow. He'd cried all his tears until he had no more and continued crying dry nothingness, like dry-heaving his heart out of his own chest. His head ached. His stomach hurt. He hadn't eaten since Leo left. He wasn't sure how many days ago that had been, exactly. Time was irrelevant.

Time had always been just a small thing that happened, ever since he was young. The world was just as it was, time being some vague concept of getting older, of gaining and losing things. He felt himself sinking deeper into a bottomless pit. Even before Leo told him his sweet Anna was gone forever, he'd felt the floor become softer, his steps sinking in until it swallowed him up whole.

Arthur realized he was now standing, his body taking him up the stairs. He knew where it was going—to Anna's room. He wanted to stop, but he was now just an infinitesimal speck inside the body people referred to as *Arthur*. He was not in control. Maybe he never really had been in control. Power and control were another illusion, and now all that was stripped bare and he was revealed to himself. His body ambled through the motions of *Arthur*. The person Arthur thought he was had been lost somewhere deep inside. His body opened the door to Anna's room and stood in the opening. It could've been a second or a thousand years. Time was no more.

Arthur's body sat down on the bed its daughter would never see again. It felt the coldness of the blankets. It lay down its head on her pillow. "I'm so sorry," it whispered to the room, hoping Anna could hear it, wherever she was. "I shouldn't have let you go. I should've gone instead, or gone with you."

Arthur woke up some time later. It was night now. The soft light of the moon peeked through the window, illuminating just the dim outline of the room. He was curled up on the bed. His body felt so heavy, the sheer weight of that body trapped it firm against the mattress. "It's not fair." He whispered, honestly. It wasn't a complaint, just an observation.

Arthur experimented with the idea of Arthur. What was he, really? He wasn't his body; he wasn't his mind, that was all somewhere else. The answer to what he was, what he really was, lay buried somewhere deep inside, trapped.

He thought about Anna's mother, Breonna. He had loved her more than anything, then they had Anna, and she became everything for him when Breonna passed. She had gone through bouts of depression when she was alive. Arthur remembered the times she'd lie in bed for days. He'd tried to coax her out, give her hope. Eventually she'd return and be her normal self. What was it he did that helped her? It seemed like a dozen lifetimes ago now that he was in the same sunken pit himself. He wondered if he'd even been right to try to make her feel better. Either way, she was gone, and so was Anna. The only thing left of them was their belongings. Just things. Empty, hollow things. "Like me," He said to no one in particular. He gave an empty laugh that seemed to echo through the empty house.

Arthur didn't want to leave that feeling behind, didn't know if it was possible to get out from under the overwhelming heaviness he felt. He just needed to feel it. Alone.

Arthur woke up again some time later. It was still night. He wasn't sure if it was the same night or the following one. His stomach clawed at him from the inside. His body's stomach would not be ignored. He rose up, every inch of him too heavy to move, like his bones were frail beams barely holding up the scaffolding inside his skin.

Arthur floated above his body, watched it travel down the stairs, into the kitchen, and slice bread. It spread almond butter on the slice and ate. Who was that man? He was familiar, yet completely unrecognizable. It moved to a mirror and looked at itself. Watching, analyzing, waiting for something, for the face to make sense. It looked back at him blankly. It was full of odd curves and lines. "This isn't me," the reflection said.

Arthur's body lumbered about the house, unsure of a specific trajectory, just moving to do something other than nothing, which he knew was a nothingness in itself. A pain shot in its foot. He yelped and looked down. He'd stepped on a Lego piece. "Anna!" He yelled to tell her to pick up her things again, then remembered she wasn't there. She never would be again. He wandered back to the kitchen and looked at the knives. He could join her, join Breonna. *But where would they even be?*

Arthur trudged back to the couch and lay down, facing the great window, a faint outline of himself reflected at him, surrounded by the darkness of the night outside.

It was light when Arthur woke up. Sometime around midday, based on the shadows outside. Arthur sat up and took a deep breath. He still felt heavy. Everything felt heavy. He stared at his feet for a while before his eyes adjusted to the harsh sun. He looked out the window across the property. The flag was up. He wondered how long it had been raised. Moreover, who had raised it? He rose, his joints ached. How many days had he spent lying around?

Arthur looked at the clock on the wall. Time didn't really matter, but he still felt the need to measure its passing. The clock was stopped.

He trekked to the kitchen to turn on the lights—they were out. He strode to the refrigerator and opened the door. It was still cool, but the light inside was also dead. He turned the knob to the coldest setting and the refrigerator still remained off. The power was out. He wondered if that was somehow connected to the raised flag outside. He put on his shoes, grabbed his crutches, and stepped outside to escape the hollow, empty house and see who was there.

CHAPTER SEVENTEEN

Leo?" Arthur's voice stirred Leo awake. He'd somehow let himself fall asleep, unsure how long he'd been there. A wave of shame moved through him realizing he let himself rest, both because of Steven, and the fact he did it outside where any danger could sneak up on him, but his body was thankful for even a moment's rest.

He stood and turned to Arthur. "The power plant--" he started.

"Yeah, afraid you might be here about that. What happened?"

Leo slumped his shoulders and looked to the ground, unsure where to start.

Leo told Arthur about the fires and losses and more of the new zombies as Arthur let him in and closed the gate, leading him towards the house. Leo stopped them, not wanting to walk up the hill to the house. "We need you there at the plant to help fix the pipe. Any tools you'll need, gather them now and we'll ride."

Arthur shook his head. "I can limp around without my crutches, but there's no way I can ride a bike that far." Arthur quickly turned to look towards the shed. "Unless—yes, I have the frame from an old boat trailer. Wouldn't take me long to retrofit to attach to your bike. I'd want to add a few bits so we can carry my tools."

"How heavy would that be? Could I even pedal it up a hill?"

Leo asked.

"Oh, it was for a small craft, though uphill isn't as worrisome as downhill. I'll makeshift a braking mechanism for the trailer, the ones on your bike won't cut it, plus those are harder to come by. Only take me a few hours. You can wait in the house if you want while I--"

"You don't think it'd be faster if I help?"

"Nah, I'm accustomed to working alone, anyway." Arthur said, waving Leo away "Go. Rest."

"Actually, in that case, I'm gonna make one last trip to my old place."

"What do you mean one last trip?" Arthur asked, concern in his voice.

Leo wanted to look away, but he held his gaze at Arthur, "I don't think I'm ever coming back. Whatever lies ahead to the east, I doubt I'm coming back, one way or another." The reality of his words landed on his heart for the first time.

Arthur nodded. He held his hand out to Leo. They shook. "Well then," Arthur said, "see you back here in a few hours. We leaving in the morning?"

Leo shook his head "No, we leave the second you're done. Even if its night, there's no time to waste."

"I see. Well then, I best get started."

Leo let the downhill gravity do most of the work. He wasn't looking forward to having a trailer on his bike again, much less a large, clunky trailer. He'd gotten too used to riding alone, unencumbered. He figured he'd savor his last trip as a solo rider. When he got back to the flat part of the valley, he pedaled again. He didn't need to rush at that moment as he was likely to make it back before Arthur completed work on the trailer.

He neared the street with his apartment complex, looking at the buildings surrounding him. He'd seen them his whole life, and was taking them in now, likely for the last time. A sudden pang of sadness shot through him, as if he were missing something. The thought made a great hollowness well up inside him. He rode up his block. It looked exactly how he'd left it, how he'd always seen it, yet it also looked greener. Perhaps the plants had grown, or maybe he was just nostalgic for the place he was still in. He wanted to shake the feeling, but as he rode up to his complex, the idea only spread its roots deeper inside him.

Leo sighed and opened the gate, riding to the carport. *He had a job to do,* he told himself. He climbed the pole to the second floor and marched straight to the room with his sketches. He looked around the walls at all the people he'd known and loved. He would not leave them behind, too. He walked around the room removing the pins from each sketch, collecting them, his friends, into a stack of memories. Sheets of faces, simulacrum of his past.

He felt an anger amidst the sadness at the realization he still didn't know who had taken the last image of his father. *The world was unfair sometimes.* After collecting the last sketch from the wall, he held the stack in his hands. It seemed too light for all the people it represented, like his memories no longer had weight. He looked around at the empty walls. The room seemed larger and emptier at the same time. He bent down and put the sketches between more sheets of paper and tied a string around them, to protect them from whatever they'd experience on the road ahead. He couldn't protect those people in life, but he'd keep his paper memories of them safe as best he could. He grabbed a few art supplies and put everything in his backpack. He walked through the apartments, through the holes in the walls separating each space his parents had made when they first claimed the apartment complex as their own decades earlier.

His parents had made a suitable home for themselves, a wonderful home for Leo. He'd been as good a steward of the building and their memories as he could be, but the structure no longer served its purpose. He wished he could at least harvest some of his vegetables, but they were several weeks away from being ready to eat. *There never seemed to be enough time.* He stuffed several changes of clothes along with a few other items into another backpack. He thought about all his things in all the rooms, and all he really needed to survive he could carry on his back.

One last trip to the roof, to look at the view. He did his normal perimeter walk. Trees peeking over roof-tops punctuated in the distance by the occasional hill. It wasn't much, but it had been everything to him. He never got around to burning that zombie he spiked and dragged to the burn pile. He didn't dare light it now, just in case the flames spread. Leo may never see his home again, but he wanted to hold the idea in his head that it might just go on existing in his absence.

After taking in the view for the last time, he climbed back down, making sure the hatch was sealed tight. Even if he may never return, he didn't want the idea of the whole place rotting to fester in his mind. He walked out the door, locking it behind him. He held the key in his hand.

He wondered if he should take it with him. He thought it seemed silly, despite still holding the key to the downtown place, then he considered stopping there for fruit and a few books. It wasn't far out of the way and wouldn't put them much behind schedule, it would just mean riding later into the evening. He left that decision for future Leo. Present Leo walked back down to the carport and set the key on top of one of the horizontal beams holding up the structure. If he ever came back, it would be there waiting for him. Otherwise, he no longer needed to carry it. The key seemed bigger than the entire complex as he set it down. It would all be behind him soon.

CHAPTER EIGHTEEN

After Scout locked the door behind Leo, she jumped off the block below the panel and waved for Sarah to follow. "So. Just us girls. Well, except for your brother, I guess, but he's drunk, so..."

"Is he okay to drink that much vodka?"

Scout shrugged "I mean, it's not great, but it's a lot better than feeling like his arm's on fire, right?" She glanced back at Sarah, who looked away to avoid her gaze. "Look, chickie, the world's a big ass bitch. You're gonna lose people. You know that, right?" Sarah's footsteps stopped crunching behind her. Scout stopped and looked back. Sarah held her face in her hands. "Oh crap, yeah, you just became an orphan. Sorry. I didn't mean to be all—you know."

Sarah began sobbing, the weight of the world compressing her body, squeezing all her emotions out of every pore.

Scout looked around, awkwardly. "Um. Hey, I think you need some time to be alone or something."

"No. I need to talk to this doctor. I can't lose anyone else." Sarah said after several deep breaths, forcing herself to stop crying. She wiped her eyes and continued on to the radio room.

Scout let her pass, then joined along.

Scout flipped a couple of switches connecting the radio to the solar cell. There were a few around the compound, and a couple on the roof and walls, all wired on separate circuits for emergencies. They were useless at night, unfortunately. The batteries that stored the power for nighttime use had all aged out of their functionality long before Scout was born. She understood the concept of batteries, but could only imagine their convenience.

Scout jumped on the radio and called for the doctor again. They waited quietly for twenty seconds before awkwardness set in. Scout nodded. "So..."

Sarah stared at the radio, willing it to talk. She looked to Scout. "How long have you been running this place on your own?"

Scout sat up straight. She hadn't expected personal questions. "Oh, uh. You know. Couple of years, I think. Hard to tell, you know?" Scout nodded slowly to herself, her eyes drifting down in memory. "Over two winters, anyway."

Sarah saw Scout in a new light, as a little girl doing her best to be an adult. She realized how painful those last two years must've been. "How'd you manage it?"

Scout looked back at Sarah, scrunching up her face. "Whatdaya mean?" She asked, cocking her head. "I just did what they taught me to do, only more of it, and every day."

"No, I mean... being alone for all that time?"

Scout shrugged. "You know. Just did it." Scout spun around in her chair and fiddled with the radio nobs, switching them around, then back to their original settings.

"You must've felt so alone."

"Look," Scout spun her chair around to face Sarah. "I'm not gonna give you some story. Did I love my family? Hell yes. Do I miss them? Every damn day. Do I need to dwell on it?" She lifted her arms in a shrug. "If you're lookin' to ask how *you'll* manage? You just gotta keep moving forward. That's it. If you're not doing your job and going forward, you'll let the grass grow all over you, breaking you into pieces, and you'll lose yourself to nature like the rest of the city.

"Know why I keep the grass and weeds off the street around here? Same reason my parents did. Same reason my uncle did before them. It's just what needs to be doing. It keeps the world from swallowing you up whole. If we stopped doing that, if we neglect it, then boom, we're all gone. That's it. That sound good to you? Just do the damn work." Scout jumped up and walked out of the room, slamming the door behind her. Sarah sat in the silence. Scout reminded her of her little sisters. Sometimes they'd get so frustrated and felt like they had no escape from the rest of the family and they'd explode, say something mean, and run to the far side of the stadium. Sarah would let Scout take the time and space she needed.

Sarah jumped at a noise from the radio that almost knocked her to the floor. It crackled to life with a man's voice in a British accent. "Power Scout? This is Dr. Clark responding to Power Scout if you're there. Over."

Sarah regained her balance and walked to the radio. She picked up the handset and spoke into it. "Um, yes, this is not Power Scout. I'm with her, though. She stepped out, but I'm the one with the question."

After a long silence, the voice returned. "Repeating, this is Dr. Clark for Power Scout, respond if you're there, or I'll try again later. Over."

Sarah spoke into the hand piece again "Hello? Do you hear me?" She waited in silence. Then she yelled at the hand piece, her knuckles tightened around it as her voice rose. "Can you hear me? I'm on Scout's radio thing! I need to speak with you, doctor! Now!" She paused.

The voice returned. "Who is that? You cut in mid-sentence, is your radio working? Maybe squeeze the button harder when you talk. Over."

Sarah looked at the hand device. She cringed, realizing how the thing worked. She squeezed the hand piece and spoke into it slowly, over-enunciating. "Hello. This is Sarah. I'm at the power plant with Scout. I need to speak to a doctor." She let go of the button and stared at the speaker, waiting for the voice to return.

"Hello Sarah, this is Dr. Clark. Is Power Scout okay? Is she hurt? Over."

"Um, no. She's fine. It's my brother. His arm is crushed bad." She waited a moment, then added, "Over."

"Okay. Well, not sure what I can do without seeing it, describe what happened. Over."

Sarah explained the circumstances into the hand piece, praying the doctor could fix her brother.

Twenty minutes later Sarah walked out of the radio room. She squinted, using her arm to block the sun as her eyes acclimatized to the bright world outside. The gravel under her feet somehow seemed louder, the world assaulting her with its mundanity. She walked through the middle of the compound looking for Scout, spotting her legs dangling off a ledge just above eye level, facing away from her. She ducked under the metal walkway, stepping around Scout's gently swaying legs. She stepped out the other side and looked up. Scout looking straight ahead, stone-faced. Sarah could tell she had been crying. Sarah climbed up the steps to the platform and sat next to Scout. They sat there looking ahead at the wall with the door to the complex.

After a moment, Scout exhaled sharply out her nose and said, "I'm sorry. If I offended you, I mean. I just--" she shook her head and looked down with a sigh.

"I know. Sometimes things just suck." Sarah kept her gaze at the wall. "I spoke with the doctor."

"Oh, yeah?" Scout perked up. "Any good news?"

Sarah shrugged. "Only maybe. If Steven's arm isn't infected or bleeding internally too much, he could survive, but he'll heal all wrong and we'll have to re-break it to heal correctly."

Scout shook her head. "Crap. That's bad, right?"

"Pretty much, yeah. The sooner we get to the doctor, the better his odds."

"At least it's a straight shot, right?"

"Well, maybe it would be, but... he's seeing the new zombies too, so... we'll definitely have to get past them first."

"Oh. Yeah. That's no good."

Sarah slumped forward, resting her elbows on her legs and her head in her palms. "This isn't how life should be. All of this. Why do we even try?"

Scout leaned over and put her arm around Sarah, feeling her back pulse as she cried.

Crying made Scout uncomfortable no matter who was doing it. The only time she'd seen her family cry was her father after her mother died, but only for a moment before he disappeared to his room. When she had dropped a wrench on her foot, he taught her to curse at the pain, to scream at it and scare it away. The method had more or less worked for her through the years.

Listening to Sarah cry made Scout uncomfortable, but she figured her father's advice may not be the best method for every situation.

A while later Sarah stopped crying and lay down on her side on the metal platform. "Thank you."

Scout shrugged. "Meh. It happens." She played her lip between her teeth for a bit, then added, "I lost my parents pretty close together, too. It was the worst. I see them here everyday all over the place. Not, like, *actually* see them, I mean the whole place reminds me of them, you know? Like they keep dying in front of me a thousand tiny ways." Scout closed her eyes and took a long, slow breath. "I guess that doesn't really help, knowing the pain doesn't stop, but you still have your brother. And your sister. And Leo." Sarah remained still on the metal grate. Her head made a small, slow nod. "When's the last time you had a nice hot bath?"

Sarah opened her eyes and looked to Scout. "What?"

"A hot bath. It feels damn good. You could use one right now."

Sarah rested on her elbow. "But—how?"

"Fool, I got steam shootin' up from the ground! Come on, let's get you a bath." Scout jumped up and held her hand out. Sarah smiled and took it, rising to her feet.

"Oh, but Steven and Dinah--"

"They're fine. Dinah can take one when you're done. Right now you need some you time. I'll make sure they're fine."

"Thank you so much. I don't want to keep you from things here, though."

"Meh, I'll play catch up when you guys are gone, don't worry about me." They approached another door near the northwest corner of the complex.

Sarah wanted to say she did worry about Scout, but the thought of a hot bath took most of her focus. "You know, every month my parents would boil water and we'd wash up in a tub. Littlest ones last."

"Oh, this'll be much better." Scout opened a door, and they entered a bedroom. It had counters around the sides, mirroring the first room Scout had brought them to. She figured they must have been break rooms in the distant past. That one was converted into a bedroom. Scout continued on, opening another door inside. "Right this way." She held her arm out, signaling Sarah to go ahead.

Sarah entered. It was a bathroom, like in the old days. A sink and toilet, a shower stall, and against one wall was a large copper tub resting four dainty feet on the tiled floor. "Oh wow!"

"Damn right, wow!" Scout smiled.

"This is—it's beautiful!"

"Now imagine it full of hot water, and you inside."

Sarah held a hand over her mouth. "I've never taken a bath like *this* before."

"Yeah, it's pretty sweet. One of the perks of the place."

Scout showed Sarah how to work the hot and cold water taps and how to unplug the tub when she was finished. She pulled some towels out of a cupboard and left Sarah to enjoy her bath in peace. Baths were one of Scout's favorite things, and she was happy to share it with someone who desperately needed it.

Scout left to check on the little ones. On her way, she wondered how Leo was doing and when he'd be back. If they couldn't get the pipe fixed and the power back on for the city, her future was just as uncertain as Steven's.

CHAPTER NINETEEN

Leo rode up the streets to the hill in the late afternoon sun. He regretted spending so much time at his old place, wondering if he could have helped Arthur and sped things up. *Oh well*, he thought. *That's all in the past now, too.* He pedaled up the hill on the winding road towards Arthur. The whole place seemed smaller without Anna there, and somehow also larger and emptier. That little girl filled up the compound. Arthur seemed to handle his loss well, at least in front of Leo. *Who knows what he does when I'm not there*, he thought. *The times when you're alone, that's when you really feel the pain and loss.*

Leo was almost at Arthurs when he heard a strange bang, not quite a gunshot. Fear radiated through his spine at the realization Arthur was in trouble. He suddenly felt silly. *Of course he'd hear those kinds of noises, Arthur was working on the trailer.* Leo had been on edge for what seemed like a month straight. He told himself to relax.

He pedaled up the last bit of street to the front gate, but something else was wrong. The gate was still closed, but the flag was raised. *Is someone else there? Who raised the flag?* He heard another bang behind the shed. Leo yelled inside, unsure if Arthur had on some kind of ear protection.

From the shed, Arthur's voice cried out, "They're here!"

followed by a reverberant thud. Leo jumped on the wall next to the gate and climbed up. He suddenly felt foolish again. *If he could climb over the wall that easily the new zombies could too.* He jumped down on the other side and ran to the shed. He saw one of the new zombies on the ground around the side, blood and brains splattered against the wall. He ran around the back, to the open air section under the roof extension. He grabbed an axe hanging from the wall to his right. He advanced inside the shed, never having seen the inside before, realizing it was more of a small pole barn. Leo heard Arthur yell, followed by more loud thunks.

He almost tripped over another one of those things on the ground, its eye smashed out of its skull, lying semi-attached in a spreading crimson puddle. Arthur was up a ladder in the loft, and one of the new zombies was doing its best to scramble up after him. Arthur swung a large wrench wildly. It scraped the zombie's head, leaving a strip of flesh and hair dangling from its scalp. It reached up towards Arthur with crushed hands, fingers sticking out at odd angles. It wrapped its wrists around the ladder rungs, trying to climb up. Arthur glanced at Leo, then looked back down at the zombie.

"I'll keep him distracted!" Arthur yelled as he jabbed at the zombie's face with the wrench. The zombie reached at him, but its impotent fingers were useless. Leo walked lightly across the room, bringing the axe behind his back. Arthur yelled at the zombie to hold its attention, allowing Leo to swing hard at it. It jerked its head to the side without warning, making Leo's swing land off-center, slicing its ear and right side of its face off, the blade dug deep in its shoulder as it tumbled to the ground from the force of the impact. Leo's tight grip on the handle jerked him down toward the maimed zombie on the floor, scrambling to get up.

Leo kicked his foot out on the thing's back to get enough force to pull the axe out of the thing's shoulder and reeled back. The zombie rolled over to look at what hit it. Leo swung the axe down right in the middle of its confused face. Its eyes still staring coldly right at him as the top of its head fell clean off the rest of its body with an uncomfortable wet suction sound. Leo stood there for a moment to make sure it was dead. He looked up at Arthur. They remained like that for a moment, breathing in relief.

"Are there any more?" Leo asked.

"I—I don't know. I don't think so." He said, dropping the wrench to the floor, letting the zombie's dead body break its fall. He climbed down the ladder.

Leo noticed Arthur keeping the weight off his left foot. "Are you okay?" He asked, really wondering if Arthur had also been bitten.

Arthur eased himself down to the ground and shook his head. "They were right at me. I was working on the trailer and noticed the flag was raised. I thought you'd returned. I went to the gate, but didn't see you there. I felt—it just felt wrong. The flag don't go up on its own. Then they sprang over the wall. They were waiting for me—ambushed me. Only I didn't walk into their trap, so they had to rush me. I ran to the work shed, and..." He shook his head, catching his breath.

Leo stepped to Arthur, gripping him on the shoulder. "Did one of them... did they get you?"

Arthur looked up, confused. "Get me? No! My leg's still healing. I was able to kill two of them, but the third one grabbed my foot while I was climbing the ladder, so I jammed down and kicked it in the face. Felt like it broke my foot again, the pain was so bad. But no, they didn't get me, I'm all me."

Leo hated he'd asked, but knew the question was necessary. If it was too late, he had to know.

"Anyway, I'm almost done with the trailer. You wanna grab your bike and we can finish it up?"

Leo nodded and walked to the gate. The grass crunched gently under his footsteps. His heart was still beating fast in his chest. He opened the gate and brought his bike inside. *Those things knew to raise the flag,* he thought to himself. *How had they known? Did they follow him?* A jolt passed through his spine as he realized they must have been watching. Waiting. *Since when do zombies wait and plan? What made them do anything they've gotten up to these last couple of weeks?*

Leo noticed something out of the corner of his eye as he walked his bike to the shed. A light from the top of the hill. He yelled for Arthur, "the house is on fire!" He ran to the shed. Arthur met him on the north side near the smashed zombie and looked to his house. The flames rose from the far corner, which meant they'd already consumed Anna's bedroom and were spreading quickly.

"No. NO!" Arthur yelled and took two pained steps towards his house which was quickly growing into an inferno, a bright red and yellow spot on the hill, directly opposite the sunset, mirroring the array of reds and oranges filling the other half of the sky.

Leo stopped him "No! Arthur, wait! The fire—it's not natural, someone set it just like the others."

Arthur looked to Leo with wild eyes "You mean--"

"There must be more of them." Leo said, pointing to the zombie on the ground. "I'm sorry, but I don't think we could save your house, even if we had time."

Arthur slumped at the realization. "Then let's get the hell out of here before more come." He looked up at his house, holding back his tears. He turned away from the fire and walked to the shed.

Leo backed his bike to the front of the trailer. It already looked heavy and daunting for Leo to think about pedaling it uphill, much less stopping it going downhill.

Arthur worked on attaching the trailer to the bike wheel. "Load my tools while I do this. I got 'em separated already. The ones I'll need are right there, I'll get this connected." He nodded his head at a pile of gear.

Leo loaded them onto the trailer. He could hear the house crack and collapse in on itself as it burned. He knew Arthur could also hear it, probably feeling each sound in his stomach. His entire life was slipping away, just like everyone else's Leo knew.

Arthur rose and tossed the tools from his hand into a wood bin he'd added to the trailer. He reached out and grabbed the crutches he left leaning against the wall. "Guess I'm back to these for now. I'll go open the gate. You wheel that behind me, see how it feels." Arthur crutched his way around the side of the shed to the gate. Leo knew he'd be watching his home burn the whole way.

Leo got on his bike and pedaled. He dropped it in the lowest gear and had to stand on the pedals, putting his whole weight into each stroke to move it across the deep grass. He hoped it would be easier on the road, but even then he'd still have obstacles to get over. *This will be a hard ride*, he told himself. *A really hard ride*. He turned wide around the shed, checking the trailer's turn radius. It was decent, just required a slightly wider berth than his old trailer.

"Hurry!" Arthur yelled from the gate. He pointed towards the house. It was completely in flames, but that wasn't what concerned Arthur most. A figure approached them down the hill. It was hard to see with the flames behind it, but Leo had little interest in finding out who or what it was, knowing whatever the answer, it was almost certainly the cause of the fire. He pedaled harder. Arthur struggled to swing the gate open with his crutches.

The figure began running down the hill towards them. Leo could only go so fast across the lawn, but he wasn't about to leave without the bike and trailer.

Arthur struggled in his rush to open the gate enough for the trailer to pass through and fell to the ground. Leo made it to the opening and stopped with the trailer beside Arthur, struggling to get up with his crutches. The figure was closing in on them, and Leo could tell it was one of the new zombies by its shambling silhouette. He almost thought it was grinning as he glanced at it. He hopped off the bike and ran to help Arthur onto the trailer.

Leo hoisted Arthur over the side, tossed his crutches on the trailer, and ran to his bike. He wasn't sure if they could gain enough speed to get away from the thing running at them, but he'd give it his best. He started with both feet on the ground beside the bike, pulling the weight of the trailer, which sank deeper into the grass under Arthur's added weight. He tried to pick up speed before turning downhill on the street. He figured the slope would be on their side, at least. He jumped onto the bike and dug his feet down to pedal as he turned.

"It's getting close, man!" Arthur yelled, scrambling through his supplies looking for a weapon. He came up with two long screwdrivers. They'd have to do, but only if it got too close for any other option.

The zombie closed in, just a few yards away and gaining. "Fast!" Leo heard behind him.

"I'm going as fast as I can!" Leo yelled back.

"That wasn't me!" Arthur yelled. "That thing said it!"

Leo really hoped the wind rushing past his ears distorted Arthur's words, because talking seemed one too many skills to add to a zombie's repertoire. He glanced back to see the zombie within feet of the trailer, its teeth bared, eyes blank like a shark. "Go fast!" It said, excited at the chase.

Arthur pulled himself as close to Leo's end of the trailer as he could, away from the thing chasing them. "Go, go, go!"

"Where. Go?" The zombie growled. "Home. Gone." It lunged at the trailer, grabbing the back end. Leo's bike jerked back at the extra resistance. The zombie hoisted its head up above the rear of the trailer, putting its weight on its legs as they dragged behind on the ground.

Arthur pulled his own legs under and behind him, facing the zombie as it clawed its way closer towards him. Leo swerved to avoid a section of road that had buckled up from tree roots. Arthur lost his balance and came down hard on his hands on the expanded metal floor of the trailer. One of the screwdrivers bounced away, and he reached out, grabbing it just before it tumbled off the side. "Watch it!" He yelled to Leo.

"Sorry," Leo said "I'll warn you next time."

"What is this thing?"

Before Leo could respond, the zombie said "What...is you?" It pulled its torso onto the trailer, legs bouncing and shredding against the pavement.

Arthur recoiled at its question, then lunged at it with the screwdrivers in his hands. He came down hard on its left wrist, piercing it through, the screwdriver head plunging through one of the holes in the expanded metal floor. The zombie reacted by using the leverage to pull its body closer and lunged at Arthur, reaching out and grabbing his hand, still holding the screwdriver handle. It bared its teeth, bringing its head to Arthur's hand. Arthur yelled and brought down the other screwdriver hard onto its head. He pierced its skull, and it became limp, its legs still dragging on the ground behind them, body stuck to the trailer via the screwdriver in its wrist. Arthur leaned back and caught his breath. "I got him... we can... we can stop now."

Leo squeezed the brakes on his bicycle, making him swerve violently, almost throwing him off the bike. In the space of a second he released the brakes and brought the bike back upright, aiming straight ahead downhill. "Um... I can't stop! The trailer's pushing too hard!" Leo searched for a smooth, grassy area ahead to slow them down, but saw nothing but trees along the sides of the windy road.

"Oh, right!" Arthur said. "I got this." He stretched his arms across the trailer to a small box tethered to the trailer's tongue with a long, thick wire. He pulled a knob and the trailer wheels seized with a high-pitched screech. Leo's body jerked into the handlebars as the bike under him suddenly slowed with the trailer.

"Holy—watch it, man!" Leo said. His right forearm was bleeding from where he'd rammed into the handlebars.

"Sorry, Leo, shoulda warned you. Guess we're even now."

Leo laughed. "Yeah, guess so."

"Ok, I'm gonna slow us to a stop. I wanna get this thing off the trailer."

Leo joined in, braking his bike, figuring out how much to brake without losing control. They came to a stop and Leo stood up, wiping the blood from his forearm on his shirt.

"Now, since we're still on a hill, you'll need to find a rock." Arthur said, sitting up, still pulling on the knob. "Put it in front of the wheel to keep it from rolling, then I can release the brakes."

Leo found a fallen branch. He held one side and stomped down on the other with his foot, breaking it. He placed the section under the wheel and kicked it tightly in place. Arthur slowly released the knob. The trailer moved forward an inch, then bounced back, relaxing against the wood. They looked at the zombie, and at each other for a long moment.

Arthur broke the silence. "What the hell was that about?"

Leo shrugged. "That's what I'm saying. They're changing. They're different now."

"It talked!"

"Yeah, I guess they do that now." They stared at the zombie. An owl hooted somewhere overhead. Night was fully set in and they were far from shelter. "We should keep going."

Arthur nodded. He pulled his screwdrivers from the zombie. He leaned over the edge of the trailer and grabbed some leaves, using them to wipe the blood off his tools.

Leo rolled the zombie over and examined its face. It didn't seem different from the others, relatively new, no longer than a few months turned. The difference between the new zombies and the old ones was all inside the creatures, which gave Leo a shudder. If they could think and talk, and maybe even reason, then the difference between those things and the living just got murkier. Leo rolled it over to the ground beside the trailer. It landed with a thud.

Arthur sat up, putting his tools in the box, and looked at the zombie. "Man, its legs are shredded. Even though it could talk, it was still a crazy damn zombie. Those things are all screwed up." He shook his head.

Leo bent down and reached in the zombie's pockets. He pulled out something small and opened it, showing it to Arthur.

"A match book?" Arthur said, scrunching up his face. "How'd he get one of those? I haven't seen one in years."

It was half full of matches. Leo closed it and put it in his own pocket. *So the zombies were the ones starting fires. But why, exactly? How'd they learn to do that, and where had this one gotten the matches?* Leo had too many unanswered questions bouncing around in his mind. He nodded to Arthur and walked to the bike. He paused.

"Oh, uh, you wanna get the block? I can hold the brakes again." Arthur said, holding up the brake box knob.

It took Leo a moment to remember what Arthur was talking about. He grunted a yes and trudged to the wheel, kicking the branch away. He picked it up and tossed it on the trailer "Just in case."

Arthur nodded. "We'll have to work it this way with me having to brake the trailer for now. I didn't have time to make an attachment for the bike. Those things kinda hijacked the situation."

Leo said nothing, just aimed them down the hill and avoided roots and plants in the road.

"Oh, I also made it so you can have two bikes pulling the trailer. I just have to finish putting that bit together, but that can also be an option, you know, in the future. I figure it couldn't hurt to have more torque pulling this beast."

Leo nodded.

"You okay?" Arthur asked.

"Yeah. Yeah, I'm fine." He wasn't, though. His mind kept turning over the idea that the zombies were becoming more and more like people. That scared Leo, and he couldn't figure out exactly why. He'd known they'd been getting smarter for a few weeks, but the thought they might become like people unnerved him, distracting him from his tired achy legs. *But now that they could start fires on purpose*, he wondered, *would it be as big of a game-changer as when man first learned to use and control fire?*

They rode into the night on the highway towards downtown for several hours. Leo took his usual exit, telling Arthur they'd take a pit stop to rest for a bit before going to the power plant. He'd been awake for two full days and his legs were losing all efficacy on the pedals. His mind spun away from him. He'd take them to the downtown office to rest and collect apples. It would also give Leo a chance to grab more of the books he wanted to read. He wanted to say goodbye to his little downtown oasis, making peace with the likelihood that he'd never return to the city again.

CHAPTER TWENTY

Scout left Sarah to enjoy her bath and went to check on Dinah and Steven. The two seemed so weak and lost to her, the whole family did. She figured it was because they were raised in a protected world. Scout laughed at having those thoughts when she lived in a veritable fortress. She, however, was trained from very early to take care of herself. She had chores and responsibilities as long as she could remember. She realized now that her parents were training her to take over the power plant. Though none of them planned on it happening as soon as it had. *Death is like that*, she mused. *Somewhere far off one moment, then suddenly it's staring you in the face, like a cold dagger.*

She had only three memories of her uncle. He had died when she was very young. She had never fully understood what had killed him, though. He was older, sure, but her parents were vague about it. She had assumed it was because she was so young when it had happened, but wondered why she hadn't asked them about it when she was older. She knew she never really had enough time. Everyone was busy doing something else.

She stopped outside the door and looked around the complex. It had gotten dirty in her parent's absence. She'd done her best, but there were limits to what one person could do. With everything that needed doing on a regular basis, she needed someone else there with her. A chill shot through her at the realization that she really did need people. She was raised to be independent, even though she completely depended on the power plant itself, even more dependent on the people who brought her food only because she kept the place going. Sure, she'd kept her distance between the outside world and the life within her walls, but the two worlds were far more intertwined than she was happy to admit. That dependency was shattered by the fact there probably wouldn't be any more meat coming her way. That scared her.

The loss of her family made her heart ache. She allowed the feeling to move through her, letting it pass out of her. She took a breath to cleanse herself, then opened the door and entered the room.

Steven slept with his head on the table, a small puddle of drool around his mouth. Dinah leaned back in a chair with her feet up against the side of the table. Her head turned as Scout entered. She was understandably bored. Scout waved for Dinah to follow. Dinah scowled and gestured to Steven. Scout swiped her hand to say it was okay and cocked her head at the door for Dinah to follow. The youngest Jackson removed her feet from the table and hopped gently to the floor, trying not to make a sound.

"What are we doing?" Dinah said once outside, eyes adjusting to the sun.

"I wanna show you around the place. You helped grow crops, right?"

"Yeah, but—what about Steven?"

"Oh, he's fine. We'll check on him later." She led Dinah to the nearest raised bed full of corn. It was taller than both of them and still not done on its journey towards the sky.

They talked about the methods the Jacksons and Scout used to grow their food. They strolled around the grounds talking about different crops, some of the bugs they had problems with, and ways to combat them. Scout talked about the slugs that kept plaguing her spinach. Dinah told her about how that was one of the other reasons her father made beer. "He'd pour it around the problem areas to keep them away, and the slugs avoided the beer even more than the rest of my family. Mom said, 'the slugs have good taste since they don't like his beer.'" Dinah bent down to look at the leaves up close. "If my daddy was here, he'd show you how to make some."

Scout looked at Dinah, hunched on the ground, observing the leaves. She bent down and put her hand on Dinah's shoulder. "That would've been nice." She didn't know exactly what to say, but felt like Dinah was processing everything pretty well on her own. Perhaps their family wasn't as weak as Scout first assumed. *Perhaps everyone's the same, but in different ways.* She wanted to say something, but all she could think about was whether slugs hated vodka as much as they hated beer.

Sarah wasn't sure how long she'd been in the bathtub, but however long it was, it was working. She didn't know if she'd ever been that relaxed. She wondered how Scout could be so full of curses and anger when she could take baths that wonderful whenever she wanted. *Then again, if that's how Scout acted with baths, how would she be without them?* Sarah rubbed her fingers together, enjoying the deep rivulets of puckered skin. She could stay in the bath all day, but the outside world seeped back into her mind. She had to check on her brother, see what he needed. Dinah could also use a bath before they left for the doctor.

Sarah reached forward to the bottom of the tub, her fingers searching for the chain on the stopper. She plucked it up and leaned back against the warm metal of the tub. The cool air danced further down her skin as the water slowly lowered, disappearing down the drain. *How did Scout keep the plumbing working*, she wondered. *Must be part of the reason she ran out of pipe for the steam.* Back at her home—back when she had a home, they had used a septic tank. Every year they'd pump up all the sludge and liquid and mix it in with the soil. It was a horrible process, and the whole stadium smelled like death for a week, but it allowed the crops to grow, and for her family to use indoor plumbing. That was all gone, as quickly as the water down the drain.

As the level dropped and cool air enveloped her skin, the feeling of weightlessness drained, too. Gravity seemed to increase on her body, pulling her down stronger and stronger towards the earth with each passing minute.

As the water covered the bottom inches of her body, the tub itself seemed to be pulling her down, holding her tight, not letting her go. The air felt good against her warm skin. The drain gurgled as the last inch of water spiraled away. Sarah sat there for another minute, just feeling the air and gravity. It was the best bath she had ever had. She hoped she'd be able to do that again before it was her turn to follow her parents. Before then—she'd have to be the parent to her younger siblings. *Life may be unfair sometimes, but fair or not, you just have to take what it gives you and keep moving forward.* All that unsureness and weakness from the previous twenty-four hours had washed down the drain. She was Sarah again, and that was enough. She rose and dried herself.

Scout and Dinah finished their lap of the complex and exhausted their knowledge on plants. Scout moved on to describe how the geothermal plant worked, at least how it should work when all the parts were in place. From nearby they heard groaning and uneven footsteps on the gravel. They instinctively tensed and faced the noise to see Steven groggily ambling towards them. "Where do I pee?" he asked.

Scout led him across the compound. She noticed he had a constant grimace, either from the arm pain or the alcohol in his stomach. As they walked, Sarah stepped out into the open air. She looked refreshed. Scout was proud of her part in that transformation.

Sarah spotted the three walking towards her. "Oh, he's up. How are you feeling, Steven?"

The boy groaned and shook his head, "I have to pee."

Sarah held in a laugh, thankful he wasn't focusing on the shooting pain in his arm. "You think you can do it by yourself?" She hesitated, then added, "with one arm?"

"Gah, I'm fine."

Sarah let him pout, basking in the afterglow from her bath. "Oh, and Dinah, you should take a bath too. We may never see one this nice again."

Scout smiled and said, "Unless you stay here with me, then you can have one every day."

"Don't tempt me." Sarah said, leading Steven to the bathroom.

Scout laughed, realizing she meant it as a genuine offer more than the joke it appeared to be. "Come on Dinah, let's get you a bath."

Late afternoon, Scout and the Jacksons brought chairs outside and lounged in the growing shade covering the compound. All but Scout had bathed and luxuriated in the warm, clean feeling. Sarah helped Steven, who was more embarrassed than pained by the process. His head bobbed as he fought vodka induced sleep. Dinah curled up on Sarah's lap.

Sarah looked at Scout, the young girl hiding the soul of an old pirate. It suited her. "This is a really nice place you have here."

Scout waved away the compliment. "Yeah, let's hope I can get it going again or it just was a nice place." They sat in silence, staring off at nothing in particular. "I was serious before, you know. You're welcome to stay."

"Oh, thank you for the offer." Sarah said. Dinah adjusted her position, half awake in her lap. "But we have to get Steven to the doctor first. After that, who knows?"

That phrase bounced its way around both their minds as they sat in silence. *Who knows.* Everything was up in the air. They just had to do what they had to and hope it all worked out for the best. If they didn't have hope, then they really had nothing.

Sarah suddenly perked up "You think Leo should be back by now?"

Scout shrugged and looked at the angle of the shadow on the wall. "You'd think so, but you'd know better than me how far he had to go."

Sarah had a jolt of concern in her stomach. "I just wish I knew more."

Scout pointed at the top of the wall "You can try the widow's walk."

"The what?" Sarah asked.

"That's what they called it. There's a ledge around the entire wall hidden just below the top. You can head up if you want. Doubt you'll see anything, though. If he's not almost back, it'd be best to hunker down for the night somewhere."

Sarah nodded. She got up and carefully set Dinah on the chair, who made a few soft protestations before curling up in a ball on the chair.

Scout led Sarah to a steel ladder that led to the top of the wall. Sarah climbed up first. The ladder curved in a U at the top, attached to the concrete floor. The inner wall had a divot in the cement surrounding the ladder, allowing them to step into a narrow two-foot channel about three or four feet deep between the thick inner and outer walls that ran the length of the perimeter.

When Scout got to the top, she gestured for Sarah to venture farther toward the center of the western wall. They stopped in the middle and looked out at the city; the sun giving it a warm glow. "Reminds me of the view from the stadium roof." Sarah said, "though here you really feel like you're in it. Back there we seemed more removed, like we were above the city."

"Yep," Scout said wistfully, "you're really in it, here."

Sarah scanned the skyline. She knew if Leo were on his way, she wouldn't be able to see him through the buildings until he was a block or two away. At the northern edge of her view, she thought she spotted movement. "What's that?"

Scout followed Sarah's gaze "What's what?"

Sarah gave a hmm "I dunno. Thought I saw something on the corner over there, like someone backed into the shadow."

A chill ran down Scout's spine. She didn't see anything, but she had an inkling she was being watched, and she didn't like it. "Lemme get the binoculars." She turned towards the ladder "You stay here and keep a lookout. Maybe don't stare in that direction, but keep an eye on it, yeah?"

Sarah affirmed, and did her best to appear to look out across the city, but the only spot she could focus on was the corner of the street.

CHAPTER TWENTY ONE

Leo slowed, letting the bike coast down the block, stopping in front of the law office. The last half hour he'd been slipping in and out of awareness as exhaustion dug its claws deeper into his mind and body. Arthur hadn't been able to rest the entire trip either from all the bumping. The cart may be convenient for *things*, but it had the tendency to rattle a person.

"Wish I had more time to add shocks or something to this thing. Man, my teeth hurt."

"Sorry about that," Leo said, struggling to lift his leg high enough to get off the bike. "Some of that was me, too tired to steer and avoid stuff, plus I'm learning the new dimensions of the trailer. Thanks for building it, by the way."

"That's fine. This the place you told me about?"

"Yep," Leo said, glad he'd kept the key with him. He climbed up the steps and unlocked the door. He turned around and looked down at the trailer. He thought about how his last one was stolen just a block away from where he stood. He considered bringing the bike inside, but the thought of going down the stairs, unhooking it, then carrying it back up, made him sick. He shook his head and prayed his utter exhaustion wouldn't bite him in the ass again.

Leo let Arthur enter first, then followed and locked the door. "Woah," Arthur said, "you weren't kidding, this place is great! I wonder how it was ignored for so long! I mean, I know there were a lot of those things lurking downtown in the early years, but man—and a fruit tree too?" Arthur zoomed with his crutches to the tree and picked an apple.

"Yep." Leo said, "The bad news is the beds are up two flights of stairs. I'm just gonna crash down here, though. I don't have it in me." He lowered himself to the floor against the wall inside the atrium.

"You sure, man? I could go up and bring you a blanket." Arthur looked at the curved staircases for a moment. "Actually, I think I'll join you. Maybe when I'm better, you can bring me back so I can snoop around up there. Right now, I'm feelin' you on the tired part." He slid down a few feet from Leo and took a bite of the apple. The crunch echoed around the atrium. Leo was already asleep. Arthur nodded to his slumbering companion and finished his apple.

Sun streamed in, giving the treetop a gentle glow, illuminating the ground floor with its penumbra. Leo slowly climbed from sleep to sounds of rustling. His eyes weren't ready for the day to start.

Arthur carried something over his shoulder past Leo, heading to the front door. "Oh, you're up." Arthur said as he passed. "I'm just gathering apples before we go. They're really good! I found a shirt and tied up the sleeves to make a pouch. Hope they won't get bruised on the ride."

Leo grunted as he brought himself up to a sitting position. His neck and back ached. He had slid down the wall onto the floor during the night and slept in that bad position for too long. "How long did I sleep?"

Arthur returned to the atrium. "It's early yet. Sun's still at quite an angle. It'd be good to get moving soon if you're up for it."

Leo stretched his legs. They were just as angry as his eyes at being asked to function, but not so much he couldn't ignore them a little while longer. "Yep. Should do." Leo groaned and lifted himself up to stand. His whole body cried out in soreness. He'd need a respite from all that, hoping it would come soon. "Crap. I wanna grab some books before we go."

"Ok, I'll gather more apples, then." Arthur turned and added, "Oh, you saw that mummy on the floor, right? I wonder if he fell through the hole in the dome, or something."

"Yep, pretty sure he did." Leo said, heading upstairs. He didn't feel like going into detail about his friend on the floor at the moment. At the top of the steps he found the stack of books he'd pulled, right where he left them. He knew it was silly to be bringing books, especially when he'd be the one who ultimately had to carry them on the trailer, but he told himself that books were never a waste. He trudged downstairs, each step its own struggle. On the last one, he heard a crowing sound somewhere outside.

Arthur stopped picking apples and asked, "What was that noise?"

The hair on the back of Leo's neck stood up. "I think—I think that's a rooster."

It crowed again. Leo and Arthur looked at each other. Leo ran to the door, setting the books on the desk nearby. "Come with me. Now." He unlocked the door and opened it slowly, peeking his head outside. His bike and trailer were still there, which was a relief, and sitting on the handlebars, basking in the morning sun sat a rooster. It almost appeared to glow in the morning light.

Arthur hobbled next to him, looking out past his shoulder into the street, adding "No way."

Leo shushed him, mind racing. He whispered, never taking his eyes off the rooster. "Ok, we have to do this smart. You still have that apple bag?"

Arthur held up the new one he'd made, half full of apples.

"Slowly empty them onto the floor. Quietly. I'll go outside and try to push him up here through the door, ok? You keep it open and hide just inside. If I can get it up here, I'll yell at you to bag it. If not, I guess I'll yell for something else."

Leo slowly opened the door wider. The rooster looked at his movement, cocking its head back and forth to get a better look. Leo turned his head as if he were looking down the street, hoping the rooster would be interested in whatever he was looking at. The bird brought its wings out and clucked a loud warning at Leo's approach, unfooled by the ploy. Leo froze. The rooster slowly brought its wings down to its side. He could hear Arthur emptying the bag behind him.

Did Blake have more than one rooster? Leo wondered. *Even if he did, odds are low more than one escaped the fire, much less the other wildlife hunting the recently freed poultry and cows. They would not understand how to survive, or they'd learn really fast.* Leo thought about how he needed the rooster for Scout, or there may be no future for chickens in the city. *No pressure or anything.*

The bike sat just off the base of the steps. As he neared, the rooster brought its wings wide and flapped more wildly. Leo shushed the animal to calm it, but he was too close for its comfort. The rooster leapt off the bike and flapped its way to the center of the street, gravity pulling it back to the ground. Leo cursed. "Arthur, get out here!" Leo took off down the steps and up the street, arcing wide around the rooster, trying to cut off its route.

Arthur peeked from around the door, seeing the rooster making an escape. He hopped down the stairs as fast as he could with his crutches. Leo yelled, "get away from the bottom of the steps. I'll try shooing him back over there. We need to get him inside the building." Arthur hobbled down the street.

Leo got in front of the rooster. It was angry and clucking up a frenzy. Leo held his arms wide out to his sides and hopped back and forth, countering the rooster's attempts to run. He inched closer. The rooster clucked and hopped, slowly flapping its way back towards the bicycle. Leo yelled, "come into the street a little. Let's force it up the steps."

Arthur nodded and moved a few feet further from the steps, holding his crutches wide, creating the idea of a pen for the rooster. Leo frantically made "chuck chuck chuck" sounds, hoping that would further encourage the rooster. It lunged at Leo, so he kicked at it, careful to not make contact. The rooster edged closer to the bicycle. Arthur waved his street-side crutch, and the rooster moved closer to the steps. Leo jumped back and forth more rapidly. The rooster flapped and hopped its way to the base of the steps. Leo and Arthur moved in close.

The rooster tried to escape through the space between the bicycle and the stairway rails. Leo jumped at the bike and shook it. The noise scared the rooster. It pecked at a tire and flapped backwards onto the bottom step. Leo hopped over the tongue attaching the bike to the trailer and motioned for Arthur to close in. The rooster screeched and hopped up the steps. Its head jerked every which way, searching for an escape, ultimately spotting the opening behind it and shot in through the door. Leo ran up the steps and stood in the doorway, making sure it couldn't escape.

Arthur made his way back up the steps, "that go according to plan?"

Leo shrugged "could've been worse. Still have to catch the thing, though." The rooster clucked inside the building, and Leo felt comfortable it wouldn't escape. Then he heard another sound up the street. A long shadow stretched on the ground ahead of a figure running towards them. "Get inside."

Arthur looked to the sound, squinting through the sunlight streaming behind it. "You sure?"

"You got the last one. It's my turn now." Leo stepped down to the street. "You figure out how to catch us a rooster."

"You got it, boss." Arthur hobbled inside and closed the door.

Leo ran to the back of the trailer, digging through a bin, finding the screwdrivers Arthur used successfully the previous night. The figure approached. One of the new zombies, based on its speed and uneven gait. *Damn noisy rooster*, Leo thought to himself. *Stupid me for trying*. He looked around for anything else to help him.

A rotting car frame sat parked across the street, its rusting metal collapsed in on itself. The zombie was half a block away. Leo ran to the front of the car and picked up the bumper, pulling it towards him, doing the same with the rear bumper, hoping to add obstacles for the zombie. He repositioned the screwdrivers so he could slash at it more easily, the one in his right hand facing up, his left facing down.

The zombie bared his teeth, face covered in fresh blood. It ran around the rear end of the car, Leo ran around to the front, jumping over the bumper on the ground. He looked back. The zombie made it over the bumper without a problem and continued its pursuit around the car. It stepped on the front bumper, lunged forward, and caught itself, not losing speed. Leo made it around the back of the car and to the side, completing a full lap around the rusted out car. He continued forward towards the front of the car. The zombie paused at the back corner and turned around towards the front. Leo glanced behind him and almost fell.

They stopped and stared at each other. Leo felt a sudden rage at the zombie for figuring out how to double back. Leo breathed hard to catch his breath and realized the zombie was doing the same. The old zombies didn't have much connection with bodily functions other than eating, but the one staring back at him breathed, both of them catching their breath. He wanted to ask the zombie if that meant it could also get tired, that maybe they had other similarities, and the new zombies hid some weakness in their newfound abilities.

The zombie stepped towards Leo at the front end of the car, Leo countered to the side of the car. The zombie stopped. It yelled at Leo somewhere between a "no" and a snarl. Leo took a step away from the car. The zombie held still. Leo's mind raced to find a way out, feeling like he'd somehow become a stupid cornered rooster.

The zombie yelled and climbed over the rusting, caved in hood. Leo ran around the back of the car, still hoping to keep the metal hulk between him and the monster.

The zombie fell off the hood, scrambled to its feet, and chased Leo around the back end. In its fumbling, the zombie's foot hit the rear bumper Leo had placed earlier, and it tumbled to the ground.

Leo spun and ran at the zombie as it slammed its arms against the ground to push itself back up. Leo kicked, making contact hard on its chest. He could hear a crack as the zombie flew a few feet away onto its back. Leo continued forward, happy to discover the crack wasn't from his foot, but the zombie's ribs. Leo jumped, one foot landing on the zombie's face, holding it to the ground. Its arms clawed wildly. Leo stomped his other foot on one of its hands and jammed the screwdrivers at its head with all his strength, the left going through the bottom of its jaw, the right at the top of its head. The one from above did not pierce the skull, but the bottom made it through far enough for Leo to bruise his hand against the zombie's jawbone. It became limp.

Leo remained still for a moment before pulling the screwdriver out and wiped it on the zombie's clothes. As he did, he realized there were feathers in the fresh blood on its face. "Chickens?" Leo asked the corpse. It must've managed to catch and eat one. That, or something else had killed a chicken, and it had eaten the leftovers. *So they don't just eat people, now.* Leo wondered when they would stop surprising him with new things and go back to being as mindless as they used to be.

Leo crossed the street, tossing the screwdrivers back in the bin. He walked up the steps and entered the office building. Arthur popped out from one of the rooms with a wire in his hand. "Oh good, it went well then?"

"These things, man. They're not normal."

"Yeah, what is, though, right?"

Leo shrugged.

"Anyway," Arthur said, handing the wire to Leo. "I made you a poultry catcher."

Leo took it.

"Found a hanger. I bent the end as a hook and straightened the rest for distance. You can use it to grab its foot. At least, I think you can."

Leo was impressed, and hoped it would work. "Ok, I guess we corner it again. I'll meet you in the atrium." Leo picked up the makeshift sack Arthur made, handing it to him.

Being cornered once, the rooster was in no mood to let it happen again.

After twenty minutes of chasing an increasingly angry rooster, they got it into a proper corner. Leo swept the wire under it, hooking one of its legs. He lifted it up and grabbed its feet with his other hand. The rooster flapped wildly. Leo tried grabbing the wings, but the bird pecked hard at his hand. Leo cursed, his wound bleeding immediately. Arthur held out the bag and Leo thrust the rooster at it, but its wings were spread too wide to fit. Leo held the furious bird at arm's length as it flapped, kicking up dust. Leo grunted and yelled for Arthur to hold the bag at Leo's left side. Leo pulled the bird in under his left arm to hold its wings close to its body. It pecked at his hip twice before Arthur could get its body into the bag. He held the end closed. The Rooster struggled inside, giving sporadic paroxysms of impotent flapping and crowing, refusing to concede the fight.

INTERLUDE THREE: SIDEKICK

A few days earlier...

Why is this so bumpy? Sidekick thought to himself. *Why isn't the hairless two-legs carrying me? He is my preferred pet. He feeds me.* Nobody really listened to Sidekick, something he'd dealt with his whole life, being fifth of the second brood of Jaleel. If he were born just a few minutes earlier he would have been first, though as far as he knew, he might be the last of his line. That may all be in the past, but at times like this, that ancient irritation was hard to shake.

He knew it wasn't entirely his pet's fault that they did not fully comprehend his demands. After all, they were big, dumb, simple two-legged creatures, not intelligent like him. He was hungry, had been for some time. The little one with long hair carried him. She squeezed him too hard. Not as bad as when that building was on fire. "What was that all about, anyway? You seem upset about it." He knew nobody would listen, but sometimes things just needed to be said. He tried to sleep.

Now what? I'm on the ground? And why is everyone else on the ground around the older one? When will someone tell me exactly what's going on? Sidekick looked around. Nobody gave him an ounce of attention. He had not been the runt of his brood, and he refused to be treated as the runt among the two-legged pack. "No, of course not." He sat down, tired. The creatures had passed him around as they traveled, which made it impossible to have a satisfying sleep. Sometimes the large two-leggeds who carried him could be quite the nuisance. "Why aren't you feeding me?" he meowed in a miffed tone he hoped they'd understand.

Sidekick sensed something was wrong. He jumped to his feet and looked into the woods. "There's something out there!" He needed to get their attention. He hissed a loud, "Hey!" The hairless one, his favorite of the large two-legged creatures, heard him. The thing in the woods made another sound. Sidekick couldn't tell if it was one of the good two-legs that provide food and scratches, or if it was an angry one who'd try to eat him. Sidekick arched his back, letting the thing know he was the fiercest of the House of Jaleel, and it better not mess with any of his large two-legged pets, or they'd have hell to pay and he'd be the one to deal it out. The thing in the woods backed away. *At least it had the sense to listen to me.*

After a while, they walked on, leaving the old one on the ground. They were all quiet, which made it easier for him to drift back to sleep.

Yet another handoff forced Sidekick awake. *No, worse. They set me on the ground!* He made sure he'd remember that for the future so he could take his revenge. They were in another new place. He had a powerful urge to have his fur stroked. He stepped out of the fabric and saw his favorite hairless pet lying on the ground next to him. That was convenient, except the pet's hands were on his back for some annoying reason. He saw a strange hand moving down his two-legged's body, heading straight towards him. "Hey!" He yelled and swatted at the rogue hand, letting it know it better stay far away from him unless it held food. He arched his back for good measure. "Just try me now when I'm huge and ferocious!"

The hand was attached to a new medium-sized two-leg with bright red hair. It swung a strange stick directly at Sidekick. "What is this nonsense?"

His hairless pet said something to the red-haired one, proving himself worthwhile at translating Sidekick's words to the other dumb creatures. Sidekick knew they were talking about him, *as they should.* The red-haired one smiled and looked impressed. *Finally, someone who shows signs of intelligence.*

Then the hairless pet stood up, and they all walked away. They seemed to have forgotten about him, and though the sting of being the fifth of the second brood reared its head again, it suited Sidekick to be away from the two-leggeds in that moment. If they would not feed him, he'd seize the opportunity to explore and hunt. If he needed them for any reason (though he rarely did), he knew where to find them.

He prowled around the new space. Not as many walls as normal places, and completely open on top, like it was confused about whether or not it was a building. It also seemed devoid of food. No smell of rats or roaches. "Who would let this happen? How's a whiskered four-legged supposed to eat?" He asked no one in particular.

With no decent prospects for food, he found a nice sunny spot to lie down. The warmth felt good. It had been a while since he'd been in his cloth chariot, and the day wasn't at the right temperature yet.

Sidekick shot awake, surprised to find his body had sprung him in the air, ready for action at some loud noise. Proof his body's tactical defenses were strong. Part of the weird building was screaming and breathing smoke. He retreated to the farthest corner of the odd not-building and secreted himself against the wall, trusting his sudden move would confound the angry thing. It was still screaming, and the cloud was growing, but it hadn't followed his clever escape. Sidekick relaxed, but remained standing, ready to pounce.

After a while, the noise and cloud died down. He could hear his favored hairless pet talking to the red-haired one. *Let them deal with whatever mess they made.* He was hungry, but he'd rather give into his tiredness, especially with the sun finally nearing perfection. He curled up and fell back asleep.

Sidekick slowly thawed awake. He wasn't sure how long he'd been out, but he was satisfied with his choice. He stretched, shaking the sleep from his limbs as he stood. Sidekick needed his sleep, especially after the two-leggeds of his had been so inconsiderate the night before.

He walked around, but couldn't find his favorite one anywhere, not even with the other long-haired one his hairless pet seemed to favor. He was confused. *Had they left without me?* His favorite one had done that to Sidekick before, but he thought he taught it its lesson with an anger-defecation. *I must try harder and teach it not to forget me again,* he thought. *I should've known something was off about that one when he did not eat the mouse I left for him as an offering.*

He heard a noise that sounded like it might be food. He walked towards it and found a delicious looking white bird. Sidekick's stomach tightened and his mouth suddenly became wet as he imagined how glorious it would taste.

The bird was in some sort of cage. He neared it, which set the bird off, making a wild ruckus. Sidekick tried reaching through the wires, but the bird was too far away, and the cage too big. *Curse my perfectly proportioned body.* He leapt on to the top of the cage and tried in vain to reach his paws through the holes to the bird. *What a horrible trick to have such obvious food just out of reach.* He pounced to the ground and lay in wait, hoping the bird would try to escape. Then it would be his. His stomach rumbled. He told it to be patient, it would only be a matter of time.

Sidekick heard footsteps. The red-haired one walked towards him. *The strange building must be where it lives.* It came hurriedly at Sidekick speaking gibberish, so he ran away.

Normally he wouldn't cozy up to any of the two-legged creatures, but something about his favored pet had changed Sidekick. He wondered what it had been. The hairless one was warm when he was cold, and it fed him and provided scratches when he wanted, and understood when it was told to cease. Those were all nice, much nicer than he'd experienced before.

Sidekick wondered where his own siblings were. There were eight of them, originally, until one of the angry two-legs with dead eyes ate their mother and some of his siblings. He didn't know exactly how many escaped after they scattered. That was when he found the place with the tree that birds liked to visit. Sidekick felt hunger pangs in his stomach. He needed to eat the white bird.

He let those thoughts go and sauntered back towards the red-haired one, rubbing his side against one of its two legs. It bent down. Sidekick ran away, just out of its reach. "Not too fast," he said. *Some of these creatures can be so careless. It's hard to be a whiskered four-legged in this world.* He wished every two-legs would take their time and understand they must wait for him to be ready. Everyone was a threat until proven otherwise.

Sidekick inched back towards the red-haired one. It moved much slower that time. *Good,* he thought, *this one learns fast.* He snuck away again, more for fun than security. He turned around and came back for a third leg rub, allowing the creature to touch him. Its small fingers felt good as they rubbed behind his ears. It was like his ears always had an itch he couldn't feel until they were being scratched. Then they felt so darn good. He rubbed his body against the creature's leg. *This is one of the good two-leggeds.*

The red-haired one said something unintelligible and walked away from Sidekick, clearly wanting him to follow, which made him not want to. Curiosity got the best of him, and he reluctantly trailed behind. It disappeared into a room. Sidekick sat down and a moment later it came out with some food. "Finally!" Sidekick meowed. He ate while it watched. *It really was one of the good ones.*

After eating and allowing the two-legged to stroke his fur, Sidekick found a delightful spot under a plant in the cool soil and took a nap.

Some time later, an unfamiliar noise caught his attention. He stretched, then strode over to investigate. The red-haired one was scrambling down a ladder on the wall. It ran into a room and came out a moment later with something in its hand and headed back up the ladder. *These creatures make no sense,* he thought to himself. He watched as it joined the long-haired two-legged on top of the wall.

Tired of watching those two, Sidekick paraded off to look for the other smaller creatures. He wanted to be petted again, and climbing to the top of the wall wasn't feasible.

The one-armed one was asleep. Normally Sidekick didn't mind waking his creatures up so they could pet him, but he felt like that one in particular would not be a good return on anvestment. It always seemed to be distracted by its strange limb. He found the other small one asleep on a chair. She looked like she'd be a comfortable spot for him to sleep on, so he jumped up and nestled into the space she made with her arms. He found the creature to be conveniently sized for his needs.

He heard the other two coming down the ladder and talking, but he didn't deem it worth his time to open his eyes. *Let them squawk and walk.* He just wanted to stay in the nice warm place.

A few minutes later, he smelled it. Every one of the two-legged creatures with dead eyes had the same smell. Some less, others more, but they all had it to varying degrees, and he smelled it in the wind. He was especially annoyed at having his nap interrupted to deal with some angry creature with two legs.

Sidekick jumped off the chair and looked around. His fur always told him when something bad was near and it was tingling. He couldn't see anything, though. Then he heard it—a noise from above on the far side of the strange non-building—one of the two-legged dead-eyed creatures creeping along the top of the wall closer to the other two nice ones. It occurred to Sidekick that the angry ones had grown more cunning of late. That made him hate them more.

Sidekick yelled at the small sleeping one beside him to wake up. It did not respond. The dead-eyed creature moved along the wall, heading toward the ladder. He yelled another warning. The creature stirred, but didn't notice. *Sometimes the small two-leggeds were smarter than the bigger ones,* Sidekick thought, *but they could also be the most frustrating.* He yelled again. That time, the small one opened its eyes. Sidekick arched his back and hissed towards the dead-eyed creature on the wall. The little one beside him realized what was going on. *The little ones always listened better.*

The little two-legged one jumped up and ran to get the one-armed two-legs, and they spoke nonsense to the other two big ones. They all ran into a small, dark room and closed the door. Sidekick yelled at them for forgetting him, but the dead-eyed creature was already on the ground, running towards him. Sidekick hissed at the dead-eyed creature. He figured it prudent to retreat so he could fight from a place of advantage another time, so he ran and strategically placed himself under a large metal tank nearby.

He watched the angry dead-eyed creature bang on the door and heard the other two-leggeds yell from inside the room. He wished he could do something, but he was surprised to feel fear coursing through him. That confused him. He could retreat farther, which would normally abate that feeling, but something was different. He realized he might actually care about those two-leggeds of his. That was new to him. He missed his favored hairless pet the most. "Why does that one keep leaving me behind?"

It dawned on Sidekick that he had abandoned his own brood when the dead-eyed one attacked and devoured his family. The weight of his actions filled him with regret. Sidekick may be the last of the House of Jaleel, but without recognizing it, he had adopted a new family. He hoped that he would be reunited with his hairless pet and the other two-legged creatures he traveled with. They may be very different, and however unlikely it seemed, they had become family.

CHAPTER TWENTY TWO

Leo pedaled hard, but the slight incline combined with the heavy trailer meant it was still slow going. Arthur held the bags of apples against his legs to protect them from bruising. The rooster had calmed down aside from a few minor paroxysms from time to time when the trailer jostled over rougher patches of road. In those moments, Arthur had empathy for the chicken. His hind end was getting the brunt of the rough ride, and the extra weight of the apples made each bump hit even harder.

Other than the occasional squawking and a subtle squeak from the trailer itself, they rode in silence. Leo's other bike bounced around on the trailer behind him.

The closer they got to the power plant, the better Leo felt. He was almost out of the woods, both figuratively and literally. His legs were lighter as he turned south down with the entrance to the plant. A block away, though, he felt something was wrong.

The outer gate was open, which was concerning since he specifically remembered closing it. The closer he got, the more hollow the pit in his stomach became. He slowed down. He could see the metal door was also open, which was an even worse sign. He immediately pedaled as hard as he could. Arthur fell backwards on the trailer at the sudden acceleration. "Hey man, what's going on?"

"Don't know," Leo said between lunges on the pedals, "but not good." He turned left and brought them around the south side of the power plant.

The rooster clucked hard at Arthur, who in his focusing on the building, accidentally put pressure on the animal. He apologized to the bird. "Is that the place?" Leo nodded. "Then where are we going?"

"Just—I need to think." Leo said. He turned north on the street bordering the east side of the complex and saw a large ladder leaning against the outer wall, lashed together with old lumber and tree limbs. He looked everywhere for signs of his friends, but nothing brought him comfort. The ladder rose from the ground to just below the peak of the wall. Bits of fabric and flesh hung from the razor wire just above the top of the ladder, and a zombie crawled on the ground at its base. Leo deduced the zombie must've tried to climb over, but got stuck and fallen, breaking its legs. Leo stopped pedaling, letting the inertia of the trailer propel him to a slow stop.

Leo's mind raced. *Who could've done this? Where are Sarah and the others?* He looked to Arthur "I need a weapon."

Arthur lost color in his face as the realization sunk in that something was terribly wrong. He reached to the box with the screwdrivers, then had a better idea. He set the bag with the rooster to the side and opened a toolbox. He dug through it and pulled out a hatchet.

Leo grabbed it and took off toward the ladder. The grounded zombie gurgled with blood as it breathed and growled at Leo's approach, its body maimed from the fall. Leo marched straight towards it, feeling the weight of the blade in his hand. He lifted the hatchet and brought it down hard on the zombie's head. It flopped down, limp. Leo stood there staring at the corpse for several seconds, pressure building in his chest. He screamed at the dead, broken body sprawled on the ground. He pushed his foot down on its neck and jerked the hatchet out of its skull. He thought about wiping the blade, but he figured that wouldn't be necessary as he intended on using it again very soon. He only hoped it wasn't on a zombie that used to be one of his friends.

He told Arthur to wait on the trailer; he was going to face whatever waited for him inside. Having backup would have been nice, but in case there was an ambush, he wanted to attack on his own and not worry about Arthur's safety. He marched around the exterior wall. His mind raced with possibilities for what he'd find inside. None of them were good.

He turned the corner to the side with the entrance. He always thought it was the most secure place he could imagine, but he never conceived the notion that zombies could climb ladders, much less build them. He still did not want to think they did it by themselves. *Some insane person must've built it for them*, he imagined. *Some sort of monster orchestrated the attack.* Whether it was human or zombie in nature didn't matter much to Leo, he killed monsters.

He walked through the open outer gate. The large metal doors should have been locked, but they both hung wide open. *Only someone inside could've released them.* There was blood on the ground around the outer door. No way for him to know whose it might've been. It looked like whoever it belonged to had run away from the building toward the gate, based on the size of the drops. *Would anyone be inside the complex?* He looked through the dark room, now illuminated by the sun shining through the open doors. An errant arm lay on the floor in the middle.

The inside of the complex looked in place as far as he could tell. Off to the right, he could see chairs set in a semi-circle. His hatchet dripped blood from the unlucky zombie lying on the ground outside. *Had any more made it up the ladder and over the razor wire?* Leo gripped the hatchet tight and began checking the complex. It felt alien. He'd only known the inside and imagined it as the safest place in the world for just a short time, and suddenly it transformed back into a foreign landscape.

The pipes and tanks made him imagine he was on a colony on the moon. He wondered if astronauts were still up in space, left there when the apocalypse began. Leo shook his head. He was wholly alone.

The room Scout had first brought him to was empty. The vodka bottle sat on the table. He crossed the complex, the gravel crunch of each footstep bringing him closer to feeling stranded on the moon. The radio room was also empty. Leo continued around the rear of the complex. Another zombie lay on the ground. It must've gone over the razor wire, but overshot the wall and fell, landing on its head. A shot of rage surged through his body. *Humans were supposed to be smarter than zombies, but zombies were relentless and single-minded.* Again, nature had over-taken humanity, like the tortoise and the hare. Slow and steady, zombies would win. Leo was just a hare thinking his greater ability would win the day, but he'd been worn down bit by bit over the years. *That's the real existential zombie threat, the way they kill humanity. Not one person at a time, but every single person at once, slowly, and in the mind. There really was no escape.*

Leo heard a noise from behind one cluster of tanks and pipes. He froze, hatchet up and ready. He slowly stepped around it, imagining a zombie lurking in wait, his mind expanding it to fifty of them, a swarm lying in wait. He was a third of the way around the tank cluster when a shadow shot toward him on the ground. Leo jumped back, and the shape stopped, as scared as he was. Sidekick looked up at him. Leo gave a yelp of joy and knelt down. Sidekick ran and leapt into his hands. Leo picked him up and hugged the cat. *His* cat. He asked Sidekick what happened. The cat meowed back.

Leo perched Sidekick on his shoulder and continued on with his hunt. The extra weight and jostle of the cat made Leo take each step slower. It calmed him, made him more present. He was directly responsible for another life, and that gave him focus. He checked the rest of the rooms and again found nothing, not even signs of struggle. The lack of answers concerned him more than if he'd found bodies. He only had the trail of blood out the front.

He neared the front gate, having made a full circle of the grounds. Sidekick growled in a low tone. His claws slipped out and ready. Leo didn't mind the pain of the claws poking in his skin and was thankful for the alert. The open inner door blocked his view to the outside, and he heard footsteps slowly moving through the space between the inner and outer doors. Sidekick hissed louder, his claws digging deeper into Leo, making him wince. He pulled Sidekick from his shoulder and set him on the ground, leaving small dots of blood behind on his shirt.

A pair of feet stepped on the gravel inside the door. They stepped forward, bringing into view an old man, somewhere in his 80s. His eyes tired and sunken, his eyebrows resting over them like a drooping porch. He was old enough to have seen the old world, watched it fall, and the new one take root. His face carried the weight of all he'd witnessed.

The man's head sat forward and low, like it was too heavy for the rest of him. He turned and looked directly at Leo. The man's constant gaze looked straight through him somehow. Sidekick remained hunched on the ground.

Leo noticed the man's clothes were dirty and ragged. His sleeve ends and shirt collar stained. *Could he have survived on the road the last fifty odd years?*

"You" the man said in a scratchy voice.

Leo's head tilted at the question, holding his hatchet higher. "... yes?"

The man reached into his pocket. Leo swung his hatchet back. The man held up his other hand. His voice came quick and gravelly. "No, wait, something to show you." He pulled out a couple sheets of paper. He unfolded one and held it out, facing Leo. It was the missing sketch of Leo's father.

Leo's chest tightened. "Why do you have that?"

"Who is he?" The man demanded.

"He—why do you have that? Are you the one who took it?"

"Yes. Tell me who he is."

"Why does it matter?" Leo said. He lowered the hatchet, still squeezing the handle hard enough his knuckles were white.

"I knew him." The man maintained his constant stare at Leo with strained breaths through an open mouth.

"You—how, when?"

"Why did you draw him?" The man unfolded the other paper, revealing the missing sketch of Anna. "Why did you draw them all?"

Leo shook his head, unsure if he should answer the man's questions honestly.

The man grunted, "Did you kill?"

"What? No!"

"Who are they to you?"

"They're—they were my friends, the ones who died. I drew those to remember them."

The man's eyes flitted back and forth as he processed Leo's response.

Leo narrowed his eyes at the man, asking, "Who are they to *you*? Why did you take my drawing?"

The man closed his mouth and stood taller. "He was my friend, when we were young." The man turned the paper around to look at the sketch of Leo's father.

"You mean..." Leo loosened his grip, "before everything?"

The man nodded. "We were friends. Then everything happened, and the zombies came. I... he was supposed to join me, but..." The man trailed off. Leo noticed the man's fingers had dark stains, almost reminding him of a zombie's hands. Leo shivered from somewhere deep inside.

The man looked at Leo, demanding with his eyes, "Who is he to you?"

"He was my dad." Leo said.

The man looked Leo up and down. "Oh." He nodded. He seemed tired, but Leo wasn't sure if he was projecting his own tiredness onto the man.

"Wait," Leo said, "You're...Xavier!"

The man narrowed his gaze at Leo, sparks of memory lit up behind his eyes. He gave small nod and grunt.

"I heard about you. My parents said...well, not much, actually, just that you wanted my dad to be with you in your bunker. I never got the full story from them before they died."

"I'm sorry." the man said, looking back at the sketch of Leo's father.

"For what?" Leo asked.

"For your loss." The man said, folding the papers.

"Why'd you take Anna's picture?"

The man returned the folded sketches to his pocket. "Sorry for your loss."

"Those belong to me."

The man looked at Leo, taking strained breaths through his open mouth. "Sorry for your loss."

Sidekick gave a low hiss. Leo recognized what caused the stains on the man's fingers and face—dried blood. Leo stepped back. "Did you—kill her?"

The man shook his head, taking a step towards Leo. "I harvested her."

Leo continued backing away, the man matching his steps. "Why'd you kill her?"

"I didn't. She was already dead. I just consumed her."

Leo continued backing up, navigating his way around tanks and pipes with glances, unsure where he was ultimately trying to escape to. The man continued, calmly matching him. "Why?" Leo asked, holding the hatchet between them.

"I have to." The man said, matter-of-fact.

"You're one of those things!" Leo took off running as fast as he could around the machinery. The man raced after him.

"No!" The man yelled behind him. "I'm *better* than them. *Because I eat!*"

Leo raced back to the entrance, sprinting towards the metal door. He could hear the man's steps closing in as the sound of their feet crunched against the gravel, echoing through the compound. Sidekick took off running with Leo and shot out the door. Leo followed a moment later, grabbing the inner door behind him, and swung it hard. It clanged shut and locked as the man slammed into it behind him.

Leo tripped on the arm lying on the floor and fell back against the wall, holding his shoulder at the pain from jerking the door so hard. A beam of light shot out of the peephole into Leo's eyes. He reeled backwards and caught his balance.

The man's head blocked the light, filling the hole with rage-filled eyes. "We could've done this a better way."

"What did you do with my friends?"

"It doesn't matter. Nothing does." The man snarled. "Every last person on earth will be turned or eaten. It's evolution. Those first zombies were a step backwards, simple mindless monsters, but I'm a leap forward."

Leo looked to the outer door, contemplating making a run for it, then he looked back at the man, eyes wild through the peephole. "What do you mean?"

Anger melted from the man's face as he spoke. "The first flu pandemic happened when I was a child. The second and third, before I was fifteen. After my parents died, I started building a shelter underground. If the world was trying to kill me and everyone I knew, I wasn't going down without a fight. I meant to survive." The man examined Leo. "Your father was my best friend. I meant for him to join me in the shelter. He was supposed to be there with me, but that last pandemic came with little warning. It seemed to pass over the entire world at once, even with all the precautionary measures put in place from the prior epidemics. Your father... he just never came. I wanted to find him, but those things—I could see those ugly monsters through the window in my shelter door. My only view of the world outside, and it was filled with those things. I watched the world fade away from my hole in the ground.

"I only saw one or two living people through that window, after that first year..." He shook his head and looked to the floor. "A neighbor actually told me I was crazy for building my safe house, said it was a damn waste. I asked if she woulda said that to Noah. She was the first zombie I saw snarling outside my window. Eventually I realized I was the last human."

Leo watched the sadness and pain of decades of solitude and confinement wash over the man's face. He was surprised to feel pity for the old man. "But...you weren't."

The man barked back, "You don't know the burden! To be the last human on earth? The weight of that?"

"But there were others, you weren't alone."

"No!" The man slammed his hand against the door and disappeared from the peephole, leaving the beam of light shining on the severed arm on the floor. Leo took a step forward, then changed his mind and turned to leave. A short, sharp click froze him in his tracks. The man had unlocked the door. Leo spun and ran outside, slamming the outer door behind him as the man raced after him.

Leo rushed toward the metal fence, realizing he dropped the hatchet in his rush to escape. *No time to turn back.* He called after Sidekick, who had run across the street. The man crashed against the outer door, realizing it also locked when Leo slammed it shut. He shouted through the peephole, "You're only delaying the inevitable!"

Leo sprinted down the street and around the corner, back toward Arthur. Sidekick bounded past him. He had a head start, but he knew it would only be a moment until the man opened the door, and Leo couldn't pedal fast enough to escape with Arthur and the trailer.

He hoped having two against one would be enough.

Leo rounded the corner behind the complex and yelled to Arthur. "Bad guy behind me. Get weapons!"

Arthur jumped up and fumbled around the tool boxes, confused, but sufficiently motivated by Leo's terror to do as requested. "One of those zombies?" He pulled out a claw hammer and tossed it to Leo.

Leo shook his head and joined his friend at the trailer, trying to catch his breath. "I don't know, but he's all bad." Sidekick jumped onto the trailer and faced the way they'd come, arching his back.

The man rounded the corner and slowed down upon seeing Arthur on the trailer beside Leo. He came to a stop and panted. An ominous smile formed on his tired face. Leo and Arthur exchanged looks, neither had a plan of escape.

"I could've stayed there, you know." The man said. "I thought about it every day, told myself 'No! Be safe in here.' Over the years there were fewer zombies outside. For twelve whole years in there, I covered the window, couldn't bear to watch the world decay. It was just too much. Eventually I resented my hole in the ground. It saved my life, but I hated it. Loathed it. It made me watch the world dissolve, all alone in my prison. Even the air inside was trapped, recirculated and filtered too many times. I had to get out." The man swallowed. Memories fluttered behind his eyes.

"I opened the door. This brave new world had an unfamiliar smell. Growth and rot, a kind of sweetness to it. My neighborhood was unrecognizable. Entire buildings just gone, flora exploding from every inch. I walked until I found a building still standing, a church made of stone. It was old when I was young, and it lasted longer than anything built after.

"I went inside. The pews were long rotted away. I climbed the bell tower. I wanted to look at the world from above, see how far it stretched. A new, acrid stench filled my lungs. Decades of guano covered the stone steps. Bats had made their home in the dark, spiraling stairwell. I crept past them, careful not to wake them.

"At the top, I looked out. It was no longer a city, but a mass grave, and I was its last king looking out on a dead world."

"Again," Leo said, "You weren't the last human."

"How could I have known that?" The man screamed. He paused and calmed himself before continuing. "I contemplated jumping, just ending my life and all of humanity right there. I don't know what changed my mind, but some voice within told me I was there for a purpose, convinced me to go on. Eventually I climbed back down the spiral staircase, but I slipped on the guano. I landed on my hip, the pain was fierce, and my screams echoed on the stone walls. The bats woke up angry and swarmed, scratching and biting me. I ran back to my hole, cuts on my arms and face, hip aching. I treated the wounds with my first-aid kit, unaware it was too late for me. I'd already been infected.

"Only certain animals can carry and mutate a human virus. Something new was gestating in those bats. Maybe it began as the zombie virus, or maybe it was something else.

"That first week, I could feel something changing in me. Fevers and chills, soreness and headache. I assumed that 'hole' would become my tomb. Then, I don't know how long after, the hunger began, an irrational hunger and rage. That voice of reason grew distant, shrinking into some dark recess in my mind. When the hunger screamed so loud I couldn't ignore it, I left.

"Things are fuzzy from those early days. I was shocked to find living people, I didn't believe they were real. Some even tried to help, but I attacked them. All I remember, all I know is that after I fed on one of them—the brain, the blood—a small piece of me returned. I ate a person and regained my own humanity. I let a few of them escape alive, carrying my infection inside them. That's when I realized I had it all backwards. I was not a zombie. After they feed, they remained empty. But when I consumed someone, I became more. I wasn't human, nor was I meant to save humanity. I built my ark and survived the flood of monsters. That antediluvian world was over, humanity washed away. I was the first of my kind, and my job—my destiny—is to cleanse the world from the last sins of humanity for good." The man bared his teeth and screamed toward the sky. "Come! Come to me now!"

Arthur looked to Leo. "How do we not find out who he was yelling at, 'cause I'm damn sure I don't wanna meet them."

Leo shrugged, pulse still racing.

"And who is he, anyway?"

"He knew my father, then I guess he spent fifty years alone underground, going crazy."

"Wrong! I spent those years going sane!" The man yelled back. "Eating flesh is inevitable. You cannot have life without death, Ouroboros can only go on forever if he eats his own tail. Either I eat to regain my mind or I erode into darkness. What will you choose? You see, I don't want my brethren to eat you when they come." The man smiled. "You're for *me*. Fate has brought us together. Your father was supposed to join me, and now he stands right here before me, in your blood."

Two zombies appeared around the far corner of the power plant behind Leo and Arthur, flanking them.

"What's the plan, man?" Arthur said, glancing at Leo.

"I dunno," Leo said, scanning the street. "We can't make it to the ladder in time, and they'd be at us within half a block if we tried escaping on the bike."

Arthur grabbed Leo's arm. "But you could run, right?"

Leo looked to Arthur. "I'm not leaving you."

"It's okay, man. Live another day. These things—I'm not sure I want to live in a world with them, you know?"

"You'd rather be one of them?" Leo asked.

Arthur shivered. "No, but... we don't both need to die today."

Leo pled with his eyes, then looked up, searching for a path to escape if he ran. Leo hated his options. "You sure about this?"

Arthur nodded. "I don't have anyone left." Tears formed in the corner of his eyes. "Take care, man."

The man watched Leo and Arthur, grinning with rage, ready to strike. The other two zombies kept their pace towards the trailer. They were running out of time. Leo hugged Arthur, searching for words, but finding none. He gave Arthur a nod and slowly backed away, preparing to bolt.

"Hey!" A voice cried out. The man gave a confused look and faced the corner of the power plant behind him. Two figures rounded the building—Sarah, carrying a large pitchfork, and Scout with curved grass sickles in each hand.

"You the guy who sent those things into my place, right?" Scout yelled.

The man turned to Leo, confused, then back at Scout.

"Oh, you built a ladder. Makes sense now. I wasn't able to check when we escaped. I was too busy killing those fuckers." She held up her sickles like giant razored middle fingers.

The man snarled. "Your time is over!"

"Yeah, got it." Scout shrugged him off.

"You okay?" Sarah called to Leo.

"Yeah. You? How are the kids?"

Sarah replied, "They're safe."

Scout yelled to Leo, "Who is this guy?"

"You will address me!" The man yelled.

"In a minute." Scout said, then turned to Sarah "This guy."

"He knew my father." Leo said.

Surprise washed over Scout and Sarah's faces.

Leo heard the two zombies behind him speed up their approach. "Can this wait?" He yelled to Scout and Sarah.

Scout took off running at the man standing between her and Leo. Sarah followed.

Leo looked behind him. The two new zombies were closing in fast. He told Arthur, "I'll lead them away," and took off running toward the ruined buildings across the street. One zombie followed him, the other hesitated, and continued toward Arthur.

Leo ran in a wide arc, keeping an eye on the zombie pursuing him. It breathed heavily and said, "Come back," baring its teeth.

Leo could see Scout running to help Arthur, who struggled with the other zombie. Sidekick hissed and jumped on its leg, distracting it enough for Arthur to give it a jab.

Sarah ran after the creepy old man who made a run for the ladder.

Leo halted and turned. The zombie dove at him. Leo swung the hammer claw-side first at the zombie, catching it on the side of its head. The claw gouged out its eye. The zombie crumpled to the ground, grabbing its face and screaming in pain. Leo suddenly realized the smarter those new zombies were, the more they could still feel pain. Leo slammed a knee into its chest. The zombie yelped, still holding its hands to its bleeding eye socket. Leo looked at the creature. He thought about what the man told him and wondered exactly when it turned from a person to a zombie, and how much humanity it might still be clinging on to.

It snarled and reached its hands out, clawing at Leo's leg. It threw Leo off to the side and rolled over, yelling and reaching for Leo as he struggled to crawl away. The zombie grabbed Leo's foot and opened its mouth to bite his leg. Leo swung the hammer hard on the zombie's face, smashing its skull. It went limp, releasing Leo's foot. He backed away from the creature. For the first time in his life, Leo wondered if he was morally right for killing a zombie.

He looked away and saw Arthur struggling with the other zombie on the trailer. Arthur got a good kick in, pushing it away in time for Scout to swing the two grass sickles at either side of the zombie's neck. They dug into it like giant scissors. The zombie stumbled and fell backwards, its head flapping around on the small bit of flesh still tethering it to the body.

The man climbed up the ladder. He again cried out, "Come now!" A chill danced down Leo's spine. More zombies had emerged between the buildings all around the power plant.

Leo quickly got up and ran towards the man on the ladder. Sarah beat him there and plunged her pitchfork up at the man, catching him in the leg. He yelled and lost his footing, falling to the ground. Sarah jumped out of the way and held the pitchfork back, ready to plunge it at the man again.

"Sarah, wait!" Leo yelled. She turned her attention to Leo for a moment. The man lunged at her, but she saw him moving and plunged the pitchfork at him and jumped back in the same motion. The tines dug into the man's shoulder. The force of his body towards the ground ripped the pitchfork out of Sarah's grasp. She stepped on the handle, pinning the man to the ground, the tines deep in his flesh.

Sarah glared at Leo "What the hell?"

"Sorry, it's just—he knew my father."

"No time for that now!" Scout yelled. She pointed to Arthur who struggled to sit up on the edge of the trailer. "Grab this guy, we gotta climb!"

A half dozen zombies ran at them from all sides. Leo recognized the zombie with the yellow dress and the one with the red stripe of blood across its chest among them.

Leo sprinted, shoving the hammer through a loop on his pants. He hoisted Arthur onto his back and they ran towards the ladder. Scout ripped the shirt off one of the dead zombies and handed it to Sarah, pushing her off the pitchfork handle. Scout took her place, maintaining pressure on the man's shoulder. "Climb! Toss the shirt on the razor wire."

Sarah nodded and started up the ladder. Scout waved for Leo to climb. He set Arthur down and glanced at the old man on the ground, struggling under the tines stuck in his wounds. "Now!" Scout yelled.

Arthur climbed. Sarah reached the top and draped the shirt over the razor wire, giving her enough leeway to climb over without getting snagged. Leo leaned to the side and hung on to the ladder with one hand, helping Arthur with his other. Arthur winced and panted as he climbed, his foot aching. Sarah pulled Arthur up and over the wire while Leo supported his legs.

Half a dozen zombies closed in on the ladder. Leo shared a pained look with Scout. She leapt off the pitchfork handle and sliced one of the man's legs. He screamed. Leo realized she incapacitated him enough that he couldn't climb the ladder after them. She spun the blades in her hands to face out, small droplets of blood arced off them, then she flew up the ladder. Leo took his cue and worked his way over the razor wire right after Arthur cleared out of the way. He had one leg over when the ladder jerked to the side. His pant leg caught on the razor wire. The zombie with the yellow dress pulled at the base of the ladder below.

Scout yelped in fear from the sudden movement hanging off the side of the ladder. She continued her ascent, clinging tight to the ladder as it jostled more violently back and forth. Leo jerked his leg over the wire. It tore through his pants to the flesh on his calf. He leaned back over the razor wire to steady the top of the ladder from toppling down with Scout still on it. Another zombie made it to the base and jerked it to the other side. Scout swung wildly, dropped one of her sickles, and grasped on the nearest rung tight with her hand. She was just two steps below the top. She grunted and leapt up, grabbing Leo's hand. The sudden added weight pulled him down onto the wire. The barbs pressed through the layers of fabric into his chest. The ladder banged against the wall in a slow arc to the ground.

Leo lifted Scout high enough for her to grab hold of the ledge.

Sarah removed her over-shirt and slid it under the razor wire, adding "Let's bring her under!" She pulled the fabric up, raising the wire with it. Leo winced as the barbs dug deeper into his chest.

Scout looked to Leo and said, "I'm good. Let go."

Leo released Scout and pulled himself off the barbs. He jerked the fabric off the razor wire, shot one end underneath, and lifted up, creating a space between him and Sarah wide enough for Scout. She pulled herself up, reached to the inside lip of the wall, and pulled her top half up. She slid the rest of the way through, falling into the trench. Leo and Sarah let go of the wire. It slapped down against the top of the wall with a reverberating metal echo.

Sarah helped Scout up.

Arthur grunted and leaned against the inner trench wall. "Is that everyone?"

"Sidekick!" Leo yelled as a fresh wave of fear rolled through him. In the shadows under the trailer, he could just make out Sidekick, safe for the moment, looking at the zombies amassing below Leo. He leaned out over the wall and counted eight of them gathered below, staring back at him.

The man rolled on his back, glaring up at Leo. They looked at each other for a long moment. "*They* are the future, not you!" The man yelled from the ground, a pool of blood blooming on the dirt around him. He screamed to the zombies, "Come, feed!"

The zombies surrounded him, lapping at the blood. They grew more violent, fighting to get at their life-source. The man howled in pain as the zombie with the red stripe began sucking blood from one of the holes in his leg. The others followed suit. The one with the yellow dress grabbed the pitchfork and ripped it out of his arm. The man shrieked and recoiled at the pain. The zombie dove at his shoulder.

Leo leaned back and slid to the trench floor, listening to the man howl below. He hated the man, hated he was the only remaining connection with his father, hoped the other zombies would finish him, angry at himself for still feeling pity.

Sarah offered her hand to help him up. The world melted away, and he found himself grateful she was there with him, safe. He wanted to say he loved her, but he so rarely used those words, unsure what they really meant in practice. She pulled him up. They stood face to face. A force deep within Leo inched him close to her. They kissed, and for a brief moment, Leo felt well. Sarah held him tight, and pain lit up all over his chest. He winced and backed away, realizing blood soaked through his shirt from his wounds. "I'm sorry." He said, catching his breath.

"I hate to interrupt," Scout said, looking over the wall, "but we're not done yet."

Leo looked at the man lying motionless on the ground, wondering if he was dead, drained of blood. That question had to wait, because the rest of the zombies spread out along the ladder, lifting it perpendicular to the wall. *They're going to push it back up!* Something else struck Leo as wrong. He only counted six zombies below. *There were more before, right?* He turned to Scout and said, "The door's open!"

Scout grabbed her sickle from the ledge and leapt past Arthur, running toward the front of the building.

Leo watched the zombies walk the ladder up the wall. Two pushed at the end, the others lifting it higher, squeezing closer together toward the bottom. He heard the front door clang shut. He looked across the power plant grounds, but a structure blocked his view to the door.

The ladder bounced closer and closer to the top of the wall. Leo was thankful to find his hammer still in the loop of his pants. He looked down at the trailer and wondered how much of Sidekick's life had consisted of hiding before they met. He felt sad for the cat, then realized he'd been doing the same thing his whole life. *Sure, he traveled the streets, made deliveries, and connected people who were even more shut in than himself, but he'd become sedentary in his own life, stuck in his tiny loop.* He knew that life had come to an end. If they survived, they'd have to get Steven to the doctor, which meant hitting the road. He wondered where Sarah had hidden her siblings. He turned to ask her, but she was busy helping Arthur move down the wall, away from the rising ladder. They were both without weapons. It would be up to Leo to defend the power plant from the zombie's siege.

The ladder stopped a few inches below the top of the wall. Leo wanted to reach out and topple it over, but his chest ached at the notion of leaning over the razor wire again. He'd already hurt himself enough that way, worried he might contract tetanus, or worse. He pushed those concerns down and readied the hammer. He moved a few feet to Sarah's side of the ladder, putting himself between her and the approaching zombies. The ladder banged against the wall as the first zombie began its climb; the others clamoring up, right behind.

The first zombie peered over the ledge, hunger in its eyes and fresh blood smeared on its face. It reached its arms on the ledge and pushed its torso up first over the razor wire. Leo swung down hard with the hammer on its skull. It gave a wet smack, and the zombie toppled back, falling to the ground outside. The next zombie quickly took its place, reaching its arms over the wire, ragged sleeves catching on the barbs. Leo swung at its hand and missed, nearly burying his own hand in the sharp metal spikes. The zombie with the yellow dress followed right behind and climbed on top of the other one, smashing its body into the barbs. Leo reeled back and swung at her head, but her arm smashed against the hammer, batting it away. She yelped, and rolled down over the other zombie, sliding over its body as a shield from the razor wire. She landed headfirst in the trench. As she scrambled up, Leo swung down hard, catching her on the back of the head, driving her face-first into the floor of the trench. He swung back to give her another blow, but Sarah jerked him backwards and he swung wide. The red striped zombie scrambled over the ledge inches away, crawling over the one stuck in the barbed wire. Leo fell backward onto Sarah. He apologized, fearing he'd done more than knock the wind out of her in their fall, thankful she just saved his life.

Red Stripe scrambled towards Leo. He kicked at it, seeing another climb over the edge into the trench and the arm of one more reach over the wall right behind it. They were about to be overrun.

Leo scrambled backward, pushing against Sarah. She rushed to back away, still catching her breath. Leo pushed himself just out of reach from the red striped zombie's pursuit. It lunged at him, toppling him back to the floor of the trench. Pain jolted through his head as his ear connected with the cement edge of the wall. He yelled, swinging the hammer hard on the back of the zombie's head. It slammed hard against Leo's already injured chest. He pushed up against the red striped zombie. It was stunned, but not dead. He reached the hammer above his head and swung down hard, cracking through the top of its skull.

It collapsed on him, spilling blood everywhere. Leo suddenly felt more pressure as the yellow dress zombie scrambled over Red Stripe's corpse.

Leo struggled to get away, but the pressure from the two bodies on top of him locked him in place. The zombie lunged at Leo's face. He instinctually closed his eyes and craned his head away from the threat. The zombie jerked backwards. Leo opened his eyes to see Sarah kicking at the zombie, her hands planted firmly against the trench walls, bringing the full force of her kick against the zombie, slamming it back.

Sarah looked down at Leo, terror in her eyes that reached inside Leo's mind, scaring him. Her mouth moved and noise came out, but it sounded strange and distant, like the sound itself had been squeezed through a tube. It took Leo a moment to realize she was screaming. It took him another moment to remember what those words meant individually, then parsed their meaning together as a sentence. She was screaming "Can you move?!"

Leo opened his mouth to tell her he couldn't budge, but he no longer had enough air inside him for any noise to escape his own mouth. He was pinned under the pile, and trapped inside his own body.

Sarah yelled something else and looked away. She continued throwing kicks at the unrelenting zombies. More pressure crushed down on him as a third one clamored over the others. Their legs slammed against his somewhere below the pile. His chest hurt and his vision narrowed. His body pinned, he focused on trying to breathe under the weight. His limbs convulsed as his body hungered for air. The last thing he saw as the world closed in around him and faded away was Sarah's legs kicking overhead against the pale blue sky.

INTERLUDE FOUR: SCOUT

Scout sprinted through the trench along the south wall to the ladder at the front of the complex, wishing her family had built more than one way up or down. She glanced outside the wall to her left and saw two zombies running alongside her on the ground. She had to book it if she wanted to beat them to the doors. She banged her body into the cement wall on the southwest corner to make the ninety degree turn and sprinted to the ladder, tossing her sickle to the ground below. She flew down the ladder, jumping the last few yards onto the gravel below. She ran to the door, hoping against all odds she had enough of a lead to close both of them.

She shot past the inner door, but the zombies were already inside the fence and mere feet away, so she spun on her heels and kicked something on the floor in her rush back inside, unable to spare one moment to see what it was. She heaved her body against the inside of the door to slam it shut, as the zombie's footsteps reverberated in the metal vestibule. The door bucked back against her. The zombies had caught up before she could close the door completely. She dug her heels in and pushed hard, but something stopped it from shutting. She pumped her legs into the ground against the weight of the door and the zombies behind it, unsure why it wouldn't just shut.

One of the zombies got their arm through the opening and reached around the door, trying to get at Scout. She leaned away and felt a rush of air from the rotting flesh inches from her face, angry that she had tossed her sickle and had not stopped to pick it up. As the door bucked against her, she saw a dismembered arm on the ground smashed between the door and the frame. *That's what I kicked.* She tried to get it out with her foot, but almost lost her footing against the zombie assault on the door. She leaned down, maintaining pressure as the zombies banged their bodies against the door, and grabbed the dismembered arm smashed in the doorway by its wrist, jerking the arm onto the gravel. Something on the ground glinted at her in the morning sun near the arm when it landed a foot away. A hatchet. *Well, that's damn convenient,* she thought. She reached for it, but felt a sudden pain in her scalp. The zombie with its arm through the door grabbed hold of her hair. She screamed as it jerked her back. She reached out with her foot and kicked the hatchet closer, but it was just out of reach. The door suddenly slammed hard against her, pushing her within reach of the hatchet. She grabbed it and twisted her body around, swinging the blade at the hand gripping her hair. She made contact, and it suddenly released her, making her reel back. She lunged at the door, slamming it against the bodies. It closed with a satisfying clang and locked itself.

She leaned her back against the door and caught her breath. Her scalp ached. As the zombies banged against the metal inside, she was thankful the doors automatically locked when connected to the solar grid. She never really liked that default setting until that very moment. Her side ached, cramping from all her running.

"Open the door!" One of the zombies yelled from behind the metal. Scout shot up and spun around to see the zombie staring at her through the hatch.

"The fuck you say?"

The zombie narrowed its focus on Scout. "Open. The door!"

The only word Scout could say was, "Woah." She heard they could talk, but seeing one do it in person threw her for a loop.

The zombie banged hard on the door. "Open now!"

Gears turned in Scout's mind and she wanted to try something out. "I can't."

The zombie cocked its head and grunted "Huh?"

"I... I can't. As long as the outer door is open, the inner one stays locked shut."

The zombie glared at her.

"It's a failsafe, couldn't open it if I wanted."

They peered at each other. The fact she was having a conversation with a zombie unnerved Scout, but she continued the experiment and drove her point home. "This door, right here," she knocked on the metal, "cannot open if that door behind you—the one right there—stays open." Scout watched the zombie think somewhere deep behind its eyes. "Close that door, this door opens. Comprende?"

Scout couldn't believe it when a moment later, the zombie turned to its friend and barked something unintelligible. She listened to them go back and forth until she heard the high pitch screech of the outer door swing shut. Her heart beat loud in her chest as it looked like her stupid plan might actually work. She remained frozen, afraid any movement might break the spell. Then, the outer door clicked shut and auto-locked. She jumped with pride and excitement.

The zombie returned to the peephole. "Now! Open now!"

Scout laughed at it. "For smart zombies, you're a couple of damn fools!"

Confusion washed over its face. Scout reached up and slid the cover over the peephole. The zombies protested from their dark metal cage. Scout was filled with relief, confusion, and fear at what just happened.

Screams from the far end of the complex brought Scout back from her reverie. The cooling stack blocked her view of the action. She examined the hatchet in her hand, feeling its weight. She gave a deep sigh and took off towards the ladder. She picked up her sickle and climbed, cursing at the pain in her side, telling it to "shut up you little shit, my friends need me!" She surprised herself at referring to those people as friends. She had never experienced friendship before. The word felt foreign, but also right. She looked across the complex at the top of the wall to see the others fighting off several zombies. She sprinted north along the wall, figuring she'd be more useful attacking the zombies from the other side and pull their attention from of the others, from her friends.

Her sprinting made her side ache more. She didn't normally

have good reason to run, but her previous twenty-four hours had been surprisingly run-based. She vowed to stay in practice going forward so she would never become that winded again. She turned south down the east wall. Ahead of her, Sarah kicked at a pile of squirming zombies, saw Arthur standing uselessly behind her, but she couldn't see Leo. She looked to see if he'd fallen to the ground inside the wall, but he was nowhere in sight. *No time to worry,* she told herself, and screamed at the writhing mass of zombies. The one nearest her scrambled to its feet. Its nose was bent to the side, blood flowed down its face and chest. "Oh, my friend kick you in the face?" She said, holding the hatchet in her right hand, the sickle in her left. The zombie snarled and ran at her. "What, you gonna be a little bitch about it?" The zombie dove for her, arms outstretched. She brought the sickle down against its right arm, pushing its body off-balance. As the zombie collided against the inside wall, she swung the hatchet down hard against its skull. Its face scraped against the cement, grating off its cheek. The inertia pushed Scout back as the zombie fell limp at her feet. She jerked the hatchet out of its skull with a loud grunt and stepped over its body.

Scout thought about all the training she had growing up. Her parents would trap zombies within the fence whenever they ventured too close to the power plant, then they would have Scout put on a thick layer of padding to protect her body, and send her out into no-man's-land to face the things alone. Sometimes she despised her family for putting her through that, but as she got older, she enjoyed taking out her anger on those things more and more. She was suddenly sad; she missed her family deeply.

Sarah kicked another zombie off the pile in Scout's direction. It bounced on its back against the trench floor and looked up, seeing Scout. It rose to its feet and faced her, its yellow dress torn and covered with blood and viscera. Scout readied her hatchet and sickle and smiled. In her fighting, and in that moment, she felt her parents there with her, in the very walls of the complex itself. She felt them smiling back at her, letting her know she made them fucking proud.

The zombie snarled. Scout snarled right back, and they rushed at each other. She swung the hatchet down at an angle and kept the sickle in the air at the ready. She caught the zombie on the shoulder, thrusting it headfirst into the razor wire. It struggled to free itself, face and hair caught in the sharp barbs. It reached out and gripped Scout's right arm so tightly she let go of the hatchet. It jerked her toward it, tearing its face in the wire. Scout brought the sickle down hard, slicing halfway through its neck. It gave a gurgled yell and released her arm. She brought her knee against its chest and worked the sickle back and forth, cutting the rest of the way through. Its body collapsed to the floor, arcing spurts of blood as it ripped away from the head, left dangling from the wire, its long hair tangled in the barbs.

Scout jumped on the corpse and tugged at the hatched, pulling it free.

Another zombie climbed over the wire a few feet in front of her, clamoring over some poor sacrificial zombie pin-cushion smashing down the razor wire above the ladder. She dove forward and bent down, bouncing the zombie's body off her back toward the inner wall. It grasped frantically at the ledge, but overshot and fell to the gravel below with a wet crunch.

The zombie smashing the wire grabbed hold of Scout's shirt, jerking her toward its open, bloody mouth. It made a sudden jerk to the side as Sarah smashed its arm against the trench wall with her foot. That gave Scout enough leverage to lift the hatchet and bring it down on the zombie's face, slicing it across the bridge of its nose and eye sockets. It flailed and howled. Scout swung again, sinking the hatchet deep into the zombie's skull. It fell limp against the wall. She looked to Sarah. "Is that all of 'em? Where's the weird guy?"

Scout leaned over the wall. The old man lay motionless on the ground next to another dead zombie. "Looks dead to me, like they drained him. Fuckers gettin' weirder every day." She looked back to Sarah, who was trying to roll the top zombie off the pile in the trench. She realized the one on the bottom wasn't a zombie at all. "Leo?" she asked between breaths.

"Grab that one's feet." Sarah said and grabbed the zombie by the arms. They lifted it toward the inner ledge of the wall, struggling to get it high enough. Sarah rested one of its shoulders on the ledge and grabbed its red hood, hoisting the torso high enough that gravity took over and slid the body over the ledge to the ground below.

Sarah brought her ear to Leo's mouth. "He's still breathing."

"What happened?" Scout asked, piecing everything together.

"The wire ripped his chest pretty bad." Arthur said from the corner.

"That why he passed out? From blood loss?" Scout asked.

Arthur shrugged. "That or he couldn't breathe under the weight. Those things all piled on top of him."

"How do we get him down?" Sarah asked, confirming Leo still had a pulse.

"I got an idea," Scout said. "I don't like it, but it could work." She looked to Arthur "Think you can get his arms with your hurt foot?"

"I'll do my best."

Scout had Sarah lift Leo's legs while she helped Arthur lift his arms. She bent over and made her way under Leo, pushing her torso up against his, back to back. With her supporting the bulk of his weight, that eased Arthur's load enough he could limp on carrying the weight of Leo's arms and head. They made their way around the trench to the ladder.

Scout hoped she would never have to spend that much time on the widow's walk ever again.

CHAPTER TWENTY THREE

L eo was lost in flashes of sky and yelling, then a sudden fire burned across his chest. He screamed at the pain.

"Yeah, I bet that burns like a bitch." Scout said.

Leo tried to ask what was going on, but his chest burned with every breath so hard he couldn't hold in oxygen long enough to speak. He was inside a room, the air bit at his nostrils.

"Scout's cleaning your wounds with the vodka." Sarah said somewhere outside his field of vision. She took his hand. He squeezed back hard, vision blurred from tears filling his eyes at the searing pain that felt like his chest was split wide open. He got out a "What--" before the pain stopped him mid-sentence.

"There," Scout said. "Done with that part. Now I recommend you drink some of this yourself before I move on to your ear, I'm guessing that'll feel even worse."

Leo tried to sit up, but the pain was too much. Scout held the bottle over his mouth. He opened wide and gave her a nod. She filled his mouth. He swallowed. The liquid burned the entire route down to his stomach.

"Ok, here comes the bad part."

"Aren't we past the bad part?" Leo asked, his voice hoarse.

Scout laughed. "Sadly, no. Here, you may want this too, say ahh."

Leo gave a confused, "huh?" and Scout placed a piece of wood between his teeth.

"That's to bite on. Trust me, it helps." Scout gently tilted Leo's head and nodded to Sarah to hold him down. "Ok, take a deep breath. The pain will come on 3. Okay? 1…2." On 2 Scout poured vodka over Leo's torn up ear and cheek. The searing pain blinded him again, his teeth clenched hard on the stick in his mouth.

"Sorry," Scout said. "It's an old trick of my dad's. You did pretty good, considering."

Leo shook at the pain, the cold vodka and warm blood dripped down the side of his head. "Now don't go touching those, they need time."

Sarah bent down close to his face. "It's ok. Your wounds actually look better than we expected with all the blood. Just a few scratches, and your ear will heal fine."

Leo turned to his side and spat the piece of wood onto the table. As Leo's sight returned, he pieced together he was lying on the table in the dining space. He breathed through the pain, gathering his strength, not yet ready to sit up. "How long was I out?"

"Not long." Arthur said.

"But long enough to make us carry your ass down here." Scout said with a laugh and waved to Sarah. "Ok, we'll leave you to your beauty rest. C'mon chickie, we got a couple more zombies to kill."

Leo reached out his arm for Arthur to help him sit up. His chest and his ear sent out small shots of pain in rhythm with his pulse. "The kids?"

"I assume they'll get them after they kill the other zombies?"

Leo nodded and continued his breathing, inventorying his body, cataloging the pains. "Sorry I got you into this."

"Man, shut up. Those things burned my home. I never want to go back there. It already felt lonely after Anna…" Arthur sat on the table and looked at the wall. "No, you saved me. From them, from…" He shook his head. "Anyway, I guess I help Scout now. Once we get the trailer and tools in here--"

"The kids. Sidekick!" Leo yelled. He eased his feet to the floor and steadied himself on the counter. He was light-headed. He hoped it was just from blood-loss and shock, or the vodka coursing through his system. Either way, his mouth was dry. He made his way to the door.

Arthur slid off the table and followed. "I guess I should go watch the back of the building, make sure no more come over the edge."

Leo opened the door, the sun blinded him. He heard Scout talking to his left.

"Come here, just for a second. I have something to tell you." She spoke at the door. Leo's eyes adjusted enough to see Scout thrust a small rod into the peephole. It lifted as if pulled down on the other side of the door, then she jerked it back out. "Yeah, suck it!" She screamed, then looked to Sarah. "See what I mean? Gullible, right? Ok, you try."

Sarah walked to the door. "Hey, come here." She gave a questioning look to Scout, who encouraged her to continue. "Come on, there's, um, something I need to say to you." She looked through the peephole, then furrowed her brow and shook her head at Scout.

"Really?" Scout said and walked to the peephole. "Damn, they ain't that dumb, after all. It's staying back. Guess those shits learn, and fast."

"What's going on?" Leo asked as he approached.

"Oh man, you wouldn't believe it, but I got these idiots to lock themselves in there. I just tricked one into letting me stab its brain through the eye, but this other one's being a real bitch." Scout said, yelling the last part at the door.

Sarah handed the rod back to Scout and walked over to Leo. "Should you be up?"

He shook his head. "Probably not, but we gotta get the kids. I need to know they're safe, and Sidekick too." He hugged Sarah and winced as the pressure made his chest bloom with pain. He pulled away. He could feel something different in her, and in himself. The thing he'd seen in her eyes weeks earlier had taken him over. "I, uh..." He lost his words. Fear of losing Sarah or her siblings shot through him. Pressure mounted behind his eyes. Fear was replaced by anger at the new zombies for threatening the people he loved. "Let's finish this."

"Welcome back." Scout said with a smile. "Sarah, you mind

grabbing us some knives from the kitchen?"

Sarah nodded at Scout. She squeezed Leo's arm and ran off.

Scout looked Leo over. Her concerns echoed his. "Think I'll get some infection from the wire?"

Scout shrugged, glancing behind him to ensure Sarah was out of earshot. "Anything's possible. We got vodka on it pretty quick, but... who knows. Good thing you're heading to the doctor, right?"

Leo grunted his assent.

Scout shook her head. "Anyway, I feel better about *your* odds than the boy, right now."

Sarah's footsteps cut their conversation short. She returned with large knives in each hand.

"I got this one." Leo said, taking a knife.

"I feel like it should be my turn." Sarah said.

Leo looked Sarah in the eyes. "Please. I need this one right now."

Sarah nodded and stepped to the door handle.

"Ok, then. You got the door, I guess, so I got the controls." Scout stepped to the panel next to the door and looked to the others "You ready?" They nodded. "Okay, on 3."

Leo cleared his throat.

Scout smiled. "Actual 3, this time. The number 2 trick is just for things that hurt. Ok. 1...2...3!" She hit the button, and a click echoed in the dark chamber.

Sarah pulled the door open. The zombie lunged forward at Leo. He thrusted the blade up at its head, stabbing into the point where the jaw met its neck. Leo pushed the zombie to the ground and released his grip on the knife handle. The impact jammed the blade deep into the zombie's brain. It spasmed twice and fell limp.

Scout laughed, "That was sick!"

Leo bent down and rolled the corpse on its back. He put his knee on its chest and pulled out the knife, wiping the blade on its shirt. Leo scanned its face, dead eyes glazed over, the clouds in the sky slowly moved across them, reflected against the cold blackness underneath. He wondered how much humanity remained, masked behind its zombie nature; how much of it was still human when he killed it?

Sarah grabbed Leo's arm, interrupting his train of thought.

"Let's get the kids."

Leo rose, shaking the chill from his bones, happy to be distracted from those thoughts. "Where are they? And what exactly happened here, anyway?"

Scout sighed "Yeah, I'm an idiot for thinking this place was safe. Seems like too many things are changing all at once."

"A few of them came through the back—up the ladder." Sarah said, "Didn't realize that until it was too late. We got Steven and Dinah and ran, but more of them were coming through the fence, so we turned back."

Scout grunted. "Basically, we closed both doors and sandwiched ourselves in the vestibule."

"How'd you get out with the doors locked?" Leo asked.

"Well," Scout shook her head. "We were trapped in there for a while, sure, but since the locks are running on the solar panel circuit, we just had to wait until sundown."

"Scout was great." Sarah added. "One of them kept reaching in through the eyehole in the door, so she grabbed its arm and ripped it off."

Scout smiled "It was frickin' nuts."

"When the locks released, she slammed the outside door open on those things. We made a break for it."

"The best part about this place is that it's not just one building. My family made a couple of hideouts on the blocks around the complex, so we ran to the nearest one with all the tools for keeping the streets clean."

"We killed the ones that chased us and stayed inside there all night." Sarah said, "We kept a lookout for you."

"*She* kept lookout." Scout added. "I figured you wouldn't be back until morning. When we heard yelling, we figured that was our cue to come save your ass." Scout laughed.

"Thank you for that." Leo said, "Thank you both. I mean it." Sarah squeezed his arm and leaned against him.

"Geeze," Scout said, "You two need a room. Where's Arthur?"

"Watching the back."

Scout yelled across the complex to Arthur, letting him know they were heading out, and to unlock the front door when they returned.

He yelled back that he was making certain the zombies on the ground were also dead.

Scout and Sarah grabbed the legs of the zombie Leo had just killed while Leo grabbed its arms. They carried the body outside and across the street, tossing it on the ground. They did the same for the one in the vestibule, then Leo followed the other two around the corner and down the street to what looked like just another building with a collapsed roof. As they neared, he realized a bit of rusty corrugated metal hid a secret door. Scout knocked on it twice and said, "All's clear."

Leo heard small footsteps walk to the door and unlock it, it swung open revealing Dinah, eyes red from tears. She ran and hugged Sarah.

They entered the dark room inside. Tools hung on the walls. Steven lay sleeping on a cot, his eyes darting back and forth under his lids. He didn't look as bad as Leo feared he might. He still had color in his face, so blood loss wasn't an immediate concern. *Still, it'll be a rough ride to the doctor. Not just for the kids on the trailer and Steven with his wounds, but because of the unknown that waited ahead of them.* He didn't know how many more of those new zombies were out there. They'd eliminated about a dozen in the last week, but like any infestation, when you find one, you'll find more, especially if they were heading deeper in the direction those things had come from. Leo had only known his city, but he knew his father had settled there after moving west, apparently leaving behind his old friend who had become the first of the new breed of zombie threat. Leo wished he'd spent more time talking with his father about his past. There was so much he didn't know.

Sarah joined Leo at his side. They put their arms around each other's backs. They stood there for a while, watching Steven's fitful sleep before Leo leaned over and kissed Sarah's forehead. "I need to get Sidekick and the trailer. You want me to help you with him first?"

Sarah smiled at him and shook her head. "No, we'll let him sleep a little longer." She pulled Dinah in close to her. "We'll wait here."

Leo left the safe room and headed down the street to his bike and trailer. Scout ran to join him. "So when are you taking off?" She asked.

"Why?" Leo said, "You kicking us out?"

"Well, there's always use for you here."

"Oh," Leo said "You want help fixing the plant."

"I have to talk to our friend in there first. I think we can handle it, but who knows." She said, looking to the ground "No, just figured you might want to stay tonight, though you guys are always welcome back, you know."

A smile crossed Leo's face. "Thank you."

They rounded the corner. Leo felt another rush of happiness as the trailer came into view. But first, he wanted to make certain the old man and zombie at the base of the ladder were no longer threats. The bottom dropped out of his stomach. The man's body was gone. He ran to the spot on the ground. The grass indented where his body had been, spattered with blood.

"The hell?" Scout said, pointing to the dead zombie on the ground. "I saw them! They were here, only that one still had its head."

The body of the zombie Leo knocked over the wall was in a heap on the ground, its head removed. Scout's other sickle lay on the grass next to the decapitated zombie. *No, that's impossible,* Leo thought. He wanted his eyes to be lying.

Scout picked up her sickle from the ground and pointed to the street. "Bastard left a trail!"

Leo looked at the grass and saw a trail of blood. He gripped the knife in his hand tight. Scout swung a sickle in each hand. They followed the trail, rage filling both their minds. The trail of blood led them across the street and down a few buildings to an alley. They made their way into the shadows to find the decapitated head split open and discarded.

"He ate the brain." Leo said.

"How'd he even get this far with his wounds? I thought those things ate into him before."

"No." Leo said. "No, they just drank his blood."

"What, like frickin' vampires?"

The thought struck Leo as odd, but he had no other explanation. "I mean... I don't know. He said that feeding on people gave him power, or something. The brain must give them more, like other zombies, but... the blood must do something for them too."

"You're telling me these zombies are vampires?"

"I don't know what they are anymore."

They continued down the alley, but the blood trail stopped at the skull-husk. They searched the adjacent blocks, but found no sign of the old man.

Unsatisfied, they returned to the trailer. Leo knelt down on the ground. Sidekick hid under the trailer behind the wheel nearest Leo. Sidekick stared at him like he no longer trusted humans. Leo reached his arm out and said softly, "Come on Sidekick, it's ok. The bad things are gone, just us here now."

Sidekick batted his hand away with its paw. "Oh man," Leo said to Scout, "that whole thing must've really freaked him out. Normally he prefers being held." Leo reached both hands in and grabbed Sidekick. The cat hissed, but soon relaxed as Leo held him close against his chest, stroking his fur. A moment later he began purring. Scout stared at the cat. "This really is the first cat you've seen up close, isn't it?"

Scout gave a small nod. "Just feral ones here and there. Never trained. They're fascinating."

Leo held Sidekick out. "Would you mind? I gotta wheel this thing around to the front, anyway."

Scout looked to Leo for permission, then lifted Sidekick in her arms, holding him to her body as Leo had. Sidekick resumed his purring.

That afternoon they brought the ladder inside the complex and set it against the back wall, giving Scout a second way of getting to the widow's walk in case of emergencies. They took turns keeping lookout from the top of the wall, but there were no signs of the old man or zombies new or old. Based on his injuries, they assumed the old man was either dead somewhere or would need a lot more time to heal.

Scout released the rooster into the hen cage. They got along together nicely. She hoped to have more soon and made plans to clean out the raised planter bed that had been destroyed by the burst pipe and grow some grain there to feed her future food source.

Leo helped Arthur set up his tools and get to work fixing the broken section of pipe with Scout. They got everything back together and let the connections cure overnight.

That night they prepared a feast, because sometimes survival itself was worth celebrating. Besides the grand meal, they all experienced the effects of vodka. They discussed the new zombies and what the old man had said to Leo, how he knew Leo's father, locked himself away for half a century going mad, and once he was out, became infected with the new strain of zombie virus from a bat.

Scout stopped the story at that point. "Wait, he has to drink blood and eat brains because he was bitten by a bat? Those things freakin' *are* vampire zombies. Or zombie vampires? No wait, they're zompires!" Everyone chuckled at first, but the weight of the new threats those zombies posed descended on them all. They discussed what dangers may lie ahead on the road for Leo and the Jacksons, and for those remaining at the power plant.

After a dark silence, Arthur held up his glass. "Seeing the road ahead populated with unknowns, I think it fitting to make a toast." The others joined, raising their glasses. "Looking around at all of us, joined together around this table, I can't help but be thankful... for so many things. I've spent my years with very few people. We all have. I don't regret my choices, and I hope none of you do either, but when I look at you all here, I'm reminded of a few words Shakespeare wrote centuries ago and chose to put in the mouth of Miranda. 'How beauteous mankind is! O brave new world, that has such people in it.'" A tear rolled down his cheek. He blushed and lifted his glass.

They clinked glasses and drank deeply, laughing into the rest of the evening.

After dinner, Sarah led Leo to a room he hadn't yet seen and introduced him to the pleasures of a hot bath. She demonstrated how to turn the tap on and how to unplug the tub. The look on her face confused him, something new was in her eyes and it excited him. She kissed him and slowly lifted his shirt over his head. His heart raced as fast as his mind. His confusion and excitement must have shown on his face, because Sarah put a finger to his lips and shushed him with a smirk. He blushed as she began removing her own clothes.

Moments later they faced each other, completely naked. Neither of them had ever been intimate with another person. The kissing and handholding they'd done the last few days was the extent of their entire romantic experiences to that point.

Sarah pulled Leo's body against hers and kissed him. Her skin percolated with goosebumps. She wrapped her hand in Leo's and stepped into the bathtub, steam rising up from the water, compelling him forward. Fear and excitement pulsed throughout Leo's body. He stepped over the edge, joining her in the water. They explored each other and discovered themselves long enough for the water to cool around them. They weren't ready to be done for the evening, so they ran a little more hot water into the bath. *Brave new world, indeed.*

They all slept well and woke to the call of the rooster in the morning. Leo and Sarah packed what little they had onto the trailer. Dinah's energy showed how nervous and excited they all were to embark on the new adventure and head east to the doctor. Steven was in positive spirits. They all hoped that meant his arm was healing, though it was obvious his bones weren't in line, though nobody spoke that concern aloud. They all wanted to focus on the good things, and the fact Steven was in less pain than he had been the day before was enough.

Arthur remained at the power plant with Scout, at least for the time being. He figured she could use the help and he could use the time to heal, and they could both use the company. Leo smiled at the thought they'd filled the missing parts in each other's lives. *Sure, it could never be a perfect fit, but it was something.* Just like Steven, he hoped their pain would be a little less every day.

After breakfast, Scout loaded food and other supplies onto the trailer, and Arthur connected the second bike to the tongue of the trailer. Leo wouldn't have to pull the weight of everything alone, he and Sarah would share the burden together.

Before leaving, Leo gave a sheet of paper to Scout and Arthur. "I used to sketch portraits of the people I lost through the years."

Scout looked at the paper, tears forming in the corners of her eyes.

"Seeing how nice last night was, I wanted to keep that moment, so instead of drawing what I've lost, I sketched what we have." The drawing was of all of them, smiling and laughing around a table. Leo had seen paintings of a dozen people in robes around a table, all sharing a meal together. He used that as the inspiration when drawing his friends. He'd seen the image in various places throughout the city, and it remained in his mind. He hoped the image of his friends enjoying a meal would live on for Scout and Arthur similarly.

"It's like the last supper." Sarah said. He held her close and hoped the previous night wouldn't be their last supper together, and one day Scout and Arthur's paths would cross their own again.

Sidekick sat several feet away from everyone else. Leo walked to him and kneeled down. "Don't worry, I didn't forget you." Sidekick purred as Leo ran his hand over his fur. "I guess you can tell things are changing again. I don't know if you'd prefer to stay here, but I'd like to bring you with us on the road. It may not be easy, but you saved my life once. Maybe more than once in different ways. Anyway, you ready for another adventure?"

Sidekick leaned his body against Leo's hand. He looked at Leo and meowed.

"Alright then, let's get to it." Leo scooped up Sidekick and placed him on the trailer with the children.

Leo and Sarah got on their bikes. They struggled to pedal in unison and steer in the same direction out of the gate. Sarah wobbled on her bike. Leo smiled and told her it was ok. She hadn't spent as much time riding it as he had. "We'll find our stride together." He said as they turned out of the gate toward the road to the highway leading east.

Before long, they reached the edge of Leo's knowledge of the city. From that point on, they'd all be in unfamiliar territory, and they'd be in it together.

Enjoy this book? You can make a HUGE difference

Reviews are the most powerful tool when it comes to getting attention for my books, especially as an independent author without the major financial arsenal of a huge New York publisher. I can't take out ads on TV, billboards, or even park benches.

...at least until someone wants to make a TV show based on my novels.

But this scrappy indie author has something much more powerful and effective than a bottomless advertising budget. I have access to something the huge publishers would kill to get their hands on.

A committed and loyal group of readers.

Word of mouth and honest reviews of my books help bring them higher in the algorithms and to the attention of other readers.

If you enjoyed this book (and especially if you can't wait to get your hands on the next in the series), I would be grateful if you would take just a few minutes to leave a review. Even a short, one-word review helps the cause.

You can review it wherever you purchased it, and if you purchased directly from the author, (thank you so much, by the way!), go to your next favorite book seller and review the book on their site. You can also encourage your library to purchase copies for their collection. Art is made to be shared, and you can help others discover this series.

Thank you very much, you make it possible for indie authors like me to continue creating entertaining stories for you to enjoy.

Cheers!

FREE SHORT STORY

One of the best things about writing and creating a world, is sharing it with others who love it, and connecting with you, the reader. I occasionally send newsletters (generally no more than once a month) with details on new releases, special offers, updates, and answering fan questions about my books, my life, or the world in general.

If you sign up for the mailing list, you will also get a free short story following Adam and Esther after the events of this book. You can get that for free by signing up at:

http://eepurl.com/ipOjtA

You can contact me at Vincent@VMIbooks.com

Find out more at www.VMIbooks.com

ACKNOWLEDGMENTS

The idea for this novel had been in my mind for at least fifteen years, quietly whispering behind my thoughts, but I was too busy or tired to write it until a global pandemic disrupted the world and removed everything I counted on for income. For all the pain and loss that resulted from Covid-19, I would like to take a moment to be thankful for the great pause that afforded a number of people the time and opportunity to put the heat to their long simmering dreams and finally bring them to a boil.

Thank you to the skilled and willing eyes and minds of Aaron, Scott, Hilary, Allen, AJ, and Ashley for helping me steer this book to the finish line, and especially Leigh for making sure I didn't butcher the English language too much, and Kate for your keen eye and sharp mind I have come to depend on not once, but twice in this book's journey alone.

Most of all, thank you to my first reader and my last reader, the amazing, wonderful, talented, funny, generous, smart, gorgeous, and every other positive adjective one could conjure, my beautiful bride, Amanda Ives. When the world around us stopped, we continued on together.

ABOUT THE AUTHOR

Novelist Vincent Michael Ives loves hard sci-fi and enjoys endlessly daydreaming in his post-apocalyptic Zompire series. He prides himself on bringing hope to a genre that has traditionally focused on the very worst parts of human nature, and enjoys finding real-world solutions to every day problems in a world seemingly lost to the zombie apocalypse.

When he's not writing or thinking about his next meal, Vincent enjoys puzzles, video games, and just hanging out with family and friends. This Portland, Oregon native has lived in New Zealand, Los Angeles, Toronto, and London, and is always looking for the next adventure to share with his wife and soon-to-be newborn child.

Vincent encourages readers to support indie authors and shop direct whenever possible. Feel free to visit www.VMIbooks.com.